THE JANITOR'S SECRET

Another Life Altering Secret Revealed

To: Gary G. Naeyaert

From: Cornell Ray Amerson

Education start when a learning Disability
is treated, Thanks for Your Support !!!
08/26/09

CORNELL R. AMERSON

THE JANITOR'S SECRET

Another Life Altering Secret Revealed

CORNELL R. AMERSON

Published by Chioma Inspirations
www.ChiomaInspirations.com

THE JANITOR'S SECRET

ISBN 978-0-9814936-9-5

Copyright © 2009 by Cornell Ray Amerson

Printed and bound in Canada

ArtBookbindery.com
Empowering Writers to Self-Publish™

Table of Contents

Dedication

This book is dedicated to my beautiful children Xavier and Andrea, whom I adore and love immensely and thank my Heavenly Father for the enrichment they bring to my life and the lives of others. I pray to the Heavenly Father to bless my children and protect them in their lives forever. I also want to provide a special dedication to those individuals, past and present, who have positively or negatively impacted on my life, making me who I am today. Finally, for those who believed I would never amount to anything: I thank my God and divine wisdom in not allowing me to except those opinions to become my reality, because if you're reading this book I am now a published author.

With unconditional love for his children,

Cornell Ray Amerson

"In loving memories of my falling father and brothers"

Acknowledgments

My journey has been a long one, filled with obstacles and hindrances. I will admit that at times I have allowed negative things to define who I am. Thankfully, my Heavenly Father sent forth three very special ladies into my life. **Ms. Robin Williams**, **Ms. Kyna Burton** and **Ms. Charity Lancaster** must be thanked enormously for the compassion they have had for their fellow human beings. These ladies have graced my soul with kindness, selflessness and respect without prejudice. It was with their help that I was able to continue my journey; it was with their help that I was able to overcome the barriers that had been set in place by so many others who had claimed to be working towards my best interests. So I thank these three wonderful ladies. They have played a crucial role in my life without seeking anything in return. It has been with their help that I have been able to write this book. Indeed, I strongly believe that it would be a crime to not acknowledge their help. So I close by acknowledging those three extraordinary and magnificent women and my mother and sisters. I pray that God will continue to bless you for being the good people you are for taking the time to lend a positive hand in the lives of others!

Sincerely

Cornell Ray Amerson

"let's not forget all the janitors and housekeepers that perished on 9/11"

Author's Background

Mr. Cornell Ray Amerson grew up in Detroit, and attended Detroit public schools. Today he is a single parent father and a self-taught artist specializing in pencil drawings. He earned a trophy in a local drawing contest as a child during the early 1970s. He also builds balsa wood model airplanes and likes to invent things. He has pursued a patent for a model airplane invention, achieving some local recognition.

Mr. Amerson has worked in a variety of jobs. His first job was as a City of Detroit summer youth worker. He followed this with stints at various restaurants, busing tables and dishwashing. After this he worked as a patent draftsman for about two years, and a Recreational Aide with the Detroit Recreation Department. He found this job a great privilege, as he met a numerous beautiful people while serving proudly in the communities in which he worked. He has also worked on the assembly line at the Chrysler North Jefferson auto plant in Detroit, and he has taught a calligraphy class at a Cornerstone elementary and middle school combination at Linwood on the North West side of Detroit.

At present Mr. Amerson is working towards his dream of becoming a successful published author of great literary works, while working in the janitorial profession as a Building Attendant in the City of Detroit's Wastewater Treatment Plant.

Though Mr. Amerson faces ongoing obstacles and hindrances thanks to his dyslexia, he knows that no matter what, his determination will allow him to prevail.

Words of Encouragement

I have written this book with two goals in mind. The first is simple: to provide a good entertaining read. The second, however, is perhaps more meaningful: to provide a work of substance that will inform, expose and educate readers about the various effects of living with a learning disability. I truly hope that you will find the book to be of great value. On that note, I would like to begin this work with a question. Do you know anything about learning disabilities such as dyslexia (other than the stereotypical knowledge that dyslexia causes individuals to see the letters or numbers of the alphabet in reverse), or do you know anyone challenged by dyslexia? If you don't, that's ok. You're not the only one with a limited knowledge of dyslexia and other learning disabilities. In this book I want to show the tremendous impact that dyslexia can have on the daily lives of dyslexic individuals.

The sad and unfortunate reality is that to this day there are still many in the teaching profession who have little to no knowledge of dyslexia and other learning deficiencies, nor of how to deal with them. For example, the City of Detroit's public school system has no real plans to deal with dyslexic children or those afflicted by other learning disabilities in the classroom. This in turn results in a lack of alternative assistance or support being provided for any child challenged by a learning disability, resulting in that child probably being denied a fair opportunity in life and an ability to achieve academic success. What this leads to in the long run is a child who will very likely fall through the cracks of the education system, doomed to suffer an unnecessary lifetime of recovery. What is depressing is that this statement is not merely reflective of my own experience in life and in the

City of Detroit's public school system: this statement is based on documented material. My own difficulties originated from gross negligence on the behalf of my parents towards my overall educational development, yet this negligence was exacerbated by the Detroit public school system. To this day the school system has not recognized any responsibility for their actions – for their failure to provide me with an adequate education. The bottom line is that this book should be viewed by parents with school aged children as a warning: if parents think they can leave the education of their children entirely up to the school system – if they think they do not need to monitor and support their children's education – they will be putting their children's formal education in serious jeopardy. If you don't believe this is the case, I hope after reading this book you will reconsider, as I strongly believe what is contained within will inspire and motivate you to take a more active role in your child's overall educational development. At heart, though the story of this novel is fictional in nature, the reality of dyslexia and many other learning disabilities are not. The fact of the matter is that dyslexia and other learning disabilities are destroying the lives and futures of enormous numbers of children and adults. I know this for a fact, because I am one of those who constantly struggle with the daily demands of a learning disability, identifed as dyslexia. To this day, very few resources and opportunities exist that can help those in such a position, especially if you're an adult challenged by a learning disability.

I hope that the story I'm about to share with you will not only inspire you, but will also enlighten you about learning disabilities and dyslexia. I thank you very much for reading my book and I hope you will continue to educate yourself about learning disabilities for the sake of your children's educational future.

Cornell Ray Amerson
10-11-2006

Foreword

A student with a learning disability possesses the potential to learn at an average or above average intellectual level, however actual academic achievement in one or more specific area is significantly below that potential. Significant learning problems involve understanding or using spoken or written language. These problems often effect the way the brain processes information and may become evident in the person's writing, math, spelling, listening and speaking skills.

One of the biggest tragedies for students and adults is that they don't always learn of a learning disability until they have experienced failure and ridicule. The amazing thing about these individuals is that they are usually smart and gifted people. Too often by the time they are diagnosed the emotional damage has taken its toll.

It is not uncommon for students to receive a diagnosis Learning Disabled/Differences (dyslexia, dyscalculia, dystopia, etc) until years after they have entered school. Parents in many cases are often angered, ashamed, embarrassed and /or complacent shying away from or detaching themselves from the school setting. The absence of parental involvement can lead to still more humiliation for the student. School staffing and systems can fail students for a multitude of reasons. All too often the quiet student will get overlooked. All too often the student barely make it will be just passed on.

The reality is a learning disability is a condition and not a person. It is something that can be treated and should not dictate who you are. Society must become more knowledgeable of this condition, parents must fight for their children, and school systems must do a better job at recognizing and educating. Learning disabilities are now better known as learning differences denoting a different and more effective approach to learning must be mandated.

Tamar Richardson,
Special Education Teacher

Chapter 1

The lay off blues

One quiet night during the midnight hours I suddenly woke up in the darkness of my bedroom; terrified and drenched in a cold sweat, shaking from the effects of a nightmare." It was the fourth night that week I'd woken up with my nerves on edge and my heart beating out of control. I could barely catch my breath. I shuddered after yet another disturbing dream, while my wife slept peacefully beside me. Yet that night, despite all my objections, the dream still held power in my waking mind – the dream managed to raise its ugly head in my reality.

On the fateful afternoon of May 7th, after working for twenty five years at one of Detroit's auto plants, Mr. Jeremiah Johnson was laid off from his job. I know this for certain because I am Mr. Jeremiah Johnson. I should've seen it coming! The writing was on the wall. But I ignored the signs... So all I could do was sit in the plant cafeteria with my termination papers, and spend a bit of time with my coworkers for one last time. Some of them were good friends. It was a sunny afternoon, and the sun was shining beautifully through all the windows of the cafeteria. But it wasn't beautiful for me. Anyway, I joked and laughed with my buddies, remembering all the crazy things we'd done over the years. For a little while everything felt OK, as if the lay off didn't exist for me anymore. But then the guys I was reminiscing with, the ones who had walked over to where I was sitting with my head down, couldn't stay any longer. They had to leave me to go back to work.

So the cafeteria gradually cleared out. Everyone but me left to go back to work. I sat there by myself, looking out through one of the cafeteria windows. I tried to fight the emotions and tears, but I couldn't. I let out a small cry and a sniffle. I immediately fought them back, thinking to myself that men don't cry. But the shock and pain of the lay off was too much: an uncontrollable flow of tears came from me. I sobbed, without caring even if it did compromise my manhood for the moment.

After a while I began to collect myself and I decided it was time to go home. My shift was over. As I stood up from my chair to leave, I felt a gentle tapping on my left shoulder. Turning around to see who it was, I was surprised to see my best buddy Mr. Jerome Harper, who I thought had taken a vacation that day. Jerome and I had a long history together; we began work in this auto plant at the same time twenty five years earlier. We'd gone through a great number of things that had challenged our friendship, but no matter what, we'd remained good friends. In fact, I still view him as my brother. Before I could say anything, he spoke to me.

"I heard about your lay off, are you doing ok? I saw your eyes full of tears man!"

"Come on man," I replied, "stop that before you get me started all over again."

"Alright man." He straightened up. "What are you going to do now Jeremiah?"

"I don't know man."

"Well, if you ever need anything, just let me know, because I'll be there for you!"

"Thanks man, I know it."

"All right Jeremiah," Jerome said, looking me in the eye, "I can't take this any more. I have to go back to work. I'll talk to you later, so take care of your self."

I told him I would, and I said that he should do the same. Then, giving me a strong handshake and a traditional shoulder to shoulder man hug, my buddy Jerome walked away, holding his head up high. I walked away as well, towards the exit doors of the plant. I wandered slowly through the parking structure to my car on the fourth level. My car… ready to take me home to my beautiful wife Sophia, who had always seemed to know what to say and what to do, how to make things better.

Once I arrived home, I still felt pretty emotional. I parked my car in the garage and sat there for a few minutes, trying to collect myself. After a while, I decided it was time to exit my car and enter my home. Sophia was in the kitchen preparing dinner, and I walked up and greeted her with a hug and kiss. She smiled and looked me in the eyes – and then she saw something was wrong.

"What's the problem?" She asked.

"Sweetheart," I began, "your husband has… well some not so good news. I was laid off from my job today." Before getting any further, I felt all the emotions that I thought I had under wraps bubble up again. I began to unravel, abandoning the notion once again that real men don't cry. I fell into the arms of my wife like a new born baby that needed more than milk and attention. My beautiful loving wife took over the situation, calming me down with her patient and compassionate embrace. I felt safe in her warm hug, safe with her soothing voice and loving words of encouragement. No matter what, she always seems able to lift my spirits, reminding me to thank God daily for allowing me the privilege of marrying one of his precious angels.

I believe my wife's love helped me to keep my manhood intact. But this was least of my worries at this point, because when I came back to my senses the reality of my situation began to set in. I had to come up with a plan so that we could survive this period while I was out of work. Sadly, I had never prepared for such a crisis. It would be an understatement to say that we were in a tight situation; we had a mortgage to pay, alongside our daughter's college tuition. And we had no extra money in our savings account. Now, without my income, we were going to have to rely on my wife's income alone, with the obvious stresses of her becoming the sole breadwinner. The matter was simple. I had to get a new job. My wife's wages from her psychology practice would not be enough to cover all of our financial obligations. And when it comes down to it, it wouldn't be fair to her or me if I stood by and allowed her to take on such a monumental task alone. If I allowed that to happen, then my manhood would be in jeopardy of being canceled, right along with my status as a respectable husband. I simply couldn't allow that to happen. Not for the sake of my manhood, but for the love of my wife and marriage, the things I treasure most in this world.

So my wife and I had a long discussion about what we could do and how we would deal with me being out of work. It was a long conversation, I tell you. Gladly, our 6:00 p.m. dinnertime allowed us to pause the conversation, as our discussion had left us famished. Once we had finished eating dinner and washing the dishes, we felt a great need to watch a comedy on television while eating microwave popcorn. So we sat together on the sofa like a brand-new couple, meeting for the first time in our dimly lit living room with the sweet fragrance of a scented candle saturating the air. After watching the comedy that made us laugh until we couldn't breathe, we felt a lot better, ready for bed. Before climbing upstairs to the bedroom, we made sure to shut off the television and extinguish the candle. We proceeded quietly to our bedroom, exhausted by the day's events. We sat on the bed next to one another and embraced, kissing and staring into each other's eyes in a silent communication. My wife began to cry, telling me in a soft voice how much she loved me. With my own eyes filled with tears, I quickly responded by telling her that I thanked God every day for her.

"I love you," I said. She hugged me tightly. She looked at me and explained that she was going to support me and stand by my side; that we would weather this storm together.

"A marriage is not just about enjoying the good times, but about having enough maturity and love and respect for one another to successfully survive the difficult times and challenges. In fact, it is only through the wisdom that the bad times give us that we can really enjoy and appreciate the good times when they come. As long as we struggle together," my wife said, "and not allow outside forces such as opinions and advice interfere with us, we should be all right in our marriage and in the covenant we made with God!"

My wife became quiet once more. She lowered her head and began to wipe the tears from her eyes. All the while, she kept her beautiful smile. My wife speaking to me in that manner was so inspiring and insightful that I was lost for words. Inside, I was so happy that my wife had spoken in such a way, because it spared me the frustration of having to read her mind, having to guess how she felt about my lay off. Whether she realized it or not, her caring and compassionate speech was therapeutic for me, because my lay off had caused all sorts of insecurities and problems with my self-esteem. My wife's kind words provided a most needed remedy. I am so grateful for having a wife who genuinely loves and cares for me. In my time of need, I found it very important to know that my wife was in my corner, no matter what, and had no intention of ever being my enemy. When that's the case, that knowledge alone provides the love, energy and confidence that I use as a husband and father; that I can take to being a provider and protector of my wife and child. I am sure that over the years of our marriage, my wife and I have learned valuable lessons: in particular, that telling someone you love them is not enough if you don't follow it up with actions. You have to talk with and not at one another, make time to be with each other and always respect one another. Well I guess I'm done speaking in my mind. Anyway, I was ready to go to bed, ready to get some rest to face the challenges of tomorrow. However, before I could finally go to bed, I did allow my wife to finish wiping one last tear from my eye. With that last act of affection, we disengaged our loving embrace and took the time to say our prayers together on our knees at the side of our bed, like we had done every night, before we got into bed and closed our eyes to sleep.

* * *

It's so nice to wake up in the morning with the wonderful smell of bacon and eggs filling the house! With a beautiful sunrise and the morning birds chirping away, I got out of bed with a smile, ready to start my search for employment. All right, I said aloud to those morning birds, I am getting out of bed now. I glanced over to the bedside clock, seeing that it was 7:30 a.m. I got out of bed yawning and stretching, and headed straight for the bathroom. I brushed my teeth and took a long hot shower. After a while, my wife called me down to breakfast. It didn't take me long to comply; I was out of that shower and downstairs and fully dressed at the table for breakfast in a jiffy. Before sitting down for breakfast however, I didn't forget to give my wife a hug and a good morning kiss, telling her how beautiful she was. When I was all settled down, she presented me with a breakfast fit for a king, both delicious to look at and delicious to eat. We both began to eat.

"Good morning my dear husband," Sophia said, wearing that beautiful smile I love so much. "I pray that you have a good day and a successful job search. So what are your plans today?"

"I really don't know," I answered, "because I've not had to look for a job for twenty five years! I guess I'll start by finding and dusting off my résumé along with my ego and pride. What do you think?"

"That sounds like a good way to start to me. Well anyway," she said, "I have faith that you will figure it out. But in the meantime, let me get out of here before I am late for work! I will see you later this evening."

We gave each other a hug and a kiss, and my wife left our home for work. After cleaning the table and washing the breakfast dishes, I decided at that point to search for my résumé, my high school diploma and my other certificates and qualifications. But I tell you, after searching all day for that information, I only ended with the hope that I would be more successful in finding a job than finding my papers! I looked all over the house, not once but maybe three or four times, and still didn't find the information I was looking for. Before I knew it, it was 6:00 p.m. and my wife was walking through the door with a smile on her face, asking me how was my day! I responded in frustration with a pitiful look of embarrassment on my face.

"Sweetheart," I said politely, "I have been searching for my résumé and other papers all day, with no luck finding anything."

She continued to smile, but she didn't say anything. She went upstairs to change out of her work clothes. While she did that I went back to my search. Anyway, a little while later she came back downstairs into the living room, asking me what I wanted for dinner. I lifted my head to respond to her question, and as I did that she handed me all of the documents that I had been searching for all day. I breathed a big sigh of relief and laughed. I was so happy that all I could do was give her a big hug and a kiss and thank her and tell her that I didn't know what I would do without her!

So the following morning, after wasting the previous day searching for my papers, I was fired up and ready to start my job search. I left the house before my wife had gone to work, carrying all my necessary documentation to get myself a job. That day I drove all over the City of Detroit and the suburbs, filling out job applications non-stop. I only paused once to take a lunch break at Burger King, where it felt good to have it my way, sitting in the lobby eating my whopper and cheese, with a chicken salad, fries and a cold drink of Sprite. Once I finished my lunch and had read a newspaper for a little while, I was ready to go back out there and fill out more job applications. I kept going until five o'clock, when it was time for me to start heading home. After arriving home with a sense of pride in what I had accomplished during the day – along with the memory of what my wife had done for me yesterday in finding all my paperwork – I decided to start dinner for us and run her a bath in appreciation. She arrived home and was treated like a queen for the rest of the evening.

The next day, and the many days that followed, consisted of me attending lots of job interviews and making lots of follow-up phone calls. Yet I got no real responses and had no success finding a job. I also paid a visit to my local and outer city community employment agencies, where I found no success in finding any form of employment. In fact, all I felt that I had accomplished to this point was to waste my time at those employment agencies. I have to say it, at this point in my job search I began to get pretty tired and discouraged. I desperately needed a job. I need to help my wife with our financial responsibilities, and I was constantly aware of our mounting bills. Bill collectors had begun to call our home regularly throughout the day, which I knew was taking a toll on my wife. This saddened me to the core, yet I was unable to help my wife with our overall financial crisis. I can honestly say that all of this employment rejection created a level of depression within me that I had never previously experienced in my life. I felt like I had some sort of a dark presence within me, making me feel like a loser and a worthless man, like someone that didn't deserve to live. I felt like my dear wife deserved better than I could provide her with. Indeed, I became very much afraid that my wife of twenty years would leave me due to the stresses surrounding my inability to provide for her; I felt that she'd probably had enough of dealing with a loser like me. If that was the case then I don't blame her. Not one bit. Because really, I wouldn't be much of a man if I couldn't provide for my family. This made me feel so angry, like I just wanted to break or destroy something to feed the rage that existed within me.

My shame and frustration at not having a job or the financial means to take care of my family made me not only to feel bad about myself, but I also began to avoid my wife emotionally. I lied to her about searching for employment when I wasn't. In fact, all I began to do at that point was leave the house before she went to work, only to return shortly afterwards to watch television all day. Sometimes I would just cry, because I felt less than a man. The bill collectors would continue to call.

* * *

Five months passed, and I remained unemployed. I felt as miserable as ever, especially since my wife was now working a great deal of overtime to try to meet all of our financial obligations. Over those months we fell behind in our mortgage payments and in our daughter's college tuition. With my wife working all those hours, I began to feel a tremendous strain on our marriage, because we began to spend less time together when she came home from work. Because she was so tired, she usually went straight to bed as soon as she would arrive home from work. And I wasn't mad at her at all for that, because I knew that it was basically my fault. Sometimes I would find it so hard to believe that I was going through this. All my life to that point I had never had to suffer. I grew up in a family with loving parents. I never wanted for anything. My parents made sure I was well educated, sending me to the finest school they could find. When I left home as a young man to be on my own, I had no problem ever getting a job and taking care of myself. When I met my wife after working in the auto plant for five years, I was more than able to take care of us both, even when she was still in school pursuiting her profession. I still remember like it was yesterday how it felt so good to take care of my family. So when I wasn't able to do this anymore I began to wonder how I ended up in such a terrible place. I wondered why I couldn't take care of my wife or myself anymore. You know what? Being so down in the dumps that you just can't see the light at the end of the tunnel and you just don't have anything to hold onto sucks to high heaven. And that's where I was. It seemed no matter what I did, I just couldn't seem to recover from my state of hopelessness.

My wife came to me concerned for my well being. She reminded me how much she loved me, and was fully aware of the tremendous pain I was going through as a result of not being able to find employment. She also reminded me that she was still going to stand by my side and support me no matter what. But she did add that I had to get it together and meet her halfway.

"No matter what you think about yourself," she said, "I still believe in you. I have no doubt that you're still the wonderful man I married and I'm simply not going to give up on you that easily. So please," she cried, "stop giving up on yourself because you obviously have no idea how much it's been hurting me these last few months seeing you in this self-destructive state. It hurts that you shut me out. God for bid, if our marriage was to come to an end, I can assure you that it would not be because you've been unemployed with no income. It would be due to you pulling away from me so far that I could lose you for ever. God knows I don't want that! So pull yourself together for the sake of us. I know you're going to find employment soon enough, but our daughter needs you and I need you. You're not just my husband you're my life."

After saying that my wife reached out to me in desperation. She pulled me into her arms and hugged me tightly, as if she was never going to let me go. Her sunshine smile was gone and tears were flowing. At that point I could do nothing but return her affection with a tight hug. Eyes filled with tears. After giving my wife a long compassionate hug, I made her a verbal promise that I would get myself together and never shut her out again. Once I made that promise, I could feel her body relax; her beautiful smile returned.

The promise that I made to my wife Sophia resulted in all sorts of benefits for the both of us, after we had the misfortune of enduring all that negativity caused by my self-pity, my self-centeredness and my irrational approach to dealing with my problems. I had allowed my problems to get the best of me. They had almost cost me my beautiful wife and my marriage. I know for a fact that nothing worse could have happened to me. So I thank God that with the help of my loving wife I was brought back to my senses, reminded that the situation we were facing was nothing compared to the love we had for one another. Indeed, in any situation like this, what you use to survive will make you that much stronger, helping you to conquer the many other challenging situations to come. As my wife said to me, "Circumstances and consequences, especially when they're challenging in nature, are the true birthplace of wisdom. And don't you forget it. If you don't allow your challenges to take their course, and you don't gain the fruit of wisdom from them, then you're destined to receive only the fruit of foolishness, which will cause further unnecessary situations and challenges that are normally deflected by the fruit of wisdom."

One thing I can say about this negative lay off experience was that it was sobering for the both of us – but it was also somehow liberating. It taught us patience, and it taught us how essential it is to take life one day at a time while enjoying the simple moments that life has to offer. While my wife and I were still challenged by the drama of the lay off, we made the decision to pull together with mind, body and soul for the purpose of initiating a healing process. Indeed, we'd already begun such a process by focusing on the situations we were able to control and by praying for resolution to those life problems where we had no control. We decided to be mindful of not bringing any more negativity to a negative situation. All that does is block your blessings from your creator, if you believe in such matters. My wife and I share our spirituality, and we believe in such matters. Because of this, I know that my negative approach and my bad attitude towards losing my job just produced more negativity that made my overall situation more complicated and worse than it was. My irrational worries and narrow focus on how I could not financially help my wife and family almost became a self fulfilling prophecy for me: I wallowed in self-pity and moved slowly on filing for unemployment benefits. You know what? I almost lost those benefits because I took so long to file for them. In fact I was too late! But to my surprise a bit of luck came my way, giving me a second chance to file. Wasting no time, I got the paperwork in on time with no delay, and my life became much better because I could alleviate our financial burden with my unemployment benefits. The blessings didn't stop there! After we had paid our bills with our strict budget, we discovered some extra money left over which we could use to treat ourselves with. So for the first time in a long time we could go on romantic dates to celebrate our loving relationship. Though I hadn't yet found work, I began to look for employment using a more calm and positive approach. This would be better for my marriage and would fulfill the promise I made to my wife.

Chapter 2

On the horizon a new job

Another month went by. That made it six months since I was laid off... But I wasn't going to worry about it, for the sake of my marriage and to follow the promise I had made to my wife. Anyway, Thanksgiving was coming up! So I concerned myself with driving to the grocery market to pick up the turkey my wife had asked me to pick up a week ago. In fact, I promised myself that I was going to get that turkey before my wife returned home from work. After finding my car keys and retrieving my coat from the closet, I walked towards the door to leave the house. As I reached the door the telephone rang, so I returned to answer it. Surprising me again, it was my buddy Mr. Jerome Harper. I hadn't heard from him in a while, but there he was on the other end of the line with exciting news concerning the possibility of a job. Before I could say anything, he pointed out that the job didn't pay anything close to what I was making at the auto plant.

"But," he continued jokingly, "beggars can't be choosy. Besides, I know how hard you're searching for a job, and I want to do whatever it takes to help you. Anyway, my wife Christina provided me with the information about this job. She became aware of an opening at a public middle school on the northwest side of Detroit where she was principal."

Before allowing him to go any further, I interrupted Jerome and asked him what the job was. He hesitated at first.

"It's a janitorial position."

"Ok," I replied, "where do I apply for the job?"

"My wife said you should go downtown and fill out the job application in person immediately," Jerome answered, "if possible early tomorrow morning. Anyway, she overheard the supervisor of the janitorial staff inform one of the secretaries in her office about a janitorial position being open. If she knows anyone looking for a job should apply as soon as possible."

After Jerome had delivered this much-needed piece of information, we began to reminisce about the good times we'd had. Eventually I had to stop him, telling him about the Thanksgiving turkey I had to pick up from the grocery market.

"Ok man, I understand," he replied, "I'm going to get off this phone now and let you take care of that." Before hanging up the phone, I thanked Jerome again for the tip, and told him how nice it was to hear from him. I set my pride aside and admitted to him that I needed that phone call to brighten up my day with a element of hope, but I also told him that I didn't want my family and friends to worry about me too much.

I enjoyed the moment with a smile on my face. I walked out the door to go and pick up our Thanksgiving turkey with a little extra pep in my step. In fact, even after I'd been to the grocery store and picked up the turkey, I was still bouncing with excitement. My drive home was much shorter – I couldn't wait to tell my wife the good news! Arriving home, I saw my wife's car already in the driveway – though I was excited, I must admit I was also a bit anxious. I immediately parked my car and hurried into the house with the Thanksgiving turkey in hand. I spotted my wife cooking dinner in the kitchen. I walked over to tell her the good news, but before I could say anything, my wife asked me how I was doing.

"Why are you wearing that silly Cool-Aid smile?"

"You might want to sit down for this sweetheart, because the silly smile on my face is the result of a phone call I received this evening from my best buddy Jerome. Jerome told me about the possibility of a job! His wife Christine learned about the job today at her work, and had Jerome deliver the message to me as soon as possible. So he called me this evening. Jerome said I should go downtown and fill out the job application tomorrow morning as early as possible." I smiled at my wife. "I can't wait for tomorrow morning! I really feel this is the break I'm looking for!"

Sophia gave me a hug and kiss.

"I am so happy for you! If you don't mind me asking, what is the job?"

"It's a janitorial job. Jerome said that it doesn't pay all that well... but, that's ok with me, because I'm willing to take a pay cut if it can help us to get by. Anything is better than nothing, right?"

"Of course that's fine baby," Sophia answered, "I'm going to support you no matter what. But in the meantime, let's wait until you get the job before we start any celebrating."

* * *

The next morning I was calm – but still excited. I was more than ready for the cool but crisp November morning. Before I left the house, I ate a delicious breakfast that my wife had cooked for me. As I walked out the door, she gave me a hug and kiss for last-minute support. My goal was to be as punctual as possible. Anyway, I made it to the building in downtown Detroit where the job application was to be filled out without having to drive like a bat out of hell and unnecessarily endangering lives on the roadways! So that was good. I arrived at 8:00 am, and after I parked my car I went straight into the building and stopped at the front desk. After saying good morning to the guard, I asked her for directions to the office where I had to fill out the application for the janitorial position.

"Take the elevator over there to the third floor, walk to the end of the hallway and enter the last door to your right, marked room 335," she replied.

I thanked her and walked off to the elevator. After reaching room 335 I was greeted by a secretary sitting at the front desk.

"How can I be of assistance?"

"I'm here to fill out an application for the janitorial position," I responded.

She smiled. "Ok sir, just sign this form and sit over there and wait until your name is called. By the way sir," she added as I walked towards the chair, "you will be called in order according to your arrival. Also, please have your picture identification and social security card ready."

I thanked her walked over to the chair to sit down. While sitting there, I flipped through a magazine that I picked up off the table adjacent to my chair. Only then did I realize that I was the first one there! Another man walked through the door after a little while, and he was also told to take a seat as well. He sat down just a couple of seats away from me, two seats to my left. I took notice of his nervousness when he said good morning to me, and I greeted him politely in return. Before I knew it, he was beginning to explain the source of his nervousness. He told me his name was Melvin, and that he was worried he wasn't going to get the janitorial job.

"I didn't get much of an education," he continued, "and I think that has cost me lots of jobs in the past." At this point his nerves and lack of confidence got the best of him. He began to convince himself to leave. He stood up from his seat, with intent to walk out the door. I talked him out of walking out, but as he sat down again I could tell he was still nervous. After that, the room began to slowly fill up. Eventually, the room filled to capacity – yet it was surprisingly quiet, with only a few conversations taking place. I wondered what the holdup was. It was now 9:00 a.m. and no one had been called yet. Eventually, I put the magazine down. Finally, Melvin and I were both called up. Once called, I followed the receptionist into another office located behind the waiting room. After stepping through the doorway, I saw a room filled with cubicles, each outfitted with two chairs, a desk and a computer. Following her instructions, I took a seat at one of the cubicles. After sitting down at the cubicle, another lady sat down in the opposite chair and handed me an application form. She informed me that after I had filled out the application form, we would have an interview, if I had time to stay for that. As she asked to see my identification, I replied enthusiastically.

"Yes! I can stay for the job interview."

Once I was done filling out my job application, the interview began. Everything was going just smoothly, until a colleague of the lady interviewing me interrupted the interview with a partially filled out application form in her hand. She said to my interviewer that the client she was serving was just wasting her time.

"This guy Melvin! He has no educational background, not even a GED. But you know what? He had the nerve to write dyslexia on his job application form where it asked if he had any medical problems or conditions that might prevent him from doing the job. How dare he put such foolishness on a job application," she continued, "we all know dyslexia is not a recognized serious disorder where you need to take medication, or need to use medical devices like a wheelchair or crutches or a seeing eye dog. It's just a fancy word that lazy people use for an excuse."

After taking a breath, she finally acknowledged my presence and apologized for interrupting my interview. She then asked my opinion of individuals who decided to drop out of school! But she didn't give me much chance to talk.

"They get the system to take care of them because they can't get a job, and they blame everyone else for their decision to drop out of school! They're a burden on the overall system as well as society at large."

I wasn't sure what I should say.

"I agree with most of what you are saying," I began, "because I personally feel there are no good reasons anyone should drop out of school. I'm sorry to say it, but those who do are just being lazy or irresponsible. I don't have a lot of respect for people who make bad decisions and expect others to come to their rescue, who don't want to take responsibility for themselves."

Before I could go on, she stopped me.

"I agree with you one hundred per cent," she said. "I am so tired of dealing with that type of mentality, and we see it so often in here. You know, there are so many of them! You know what I'm going to do with this job application I have in my hand? I'm going to file it in my dumb bell file which is that small trash can that's right in that back corner of the office."

Before my interviewer could say anything to her, she had already balled up Melvin's job application and cocked her arm back like a pro basketball player. She launched a clean precision shot straight into the trash can, and then danced a little dance. She walked away, saying how she was going to give Mr. Melvin a call in the morning to tell him that he did not fit the criteria.

After the interruption, my interview resumed. My interviewer apologized for her colleague's behavior. The rest of the interview took about twenty five minutes. I felt pretty good about it, because at the end the lady gave me a firm handshake and told me to go to room 405 on the fourth floor to have my picture taken for an ID card. She also instructed me to return to this room after having my picture taken to pick up my work schedule papers which would show me the time, date and location of the job. I'd got the job! I looked up and thanked my Heavenly Father for the blessing. You wouldn't believe how happy I was!

On my way to the elevator I met up with Melvin in the hallway at a water fountain. He said he was about to return to room 335 to pick up his ID and other information from the lady who had interviewed him, as he had forgotten them at the end of the interview. Once I saw him, I began to feel kind of bad about his situation, because I witnessed his job application being tossed into a trash can. But he appeared to be in good spirits. He had a smile on his face.

"Mr. Johnson," he said, "I think the lady who interviewed me was truly wonderful. She told me to expect a phone call in the morning – and when she said that she had given me the thumbs up with a smile on her face!"

He was clearly excited. So I decided not to be a barrel of bad news for him and kept my mouth shut. Keeping the conversation short and sweet, I'm sad to say I was able to pull it off. Soon after I got into the elevator, I wished him good luck, despite the situation not sitting right with my conscience. Anyway, I made it to room 405 and had my ID picture taken. I then returned to the office and picked up my work schedule, and then I left to drive home.

I arrived home to the delicious aroma of Thanksgiving turkey cooking in the oven. Oh I tell you, your mouth would water at the amazing things that I could smell cooking in the kitchen. I found my wife in the kitchen, preparing things for the following day's Thanksgiving dinner. I tried hard to restrain myself from sampling the food, but as you can probably guess, I wasn't very successful. But at least I said hello to my wife, giving her a big hug and a kiss before I sampled the food. Boy was it delicious. When I had finished sampling the food, my wife looked at me and asked how my day was. I put on a sad face, saying that it wasn't very good at all. She was about to give me her inspirational don't give up speech, before I laughed.

"I'm just kidding!" I said. "I got the job."

Her face and eyes lit up. She wrapped her arms around me and gave me a big hug and a kiss.

"I told you everything would be all right," she said. "How special our Thanksgiving Day is going to be! It's truly going to be a thankful day after the blessing from God you received today!"

We continued to talk, play and enjoy each other's company, while I pitched in to help my wife prepare the rest of the food for our Thanksgiving dinner. But before I knew it, my conscience got the best of me, putting a damper on our joyful time. I explained to my wife what had happened to Melvin at the job interview earlier in the day. Before allowing my wife to say anything, my guilt and self-righteousness took over.

"If he hadn't have dropped out of school that wouldn't have happened," I said.

"First of all," my wife responded, "that lady was wrong for tossing that man's job application in the trash can like that. She's eliminating his chances and stopping him from bettering himself. He's just going to stay on the system, someone the rest of us have to take care of." She looked at me. "I'm also a bit disappointed in you, because you're usually more caring than that... But you're also wrong in your judgment, because you don't know where that man has been or what he's going through."

I told my wife that she was right. I felt so bad about myself and I couldn't do anything about it. So I just dropped my head in shame.

"I love you baby," my wife said, "but you shouldn't make judgments about others, because we're not perfect. I hope you gain some wisdom from all of this. But in the meantime, let's not spoil this evening! I still love you very much dear! Before we go on any further Jeremiah," she paused, "are you ever going to tell me when your work starts?"

"I'm sorry sweetheart," I answered, "I start work this coming Monday. 8:00 a.m. on December 1th. And I am anxiously awaiting that day."

* * *

So Thanksgiving Day arrived. As I was watching a college ball game on television, Sophia called for me to come and help her with some last-minute dinner preparations before our guests arrived.

"Ok honey," I called back, but it took me a little while to peel myself away from the television. Eventually I made it to the dining room and gave her a hug.

"We don't have time for that!" she said to me, blushing and laughing. After she had my undivided attention, she began to instruct me on what she needed me to do. Once we were finished with those last-minute dinner table preparations, the result was magnificent. Our layouts closely resembled a Norman Rockwell painting. She proudly stepped back for a moment to admire our last-minute dinner table preparations, looking like an artist admiring their first masterpiece. While she was admiring the visual look of the Thanksgiving dinner table arrangement with all its delightful trimmings, I began to admire my wife's beautiful visual profile. I tell you, she's a beautiful work of art. But before my thoughts could escalate into fantasy, they were abruptly interrupted by my wife asking me to do her a very important favor.

"Sure sweetie," I replied.

She continued to speak to me with a concerned look on her face. She asked me to promise her that I would enjoy this wonderful Thanksgiving Day and leave my worries behind, at least for this day. I responded by giving her a hug, telling her that she had nothing to worry about.

"I plan to be on my best behavior today, since I consciously gave myself permission to enjoy myself and have a good time. I am also acknowledging this day as a personal celebration day in response to yesterday's achievement in getting a job." Everyone deserves to have a good time in their life at some point!

"You're right, Jeremiah!" Sophia answered. "We will have a good time today."

Before we could take another moment to admire our exquisite Thanksgiving Day dinner table, the doorbell rang. Our guest had arrived, including family and friends and other special guests such as our daughter Alicia. She'd brought some of her college friends. My best buddy Jerome and his wife Christina also came, but they couldn't stay long because they had another engagement. I said that was ok, because our house was already filled to capacity. Despite the many conversations that began to saturate the air of our house, the real party celebration didn't start until I had managed to gain everyone's attention and verbally welcomed everyone to our home. I asked that everyone take some one else's hand, so that I could initiate the proper blessing of the Thanksgiving Day dinner we were about to serve to our honored guests. After blessing the Thanksgiving dinner with prayer, a proud but profound moment took place – unknown to everyone but my wife – when I walked (or even strutted, according to my wife!) over to take my place at the head of the dinner table for the traditional Thanksgiving Day turkey carving. My wife knew that moment represented more than just being a king in my own castle, it represented that I was once again the man of my house, worth the respect and love of my wife and family. I was really feeling my manhood and confidence return. It's no secret that I hadn't been feeling much like a man before that.

Soon after the ceremony of blessing the Thanksgiving dinner and carving the turkey was over, the party was on! We put on the Temptations and other Motown hits, and we ate and drank and cheered. Some of us watched the sport on the television, some of us watched a movie on cable, some of us played cards. I even let my daughter and her flamboyant friends play some of that hip-hop, rhythm & blues and rap. But I made sure it was clean music. Well, that made them feel welcome too. Suddenly, in the midst of looking around to make sure that everyone was enjoying themselves and had everything they needed, it hit me that I was actually having a good time and enjoying myself! It made me so happy to see the smile on my wife's face as she received heart felt compliments about the dinner from our family and friends. After the long but pleasant dinner, we brought our Thanksgiving party to a close at about 12:30p.m. With warm handshakes and hugs and kisses, our guests left to go home, and our daughter left to hang out with her friends. So we were once again in a quite, empty house. We were so exhausted that we decided that we would straighten things up in the morning, so we took a nice warm shower and fell straight into bed.

* * *

At about 10:45a.m. the next day we were awoken by our daughter, who had stopped by to help us clean up the house. I think she also wanted to spend a bit more time with her parents, who she loved and dearly missed. She was going back to college pretty soon, where she lived with her friends in a dorm room on campus. Having Alicia at home was a great pleasure, especially when she assisted in cleaning up the house. So we finished cleaning the house with time to spare, which meant that we could take her out to a movie and dinner. I guess we all must have been very tired from yesterday, because as soon as we returned home from the movie and dinner we all went straight to bed. The next day we were all rested and enjoying each other's company. A bit of family time before Alicia went back to college. Nevertheless, our family time was soon interrupted by a phone call at about 6 o'clock that evening, with the person on the other end asking to speak to our daughter.

"Alicia, telephone!" I called out to my daughter from across the living room.

"Thank you daddy!" she replied.

After she'd walked across the living room, I handed her the phone, saying "you're welcome baby!"

Once Alicia was done speaking on the phone she announced to us that she had to get ready and pack her stuff for college, because her friends were coming to pick her up at 6:30 p.m. to take her over to their house to spend the night together. I guess it was more convenient for them all to be together as they could then leave early on Sunday morning and ride back to college together.

"Are you guys alright with that?" Alicia asked.

"It's ok," Sophia replied, "just make sure that when you arrive on campus, you give us a call as soon as possible. Let us know you've made it there safely."

"Ok!" She said, and then she walked upstairs to her bedroom to pack her things. Moments later she was back downstairs, with a suitcase in her hand. She placed it on the floor near the front door, and then proceeded to the kitchen where she ate dinner with us. After that, we all sat down on the couch to watch television, while Alicia waited for her friends. I tell you, they weren't very punctual. They arrived at 8:45 p.m. So finally, with misty eyes and passionately telling us how much she loved us, she surprised us by simultaneously giving us a big hug and kiss on each one of our cheeks. We reciprocated her loving affection, before watching our precious daughter get into her friend's metallic blue minivan and drive off towards their house. I looked over to my wife.

"You can breathe again now honey, she'll be all right. She's with all her friends, who she grew up with. They're all as mature and responsible as she is."

"You're right sweetheart," she replied, "she's protected by the blood of Jesus. But nevertheless, I still worry about our daughter. I guess I'm just a concerned parent."

"I know, Jeremiah. I feel the same every day… and just about all day. Every time I think about our little angel, our only child, out in the world it concerns me dearly. So I guess I just try not to think about it too much, because it only makes me extraordinarily anxious." We turned and walked back into the house and finished watching our movie. And then we went to bed, not long after the movie ended.

And then it was Sunday, one day before my first day of work. My wife and I got ourselves ready for church, while waiting for the call we were anticipating from our daughter. She eventually called, and both of us breathed a sigh of relief and thanked God for our daughter's safe return to college. I think that waiting for our daughter's phone call kind of temporarily impaired my wife's attention, because Sophia misplaced her Bible while we were getting ready for church. Luckily, I could return a favor to my wife and retrieve her Bible from the cocktail table in the living room. I handed it to her and she gave me a kiss and thanked me. We then hurried out the door to the car and headed straight to church. We weren't as late as we thought we would be, especially considering the forty five minutes of traveling time it normally takes us to drive to our church. When we arrived, we realized that the morning service was still in progress. I count this as a blessing in itself, because we didn't miss my favorite pastor O'Neal Raleigh give his explosively inspirational, spiritual and motivational sermon. In fact, I haven't missed one of his sermons yet. Anyway, since we were fairly late for church that day, my wife and I had to sit in the pews near the back of the church. From there we thought it would be difficult to hear the pastor preaching, but despite the challenge, I was still able to hear everything just fine. So soon after the soulful musicians with all their instruments and the voices of the church choir finished, pastor O'Neal Raleigh stood at the front of his church choir and began to deliver his sermon for the day. This was the moment I had been waiting for, because I was in desperate need of spiritual therapy and rejuvenation of my faith after all that I had recently been through. This was particularly soon after the last six months of unemployment. I truly felt drained in spirit and soul. But that's ok, because on that day, I knew I was where I needed to be to rectify my spiritual distress. I was also looking forward to pastor O'Neal Raleigh giving me the necessary spiritual strength I would need for my everyday life. I was particularly thinking about the spiritual reinforcement I would need for my first day of work the following day, and the weeks that would follow. In fact, I was thinking about the next day so much that at that point my wife had to tap me on my legs and quietly ask me to be quiet so that she could hear the pastor's preaching.

"Ok, sweetheart", I replied, and quietly apologized for my unaware thought outburst. I'm glad my wife interrupted my thoughts, because I was so deep in them that I was unaware that the pastor's preaching was already in progress. At that point, loud cries and shouts of "Amen" and "Thank you Jesus" began to echo throughout the church – this clearly marked the beginning of his sermon for the day. So as soon as I realized what I was missing out on, I began to pay close attention to all that was being said. I didn't want to miss out on the message for the betterment of my spiritual health that he was giving! Once again I praised God, because I was more than normally impressed by the sermon delivered that day. Pastor O'Neal Raleigh is a man that is truly blessed with God's calling in his life, and I tell you he inspires everyone around him. I can feel in his spirit and I can see in his daily actions a genuine, decent, honest and honorable soul full of integrity. And if I respectfully add, I truly believe that he is representing God well in his ministry, standing above all those greedy, egotistical, self-centered, self righteous, selfish, self appointed pastors and ministers that are causing all sorts of destruction to humankind!

Anyway, soon after pastor O'Neil Raleigh closed his sermon with a prayer and ended church for the day, my wife and I maneuvered our way through the crowds of people exiting through the church house doors. We stopped for a moment and chatted briefly with a couple of church brothers and sisters that we hadn't seen or heard from in a while (due to their lengthy absence from church), before we got into our car and drove off the church parking lot. After leaving the church grounds, we headed west for the 96 Jeffries Expressway. As we drove up the entrance ramp, my wife looked over at me for a while, and asked me if I was ready for my first day of work tomorrow.

"Not really!" I answered. "I want to wear a new suit to make a good first impression on my first day of work, but sadly that's out of the question, what with our current financial situation."

My wife responded by reminding me that we had just left church, and that worrying about things without faith in God gets us nowhere.

"Were you actually listening to your favorite pastor's sermon at all today?" She asked. "Yes I was listening sweetheart, you're right."

"Ok then," she said, "I hope your temporary spiritual relapse is over now and your faith has been restored Jeremiah because I have a plan. We are going to stop at the shopping mall that's about a half mile west of the South Field expressway just on Hubbard street, and we're going to get you a new suit without worrying about the money."

"That's sound like a good plan!" I smiled. And just as I said that, I began to see the shopping mall in the distance, with all those cars parked out front. So we pulled up in the parking lot, and as soon as we had parked I immediately got out of the car and walked around to the passenger's side of the car to open the door for my wife. Once we were inside the shopping mall, we traveled from one men's clothing store to another, until I'd finally found a suit that was just the right size, color and style. So I was satisfied – but do you know what my wife did? She not only bought me the suit, but also got me a new pair of black patent leather dress shoes and a tie to go with the suit. I was so happy! I gave my wife a big hug and a kiss and said "thank you honey!" right in front of the cashier. He smiled at us and wished us a good day. So we walked back out of the mall to our car, and I again opened the car door for my wife like a perfect gentleman. I placed my suit, shoes and tie in the car, and we drove off with the intention of going straight home, because we were both so hungry after the church service and shopping at the mall. But our hunger got the better of us, and we had to make a quick stop at a small fast food chicken restaurant where the chicken is actually finger licking good. So once we were done eating our chicken dinner, we returned to the road.

We were having a beautiful conversation driving home, until my wife started to yawn once or twice, and then fell sound asleep with her head resting on my shoulder. Moments after my wife had gone to sleep, I found myself struggling to stay awake as well, what with the boredom of just looking through the car windshield at the road. So I turned the car radio on to keep me awake and make sure I wasn't too bored. But that didn't really work too well. What did work however was when my mind began to reflect on my pastor's sermon that day. Thinking about that, I began to ask Jesus to forgive me once again for the mean-spirited role I played in judging Melvin during the day of the job interview, when I set aside my Christianity and participated in a sinful attack against Melvin which was wrong. It was a serious personal, spiritual transgression. I truly believe that the pursuit of redemption is necessary in order to grow my spiritual dignity. Furthermore, I could safely say that this new level of Christianity I was feeling in my soul would provide me with the necessary wisdom and discipline to help me to restrain my tongue or restrain any actions that would take me out of the divine order or compromise my overall personal relationship with my Heavenly Father. And do you know what? Pastor O'Neal Raleigh's sermon had a tremendous impact on my spiritual consciousness, causing a profound but welcome spiritual rebirthing within the fabric of my being. I really believe I now have a better perspective on why it's so important to treat everything under God's blue skies with dignity and respect. When the pastor's preaching evolved into a heartfelt plea with eyes full of sadness and a facial expression of pure disappointment in his parishioners, he began to ask in the name of Jesus Christ for all to hear with more than a fresh ear, but with a spiritual ear. He then began to articulate his preaching in that loud but kind voice, washing therapeutic and electrifying words of tough love over us. His voice and dialect had the power to move the spirits of any church congregation, and especially when his joyful spiritual energy caused him to pace back and forth, like he was dancing in front of the altar. He began his sermon with a plea.

"In the name of Jesus Christ," he cried, "just stop all that unholy hypocrisy! Just stop those condescending behaviors and stop sinfully judging others! All of this usually causes nothing but destruction to one another's spirituality, which eventually results in people fleeing the church and becoming lost in the world forever. A wall can be created by such foolishness that will prevent others from seeking God and from growing their Christianity and spirituality by way of the church. Not only that, but such behaviors will unfairly tarnish the reputation of genuine Christian folks, making it harder in today's society for them to perform their Christian duty. This is all because of those who daily step out of line in the name of God and Jesus Christ with holier than thou attitudes stemming from spiritual arrogance.

"Oh there are those who believe that anything can be done and justified in the name of Jesus Christ," he continued. "Well I'm here to tell you that is spiritually counterproductive and not the will of God!" After this call, the pastor was compelled to make another spiritual plea to those Christian brothers and sisters engaging in such practices that cause nothing but deterioration and destruction to the overall body of Jesus Christ's doctoring and legacy.

"Just stop it now!" He cried once again. "Don't tell another living soul that they're dammed and going straight to hell. In fact, you need to seriously focus on redemption and repenting today for the sake of your own soul, you need to humbly ask for forgiveness while you climb down from your nose bleed spiritual high horse or pedestal where you reside above all those spiritual infidels that are not worthy enough to be in your divine presence, as your self-righteousness dictates to you..."

Unfortunately, I am sorry to announce that my thoughts ended at that point, as I heard my wife shaking off her sleep.

"Why are we driving past the house?" She asked me groggily.

"I am so sorry honey!" I replied. "I was so distracted by my thoughts that I simply wasn't paying attention."

I safely stopped the car and backed up into a neighbor's driveway across the street, then turned around to drive back to our driveway. My wife and I had safely made it home.

Gradually, the day became night and the evening came to a close. After we had dinner and watched a little television, our tiredness caused us to prepare for bed early. I needed to get some rest for my first day of work the next day. So we retire to bed at about 8:30 p.m., and my wife and I embraced each other with a loving hug and a passionate kiss while sitting at the foot of our bed. We briefly discussed a couple of concerns about my first day of work. We also expressed our overall love for each other, stressing how much we appreciated each other. Before we got in bed and cuddled up against one another, we first made sure our bedtime prayers were said. After the sermon in church that day had given me a much needed spiritual boost, I really felt more than ready for my first day of work tomorrow... despite the way my nerves were twisting as I lay in bed. What would the first day of work be like?

* * *

So the next morning arrived. I had no problem getting up for work, because I'd hardly slept a wink. I simply couldn't wait any longer to go to work and get started! Part of this was excitement, part of this was nerves – I wasn't used to getting up in the morning to go to work! Anyway, after taking a shower, brushing my teeth and dressing in my brand new traditional black well ironed suit, with my new shoes and tie – with a little splash of cologne – I then proceeded to head out of the bedroom and down the stairs to the kitchen. I sat down at the kitchen table and was presented with another breakfast fit for a king! After eating that delicious hot breakfast made by my wife with love and patience, she shared some encouraging words with me before I left the house. As I left the house I turned and looked into my wife's beautiful eyes, telling her that I loved her so much. I gave her a kiss and a hug and hurried out the door. I wanted to arrive at work on time!

In no time at all I arrived at work. I parked my car in the employee parking lot. I shut off my car's motor and the CD drive (I was playing a motivational speaker's CD), before I unfastened my car seatbelt and exited the car. So then I walked towards the Walter Allen Ivan combined Elementary and Middle School, located on Joy Road street east of Green Field street on the Northwest side of Detroit. This was where I was going to work. With a smile on my face and my confidence at an all time high, I walked down the sidewalk leading to the front door of the school building. I was ready and eager to start my new work day! Although the journey to the front door was short, I still managed to take in the beautiful fall weather with its slight cool breeze, particularly after what had been such a long, hot summer. I looked at the trees, with their beautiful leaves falling in the breeze and partially covering the school's nicely groomed lawn. I also saw the excitement of the parents, driving up and parking in front of the school building, then escorting their children safely into the school building. They were much like the crossing guards, who with stop signs made sure that all the children could walk safely across the street to the school. Just watching all this brought back wonderful memories of the time my wife and I had brought our daughter to school for the first time. She was just knee-high and full of energy! She had such a beautiful happiness within her, and boy she loved going to school. She really loved her wonderful teachers and classmates, and really understood that they cared for her. When we walked her up the front steps for the first time, her eyes were wide and she had such a beautiful smile. She was skipping along, asking a ton of questions. She was always very inquisitive, and she loved the attention that I guess my wife and I were very guilty of providing. I thank God for those beautiful and precious memories that I will never forget. I'll hold on to those precious memories for ever.

I finally reached the front entrance of the Walter Allen Ivan public school building. With a couple more steps, I thought to myself, I'll be walking through the door and into a new job – a new beginning. I was ready to experience everything that life had to offer. Anyway, I walked straight to the school office, where I was told to report on my first day. When I walked into the school office, I was cordially greeted by one of the school secretaries.

"Good morning sir! How are you doing today?" The school secretaries and the other office staff all smiled at me. One in particular asked for my name and how she could assist me.

"Good morning," I replied, "my name is Mr. Jeremiah Johnson. I am here to meet with Ms. Cheryl Washington, the janitorial supervisor."

"Ok! Just take a seat over there while I page Ms. Washington to let her know you are here," she said.

"Thank you!" I replied, and then I took a seat. While I sat patiently waited for Ms. Washington to arrive, I began to distract myself by observing my surroundings. I looked up at the soothing light turquoise ceilings tiles, then at the decorative light fixtures and the beautiful multicolored mosaic patterning the floors. I looked at the variety of people flowing in and out of the office, and listened to all their different conversations. I heard the noise of children in the hallways outside of the office door, changing with different bells. At this point, my observations ended as the pleasant aroma of coffee, tea and doughnuts began to saturate the air.

"Would you like a doughnut and a coffee sir?" one of the secretaries asked me.

"No thank you," I replied. My rather large breakfast was still filling my stomach. After a while, my attention was soon directed towards the school principal's friendly and familiar face – my best friend's wife. She walked into the office with a smile on her face.

"Good morning Jeremiah! How are you doing today? Are you being assisted?" She asked.

"Yes ma'am I am," I replied.

"Ok!" she replied. With her professional demeanor, she continued to walk over to speak with a parent who had arrived at the office before me. Before I could take a peek at my watch, I heard a soft-spoken woman entering the school office. She walked over to the office secretaries.

"Good morning," she said politely, "did you page me over the intercom?"

"Yes," replied the secretary as she pointed in my direction, "that gentleman sitting over there is here for you."

"Thank you!" Ms. Washington replied. She smiled and walked over to me. She extended her hand and I stood up to receive her firm handshake.

"Hello!" she said. Before I could reply, she continued to talk. "You must be Mr. Jeremiah Johnson, our new janitor. I've been expecting you, and I'm so glad you were able to make it this beautiful Monday morning." Eventually, I was able to say good morning back to her, and express to her how much I was looking forward to working at the school. She asked me to come with her so that she could get me situated. We walked out of the school office and down the hallway – I had to work to keep up with her fast-pace! As she walked, she asked me if I had ever worked in a janitorial position before.

"No!" I replied, "I have worked many other jobs, but never as a janitor."

"So what was your last job – if you don't mind me asking?"

"I worked in an auto plant for more than twenty years before I was laid off," I replied.

"I'm sorry to hear that," she replied.

"Thank you," I said. "I'm OK," I added, "I've learned to move on with my life despite the difficulties I had to face while I was out of work. I experienced a lot of mental and financial distress. But at least, while being laid off was painful, it was humbling. It taught me to use my situation and experience to grow, enhancing my spirituality and level of wisdom. I focused on all the positive things in my life, and that helped me to cope with the negative things as well. Anyway, I thank God for blessing me with this job – you just can't imagine what I had to go through before this. I am so thankful for this job and to be working once again!"

"Your attitude is inspiring," she replied, "particularly after such a difficult time."

We continued to walk down the halls, without talking very much. We passed lots of lockers, and a few children who were running late. Although I had no idea where we were going, my excitement at starting the new job was still at an all time high. In my mind I continued to thank God for the employment He had provided me with. I thought about the new beginning that was open to me, and the blessings that I believed I would continue to receive as long as I stayed in the divine order. As we reached the janitorial office, I paused for a moment to quench my thirst, taking a sip of water from a stainless steel water fountain affixed to the wall adjacent to the door. Ms. Washington stopped and turned to me before we entered the office.

"All the janitorial staff are required to report in at this office to sign in and sign out every day," she began. "This is also where you'll pick up your paycheck, and where you'll receive your assignment each day. If you have any questions, problems or concerns, you should come to this office immediately and speak to me. I'm usually in here working on paperwork on the computer, but if you come at 11:30 a.m. I can't guarantee it, because I'll probably be on my lunch break. Do you have any questions that you would like to ask me at this point?"

Before I could say anything, she once again began to speak. "It's important that I tell you this before I forget: you have a union, and whenever you need to speak to me with union representation, I'll make sure you are provided for. So anyway, do you have any questions for me?"

Before allowing her to say anything else, I quickly spoke.

"Yes! When do I get started and when can I meet my coworkers?"

With a nervous laugh she said "I guess now!" We proceeded to walk through the door of the janitorial maintenance office. Just about everyone in the office looked up and said hello. Before Ms. Washington could properly introduce me to my new coworkers, I immediately spoke up, giving a good morning salutation to all my new coworkers with a big smile, matching the smiles on most of their faces.

"My name is Mr. Jeremiah Johnson," I said, "I take great pleasure in being here. I am really looking forward to working with you guys, and getting to know you on an individual basis."

Once I was done speaking, a lady sitting against the wall near the back corner of the office put down her magazine and spoke up. After a nervous giggle she said "My name is Ms. Janice Oxford." Following this, a young man in his early twenties said "What's up man! How are you doing? My name is Mr. Cyrus Noble and the ladies call me Mr. Blanket. And that's because when I wrap my arms around a woman she tells me it's like a security blanket of loving. Ha, I'm just kidding man!" Before I could laugh, a lady sitting at a table near the center of the office (I guess she was eating breakfast and reading her Bible) interrupted. She told me her name was Mrs. Abigail Bailey. Two other ladies standing by the office's wastebasket, having a meeting of their own, then spoke up.

"How are you doing," said one. "My name is Ms. Paula Gooden and my buddy standing next to me is Mrs. Bernice Littlefield."

"Hello Mr. Jeremiah Johnson," said Mrs. Littlefield, "I hope you enjoy working here, because this is a nice place to work, in spite of the pay being not so great. Most of us have been working here for more than five years."

After I responded to Mrs. Bernice Littlefield, a gentleman with a gray patch in his hair and a voice as deep as Berry White's, sitting in a seat behind the office computer at the desk to the left of Ms. Washington's desk, looked up with a smile.

"Hello and good morning sir," he said in a friendly tone. "Mr. Jeremiah Johnson, my name is Mr. Nathan Jones, I am Ms. Cheryl Washington's assistant janitorial maintenance supervisor and will serve as an alternate when she's not here or unable to assist you with any questions or concerns or problems you might have."

"Thank you, I appreciate that," I replied. At that point I observed that one man had not yet introduced himself to me. He was a young man, sitting quietly in an office chair in the corner opposite the two ladies standing near trash cans. His head was down, as if he was purposely choosing to be antisocial, oblivious to all that was going on around him. He seemed to be sketching with a pencil on a pad of paper, saying absolutely nothing to anyone. For some reason, his behavior made me feel a little uneasy – to the point where I had to seriously ask myself what I was getting into. As I further observed this young man, I realized he was probably in his late 30s or early 40s. He was just sitting in his seat as if he was invisible and simply didn't exist in the world. His demeanor was starting to really concern me in a negative way, because one of the ladies, I don't remember which one, said in a disrespectful way to him, "Stop being so rude with your antisocial butt and speak to the new employee that will be working with us." At this point I could see that he was obviously annoyed with his co-worker, and he stopped sketching in his sketch pad and began to raise his head slowly towards this lady, looking – I'm not kidding – like a demon emerging from the pits of hell. He was something like you see in one of those scary horror movies, what with all that anger... but maybe there was also some sadness in his face and eyes. Anyway, he looked over in the direction of the lady who had spoken to him, but he spoke to Ms. Washington in a threatening voice.

"Tell that lady over there to shut up talking to me, because I am sitting here minding my own business and not bothering anyone. She better stop trying to tell me what to do, because the last time I checked," he said, "you are my supervisor, Ms. Washington." He looked aggressively at Ms. Washington. "Would you say something to her? I am tired of her saying stuff to me." He continued to talk, though at this stage he was almost mumbling under his breath. "Nobody is doing anything about it... I guess someday I'm going to have to handle this matter myself, or else no one will ever take me seriously and leave me the hell alone." He then resumed his anti-social stance.

Chapter 3

Drama in the workplace

I stood there, amazed at the drama and the animosity existing in my new work place. There I was, in my brand new clothes, trying to make the best impression I could. And there were my new colleagues. I tell you, I was sorely disappointed. All this negative behavior was leaving a bad taste in my mouth. It was unprofessional and downright deplorable. I was thinking that I didn't want to work with or even know any of these people. They could at least have waited a couple of days before airing their dirty laundry in front of me. The only thing I could think to do was to ask God for strength. This must be a test I thought, because I'm just about ready to run right out of here without looking back. But since my wife and family were counting on me – and because leaving might have brought on an even worse situation – I couldn't leave. Well, I decided at this point, I better start coping with the situation by at least bringing something positive to the table. A man has to do what a man has to do, whether he likes it or not. Anyway, what happened next made things even worse. The drama continued. When the young man had finished talking, he was met with seriously disrespectful laughter from the lady who had initiated the conflict. Even worse, just about all the other coworkers joined in at his expense. As you would expect, he became very angry and upset in return. In the face of the escalating attack, he soon realized that engaging in battle was futile. So he turned his head down again, and resumed sketching in his pad with a deeper and more disturbing concentration, ignoring the mean-spirited comments being quickly directed at him, such as "He is so stupid" and "He does nothing but get on people's nerves." Eventually, Ms. Washington lost her cool and shouted.

"Just stop it! Stop it now! If another person says anything else out of line, I will write you up for disciplinary action. You'll be needing the assistance of your union representative if another inappropriate thing is said!" she yelled. After that, she insisted that all the staff go to their assigned areas and perform their janitorial duties. She had a look of disappointment on her face when she turned back to me.

"I'm so sorry you had to witness this craziness, especially on your first day of work. Mr. Johnson I'd like to apologize for my whole staff. Believe it or not, there are some days when they all behave professionally."

I thought to myself that I had no idea what just happened. But I felt a need to respond anyway, so I said that we all have bad days sometimes. Before I could say anything else, the young man sitting there sketching in his sketch pad proceeded to get up out of his chair and casually walk towards me. I tell you that scared me half to death, because I didn't know what his intentions were, what with all that anger he'd just expressed. I tell you I even thought about just running out of that office again, I didn't know what to do or think anymore. I'd never had to deal with a situation like this when I worked at the auto plant, where my colleagues and I made a conscious effort to get along with each other. We all understood that working around each other for such a long period of time, eight hours a day, day in day out, could be unbearable if there are personality clashes. We also realized that not getting along with one another produced nothing but stress and drama. Who in their right mind wants to exist in such an environment? I know we didn't, so we chose not to. Anyway, before my runaway thoughts could continue, they were eventually interrupted by the young man's voice, asking me how I was doing. Do you know what?

He walked up to me with an extended arm and delivered a firm and respectable handshake. "I'm sorry about before," he said. "My name is Elijah Ray Anderson. I'm not that friendly, so don't try to get too close because I am not interested in friendships at work. As long as you remember that everything will be alright." Despite that addition to his introduction, in a strange way I felt all my fears regarding the young man simply dissolve and disappear as soon as he shook my hand. As soon as he had finished his introduction, Mr. Elijah Ray Anderson slowly turned and walked back to the corner of the office, where he sat down once again. He continued to ignore the few of our coworkers who had stayed behind after being told to go to their work area. Once he'd made it back to his seat, he immediately began to sketch in his sketchpad again, and a look of solitude and peace fell over his face. I stood there burning with curiosity. I could still feel the tension in the air between Elijah Ray Anderson and the others. It's sad, but they had a serious dislike for one another. Yet Elijah Ray Anderson's personal introduction, with his strong handshake and the sincerity in his eyes made me feel that he was reaching out to me. It made me feel kind of bad, because I had partly allowed my ignorance to get the best of me: after allowing my fears to overtake me, with my first thought being of anger, before he introduced himself I found myself temporarily on the side of the others. But you know what? I didn't know anything about the other workers as well. So at this point I began to reassess my opinion of them all, but most particularly of Elijah Ray Anderson. It made no sense how they were treating one another, and I most definitely didn't want to get involved in that. I'd rather go back to job hunting. Well... maybe not. My search for a job sure was frustrating. Anyway, I did decide that if I stayed here I would be sure to form my own opinions about those people, primarily based on facts and fairness. I refuse to work in a hostile environment or in any other environment that will be counterproductive to my being there. So I thought to myself that as long as I was there I would do whatever it took to create a more pleasant environment for us all to work in. My level of faith, I thought, would make this task possible, because I truly believe that there is some element of good in everyone, and that includes Elijah Ray Anderson, despite the negative opinions and attitudes I had witnessed. I didn't know what was going on with Elijah Ray Anderson, but my mind did run to speculating. I know speculating isn't always a good thing, but I did think that the young man was motivated by a deep sadness, and his rough attitude was simply a deceptive cover. I thought to myself, 'What is his story?' I felt compelled to find out.

Anyway, before I could continue my mental rumination, Ms. Cheryl Washington interrupted my thoughts, asking me if I was alright.

"Yes," I said, "why do you ask?"

"You look as if you where in a trance!" she giggled. Well I guess I was, because those deep thoughts had overtaken me.

"I'm ok and back to Earth," I replied with a smile.

"I'm glad you're ok… particularly after the unfortunate situation you had to witness this morning. I apologize once again for my staff and hope that this unfortunate incident doesn't negatively affect your overall view of the work life in this school. Believe it or not, it's not a bad place to work. You'll find this out soon enough." She wound her voice down, then changed tone. "Well, Mr. Jeremiah Johnson, since you've now met your coworkers, it's time for me to take you on a tour of the building. I'll also explain a little bit more about the rules and regulations that you'll have to follow, and what will be expected of you."

So we went on the tour, and Ms. Cheryl Washington told me all about what was expected of me, and showed me all of the areas and things that had to be cleaned and maintained. It's hard to believe it, but as the tour finished it was quite late in the day, so she said that once she had signed me out I was finish for the day. We returned to the janitorial office so that she could sign me out for the day. Upon leaving, I took the opportunity to speak to my coworkers still in the office.

"Everyone take care now," I said, "I'll see you guys in the morning." I walked down the hallway and out through the school doors, towards my car that was still parked in the school's employee parking lot. After arriving at my car, I got in and took a well-deserved deep breath. I began playing my motivational speaker CD again, and drove off. I listen to that CD all the way home. But you know what? No matter how hard I tried to focus on the message of my motivational CD, my thoughts kept returning to the events of my first day of work. First impressions are very important. I was appalled at what I had experienced that morning. The more I thought about it, the more my common sense told me that I shouldn't return to that job – I would just be subjecting myself to a whole lot of craziness. But if I don't go back, I thought, I'll just be sent back to the frustration and craziness that comes with looking for another job. And any new job might be worse than the one I already have. In a moment of despair I thought "that's it, I'm just not going back!" I thought that when I told my wife of this decision she would understand, because I knew she would want me to be happy where I worked. I arrived at that decision as I pulled into our driveway. I sat there for a short moment, relaxing the nerves in the pit of my stomach. I wasn't looking forward to telling my wife. Gradually I calmed down, and gained the courage to leave my car and enter the house. Once inside I headed straight for the kitchen, because I hadn't eaten anything for lunch on my first day of work.

After making a ham and cheese sandwich, I grabbed a cold can of pop from the refrigerator and walked into the living room to watch television. I was shocked to discover my wife Sophia already sitting on the sofa watching her favorite television program. When she saw me enter the living room she looked up.

"How are you doing sweetheart?" she asked. After she shut off the television and asked me to have a seat next to her, she asked me to tell her about my first day of work. I thought I had all my nerves under wraps, but I tell you at this point they began to unravel. I just couldn't face telling my wife anything about my first day of work. I would just rather forget about it. But that wasn't an option. I guessed that I was just going to have to tell her about my first day of work, no matter how agonizing it was going to be for me. Anyway, I set my food down and began to tell my wife about my first day of work. Before telling my wife anything, it just came to me that it might not be a bad idea to tell her about my miserable day, because only then would she be able to understand and support my decision not to go back. Then I could explain to her how I would immediately pursue another job that I could be happy with. But I tell you, I learned that I couldn't be more wrong about my decision after hearing what my wife had to say once about my first day of work. So anyway, I told her about the day and about my decision. She said straight away that she was not pleased with my decision, but that she was going to support me anyway. As she said, "a bird in the hand is better than two in the bush." She said my fears were irrational, and they weren't playing a helpful role in my decision-making. You know, she was right. And yet she didn't stop there! She reminded me of the three principles that had initially attracted her to me: my personal relationship with God, my compassionate way of helping my fellow man and my determining spirit that just won't give up on a challenge without a fair fight!

So I asked her some questions about the young man I had met that day, hoping that she could help to explain the situation.

"He sounds depressed," she said. She asked me a few more questions, narrowing down what she thought was happening. She then explained things in layman's terms.

"I can't make a proper psychological evaluation, of course," she began, "and he should be checked out by a medical doctor to rule out any medical conditions that might be causing psychological problems. But you felt that he was trying to reach out to someone, right? Well if that's the case, the bottom line is you might be what he needs. And you know what? I truly believe that things happen for a reason. I don't believe your meeting was an accident. So maybe that's the reason why you're there. Anyway, with no disrespect to the practice of psychology, I really think that sometimes psychological remedies are not always adequate. For a lot of people divine intervention and spirituality makes much more of a difference than any therapy a psychologist could provide. Anyway, you should remember that perhaps the problems aren't all on this Elijah Ray Anderson's side. Those coworkers you told me about are playing a substantial part in the problem as well."

At this point my wife looked at me, with a bit of irritation behind her smile. "Jeremiah," she said, "please remember not to take my support for granted. Be mindful not to make decisions that will compromise your overall honor and integrity." Well, it's no secret: at this point my loving wife's lack of criticizing and her down to earth insights had persuaded me to reevaluate my overall situation. So I changed my mind. I decided I would return to work tomorrow, with a new improved outlook and attitude and a desire to take on any challenges that came up. I knew that this was some sort of a divine test, which I would muster everything in my power to pass.

* * *

So the second day at my new job arrived. I hate to admit it, but I still didn't want to be there. But I reminded myself of the commitment I'd made the previous day, and I began to find things just a little bit easier to cope with. This was especially necessary after my coworkers arrived at work, and we all sat in the office waiting for the supervisor. They had the nerve to say good morning, and then ruin it by going straight back to their arguments and acting like complete fools. I tell you it was awful. They kept going like that until the supervisor arrived. Anyway, once Ms. Washington entered the office, all the foolishness came to a complete stop. She said good morning to everyone, and then began to speak to us about the janitorial agenda for next month, leading up to the Christmas holiday. She said that we'd be extraordinarily busy during the time leading up to the holiday season, because we were going to be putting up all the Christmas trees in the teachers' classrooms if they wanted one, along with putting up decorations throughout the rest of the school. We would also be doing a lot of cleaning, stripping and waxing the floors to accommodate the many classroom Christmas parties that would be taking place. After telling us about the coming month, she then moved on to the day's agenda.

"You guys are going to carry out your general cleaning duties at your assigned work areas. Mr. Jeremiah Johnson, you were going to be assigned to Mrs. Abigail Bailey for general janitorial training, but since she's taken ill I've reassigned you to work with Mr. Cyrus Noble until she returns." After she had finished all her announcements, Ms. Washington dismissed us, telling us to have a good day and that she would see us all at the end of our shift. After the morning's rough start, I was happily surprised to find that the rest of the day was quite pleasant. It was a joy to work with Mr. Cyrus Noble, as he's a guy who really knows how to enjoy himself at work. And he certainly wasn't taking his job too seriously that morning! Anyway, Mr. Cyrus Noble is a lighthearted person and a comedian, and he likes to have a good time and flirt with all the lady teachers and parents who pass through the school's hallways. And when he wasn't flirting, he was cracking jokes. He made me laugh so hard sometimes that I couldn't catch my breath. And then he'd strut through the hallways as if he was some magnificent gift to all the ladies of the world. With all this going on we managed to get little to no work done, and I didn't get any training. But at least I was learning how to not take this place so seriously.

"Man," he said, "you'll have plenty of time to learn how to clean toilets when Mrs. Abigail Bailey comes back. In the meantime, as long as I am training you we're going to have a good time." I can honestly say that he managed to keep his word, because I had so much fun that day that I hated to see it come to an end. Anyway, my day of fun did come to an end – but it did give me a new incentive to return to work tomorrow.

So anyway, I kept on going to work each day, and each day the morning would begin with a janitorial maintenance office full of fussing and fighting. The weekend came and went, and there I was, back at work the following Monday morning. By this point I was really looking forward to just one day without workplace drama. I was briefly surprised, because I almost got my wish! Everyone arrived in the office to wait for Ms. Washington, and things were going along nicely with many pleasant conversations taking place. That was until Ms. Paula Gooden shouted across the room with an arrogant demeanor, asking Mr. Elijah Ray Anderson a degrading question in front of all his colleagues.

"What does one plus two equal?" She yelled. His first response was to ignore her, and he continued sketching in his sketchpad. She repeated the question, but slightly louder and with a great deal more rudeness. This time Mr. Elijah Ray Anderson became very annoyed, and with his face full of anger he turned and looked at her.

"Don't say nothing else to me, because I am not for your bull today!" He yelled. But she continued with her verbal attacks.

"You simply don't know the answer to the question! You dropped out of school with your stupid butt!" With frustration in his face and sadness in his eyes, he momentarily dropped his head to collect himself after this verbal attack. Unfortunately, before he could respond to her the rest of the coworkers joined in and began to talk about him, make fun of him and laugh while he did the best to defend himself. I looked over at Ms. Paula Gooden, who wasn't saying anything at this point. She was just sitting down in an office chair wearing a devilish smile, proud of her success in causing all that drama, pleased at the chaos she had created. After her brief reflection on her success, she once again joined in with the rest of the coworkers. By this time Mr. Elijah Ray Anderson had enough, and had simply stopped defending himself. He began to focus intently on sketching in his sketchpad. In fact, he was focused with such intensity that the rest of his coworkers ceased their verbal attacks – except Ms. Paula Gooden. She continued to abuse him, until her attacks began to reach such a level of harassment that they were beginning to make the rest of the coworkers uneasy. I gathered up enough courage at this point to say something to Ms. Paula Gooden.

"In the name of Jesus, would you leave that man alone? He wasn't bothering you, in fact he was just minding his own business until you began to attack him with no just cause." She looked at me.

"I don't know who you think you are, because you need to shut your mouth! You need to mind your own damn business. You better hope for your sake that I don't find out that you dropped out of school as well, since you just got here!" I thanked God, because before I could respond the supervisor walked in.

"Good morning, I'm sorry I'm late!" She looked around. "Is everything ok in the office? I see many sad faces this morning. Well, I hope whatever the problem was you guys have now resolved it, and we can all move on and have a pleasant workday today."

I am pleased to report that the rest of the workday was just fine, without any further incident – though Mr. Elijah Ray Anderson's antisocial behavior did increase. Whenever

I saw him he seemed consumed with the verbal assault he'd been subjected to earlier that morning. Despite the calm that filled the rest of the workday, I could still feel in the pit of my stomach that it wasn't completely over with yet. The fact of the matter is, I knew that any peace amongst the staff was only temporary, a calm before a storm. Anyway, after shaking off those weird feelings, Mr. Cyrus and I went off to perform our janitorial duties, as directed by the supervisor. We worked up a sweat in the first half of our shift before our lunch break, and after lunch we continued until the end of our shift. When we were heading back to the janitorial office, we saw Elijah mopping a hallway. As we walked past him, I stopped to ask him if he was alright. He turned his head away from me with a frown on his face and a little anger still in his voice.

"Don't worry about me I am doing just fine!" He said as he continued to mop, doing his best to ignore me. At this point I didn't say anything further to him and Cyrus and I continued towards the janitorial maintenance office. So, tired and exhausted from all the hard work we had done, we used the little strength we had left to sign out for the end of our work shift and go home for the day.

The next day I was an hour late for work, as I had to run an errand for my wife in the morning. Despite my excuse, I was concerned that this might look bad, particularly since I had just started working there. Well, there wasn't much I could do about it. Anyway, I walked quickly down the hallway towards the janitorial maintenance office. Before I reached the janitorial maintenance office, I saw my supervisor Ms. Cheryl Washington about to walk into the school office. I called out a quick "good morning!" to her, and she turned to me and smiled.

"Good morning Mr. Jeremiah Johnson, you know you're late this morning."

"I know!" I said apologetically.

"The rest of the janitorial staff are in the janitorial office having a staff meeting with a representative from the union hall. Oh – everyone except Mr. Elijah Ray Anderson, I mean. It seems he's also running late." Once she was finished with her information, she said she would see me back at the office, and turned and walked though the doors of the school office. So I continued to walk to the janitorial maintenance office. When I arrived, I noticed that the union representative had already left – but my coworkers seemed to be conducting their own unofficial meeting. They were all huddled around and whispering with Ms. Paula Gooden, who was seated at the desk as if she was the supervisor. This little meeting ended abruptly when they saw me. I ignored what I had just witnessed, and said a polite "Good morning" to everyone. Everyone responded politely back to me, except Ms. Paula Gooden. She was wearing her devilish smile once again, and with the strange and suspicious looks on the faces of my coworkers, I became a little uneasy. Anyway, before I became further disturbed by their conspiratorial activities, Ms. Cheryl Washington walked into the janitorial maintenance office. Five minutes later, Mr. Elijah Ray Anderson and his sketchpad also walked into the office, without saying good morning or anything to anyone. He went to take a seat in the corner of the office, ignoring everyone else. Once everyone was present, Ms. Cheryl Washington began to explain our janitorial Christmas work assignment agenda in greater detail. Halfway through however, she had to interrupt her speech to stop a little meeting that was taking place between Ms. Paula Gooden and one of her partners in crime, asking them to share their conversation with the rest of us.

"No, I don't think that would be a good idea Ms. Washington," Ms. Paula Gooden responded, "please continue on with your speech." So after she had everyone's undivided attention, Ms. Washington began to issue the specific tasks she wanted each of us to perform that day. She then passionately launched into a speech about the disciplinary consequences of workers choosing not to work or delivering unsatisfactory results. It seemed that countless complaints had been brought to her attention by the school principal or other school staff.

"If any more unsatisfactory work is brought to my attention, it will be dealt with immediately. If you are reported for poor work performance, you may find yourself facing suspension and many days off work. Anyway, I'm not too worried, because I know you are all going to get the job done. Does anyone have any questions for me at this point?" Ms. Washington looked around. "Since no one has anything to say, then let me say this before I forget. We are going to initiate a two week cleaning project, beginning next Monday morning. I need you guys to be ready and on time that day and the weeks that follow up to the last day of our overall work assignment on Thursday, December 20. We are going to be involved in a great deal of work, stripping and waxing just about all of the school classroom floors in addition to decorating the entire school with Christmas ornaments and other items that will properly express the Christmas theme. We also have to keep in mind that it will be crucial to make sure that all toilet paper and hand towel dispensers are fully supplied, and all the hand soap dispensers are full to the brim. All surfaces that need it must be wiped and dusted, all trash must be removed, and all the school must be swept and mopped before and after the Christmas parties on Friday, December 23rd. That will be the last day for school students, and administration staff will also take their Christmas vacation until the new year. Finally, before you all go off to work, I have very good news to report. Our dear friend Mrs. Abigail Bailey will be returning to school sometime in the new year. I am looking forward to seeing her again. It is always such a pleasure to work with her. Well, that's all I need to say for now. So I suggest you guys go to work! I know I have taken up enough of your time. Enjoy the rest of your workday!"

My coworkers and I got up from our seats and left the office, all heading to our assigned areas. I was still assigned to work with Cyrus that day, and we worked just as hard as we did the day before. Once again I tried to speak to Elijah in the school hallway, while he was sweeping trash into his dust pan. He simply ignored me, frowning a bit as if I was annoying him. I paused for a moment and was going to say something else to him, until Cyrus stopped me in mid-thought.

"Why are you wasting your time trying to be nice to him? Can't you see that he is just mad at the world?" He laughed, and began to sing. "Let's go Jeremiah, leave that fool alone." We both began to walk away. After we'd walked some distance from Elijah's negative personality, Cyrus stopped his joyful singing and began to inform me of a new work directive for tomorrow. Ms. Cheryl Washington had said she wanted him to tell me about it if she forgot to mention it in the meeting. Anyway, my new directive consisted of me working alone for the first time tomorrow.

"Basically," he said, "you're being assigned to clean Mrs. Abigail Bailey's normal_area until she returns to work after her surgery. Now, don't be too proud to ask if you need any help, just let me know and I will be more than happy to accommodate. But I have confidence that won't be the case, since you've been trained by the best!" He began to laugh, before returning to his joyful singing. We entered a bathroom on the first floor and began to clean. That took a while, so once we were finished there we went to go and eat lunch. Before going to launch, I had to stop at my locker to retrieve my lunch box. Cyrus continued to walk towards the lunchroom without me. But you know what? I stood there at my locker looking dumbfounded, because I couldn't remember my combination! After a while I began to play with the lock, and I eventually remembered the combination. I opened the door and grabbed my lunch, but the whole process had wasted a couple of minutes of my precious lunch break. Anyway, with my lunchbox in hand I walked quickly to the lunchroom. Walking into the lunchroom, I was surprised to again witness a secretive meeting between most of my co-workers. They were congregating and plotting hard, all with serious expressions on their faces. Once they saw me, they disassembled their meeting immediately and began to sit down and eat their lunch, as if the meeting had never taken place. So I have to say, I started to get a little worried. I wanted to know what those characters were up to, and who was going to get hurt in the process. Just from the looks on their faces, it seemed that my coworkers were up to no good! It was just a matter of time before they could implement whatever scheme they were cooking up, and I knew that it wasn't going to be something in the best interests of mankind. In the meantime, the only thing I could think to do was to pray that no one was going to be seriously hurt by their bad intentions. I also prayed that someone in the group would stand up and speak out, and try to convince some of the others to not go through with any plan that would negatively affect anyone else. Unfortunately, right after my speculation something negative began to happen. It all started on the following Monday afternoon. At that point I learned that Mr. Elijah Ray Anderson was an unaware target of Ms. Paula Gooden's anger.

It was a rainy afternoon, and a teacher had complained about Mr. Elijah Ray Anderson's poor work on the second floor. He'd tried to defend himself when Ms. Washington reprimanded him, but this only made matters worse. His defense fell on deaf ears. His frustration was at an all-time high at this moment, and once again he dropped his head with a frown on his face. Asking to be excused, he proceeded to leave the janitorial maintenance office. While leaving the office, he mumbled under his breath, saying "I know my entire area was clean when I left it!" He had no idea how right he was, but the fact that he didn't talk or interact with anyone placed him at a disadvantage. I was not happy with the drama in the workplace, so I decided to exercise my Christian duty. I decided I was going to help my fellow coworker Mr. Elijah Ray Anderson whether he liked it or not. I decided that he didn't have to know what I was doing, but I couldn't in good conscience just stand by and do nothing. So anyway, with all that plotting going on, I decided I would have to become an undercover ally helping Mr. Elijah Ray Anderson.

* * *

I decided I would try to sneak some time from my busy work schedule to venture onto the second floor – Mr. Elijah Ray Anderson's assigned work area – to investigate my co-workers' behavior after he had gone. Anyway, I found out that Mr. Elijah Ray Anderson had received his write up because of the childish behavior of our co-workers. My prayers had been answered: one of the people who had taken part in those secret meetings – whose name will remain a secret – came to me out of the blue at work one day, nervous and shaking. She said she had information that she would reveal to me only if I promised not to snitch her out. I promised I wouldn't. Anyway, this individual first explained how she didn't want to have anything to do with all the drama that was going on. She then pointed out the back stairs of the school building, saying that these were being used by other co-workers, who she would not name, to sneak into Elijah's work area without being detected. Once in his work area, they sabotaged all his work, systematically working to keep him in all sorts of trouble. They hoped that this would eventually result in him being subjected to the ultimate disciplinary action, getting him suspended for a few days. "This would satisfy Ms. Paula Gooden's vengeful appetite," she said, "but you didn't hear that from me!" My informant looked up and saw a couple of teachers coming down the hallway. With a spooked look on her face, she stopped talking and immediately started to walk down the hallway. She quickly disappeared around the corner.

Once I recovered from the shock of what I'd just heard, I immediately went to the janitorial office. I wanted to share some of this information with Ms. Cheryl Washington, hoping that she would reconsider the reprimand she had given Mr. Elijah Ray Anderson. I wanted to do whatever was necessary to make things right again. But I was surprised to hear my supervisor's response, even though I soon understood where it was coming from. She spoke with an element of arrogance and anger in her voice.

"What you expect me to do is simply not possible, because you are not providing me with any concrete proof or evidence – just speculation that is based on he said she said information. I will not respond to such an allegation nor put my job on the line for it. So," she finished, "is there anything else you need to tell me before I go back to work?"

"No!" I responded. I am sorry to say that I walked out of the janitorial maintenance office with an unimaginable level of frustration lingering within me. But even though I was frustrated, I took some comfort in the knowledge that I had at least tried to do something. Because the fact is, most people don't care enough to get involved in what's right. And that's a crying shame.

Anyway, soon after my futile attempt to bring about some justice for Mr. Elijah Ray Anderson, things became worse for him. Basically, I couldn't prevent him from being given a two week suspension: those hateful coworkers managed to stay a couple of steps ahead of me. They continued to return to his work area, removing all the paper products and liquid hand soap from the bathroom dispensers. They used some of those paper products to block up a few toilets, causing them to overflow. They poured some of the chemical stripper onto a freshly waxed classroom floor, they spread litter throughout the hallways, bathrooms and classrooms, they placed a rotten and moldy half eaten apple on the top surface of a teacher's desk, demonstrating clearly the signature of a disgruntled employee in the workplace. You know what made it worse? All of this vandalism was discovered on the last day before the start of the Christmas vacation, making everything seem so much worse.

Ms. Cheryl Washington allowed the perpetrators to convince her that Elijah Ray Anderson was guilty, without looking at the facts. They said to her that he wanted to retaliate after his earlier reprimand. This surprised and sickened me, as she happily listened to those lies, while she'd dismissed my information as irrelevant rumor and gossip. So I stood there in the janitorial maintenance office hurt and bewildered at my supervisor's behavior. I lost a great deal of respect for her, as I had to watch the mental anguish Mr. Elijah Ray Anderson was going through when Ms. Washington handed him his suspension papers. She didn't even given him the chance to tell his side of the story. He tried to defend himself, but when she kept telling him to lower his voice, he realized that he was just wasting his time. He could see it in her eyes that she was trying not to hear what he was saying, that she didn't believe anything he was saying. She clearly believed the others that he was without a doubt guilty as charged. With a look of anger he slammed the janitorial maintenance office door, almost knocking it off its hinges. I saw him storm down the hallway and out through the doors of the building. He walked briskly through the cold air, grimacing through the six and a half inches of snow with tears in his eyes. He was mumbling in a low voice that he was innocent. He walked over to the Joy Road bus stop directly across the street from the school building, mumbling in the cold winter air until he boarded that Joy Road bus to take him away.

Chapter 4

The beginning of a new friendship

"Good morning Mrs. Abigail Bailey!" I called out, when I saw her in the hallway outside the janitorial maintenance office. "I'm glad to see you back!"

"Thank you Mr. Johnson, I sure am glad to be back." She walked into the office, with her Bible clenched in one hand and a breakfast takeout in the other. She sat down at the table in the center of the office.

"Where is everyone?" she asked, sitting comfortably in her chair before arranging her Bible and her breakfast.

"I guess we're kind of early this morning," I said. It was the first day back after the new year. Gradually, the rest of our coworkers began to file into the office. Once they'd all arrived, Ms. Cheryl Washington spoke to us about the spring cleaning agenda. Turning to me, she said that I was being reassigned once again. As the meeting finished, we all turned to Mrs. Abigail Bailey and gave her a welcome back hug. Everyone asked her how was she doing, and she told us that she was doing just fine, except that she was a little sore from surgery. With a big smile on her face, she thanked us for asking. At that point I noticed that Ms. Paula Gooden had not taken much part in the welcoming. In fact, she immediately left the office as soon as the meeting was over and proceeded straight to her work area with a frown on her face, as if she was mad that Mrs. Bailey was back. Anyway, when all the pleasantries were over I had the privilege of being reassigned to work with Mrs. Abigail Bailey. I would be working with her until she received further instructions from her doctor informing her that she was well enough to work alone. I had no problem with my new assignment, because it was nice to work with someone new for a change. So I politely asked Mrs. Abigail Bailey if she was ready to walk to our assigned work area to get a start on things. I jokingly told her how I had taken great care of her assigned work area while she was gone. She looked at me and we both began to laugh while we walked down the hallway together. I found myself really enjoying this walk and the conversations I was having with Mrs. Abigail Bailey. I soon discovered that she was a wonderful and spiritual person, and you could genuinely feel the love she had for her fellow man and woman – in spite of her need to say Jesus' name as frequently as she could while she had her Bible tucked securely under her left arm, like one of those designer purses. Anyway, that didn't bother me at all because she didn't come off as some radical religious fanatic who would pass out hurtful judgments. Those sorts of people usually do a great disservice to the Heavenly Father's will and to all humankind.

Anyway, our conversations and journey to our assigned work area came to an abrupt halt when I remembered that we needed to pick up some supplies and equipment, including a broom, a dust pan, a mop and a mop bucket.

"That's no problem Mr. Jeremiah Johnson," she said, "I have a key to the janitorial utility closet that's near our work area."

"Great!" I responded. So we began walking once more, and we soon arrived at the janitorial utility closet to retrieve the things we needed. But here's where things got worse: as soon as we left the janitorial utility closet we ran into Ms. Paula Gooden. With all her hateful ways, Ms. Gooden took it upon herself to use this meeting as an opportunity to step in between me and Mrs. Abigail Bailey. I think I heard Mrs. Bailey say a prayer under her breath. But then Ms. Gooden delivered a verbal warning to me. Speaking like some type of gangster – and with breath that smelled like a waste water treatment plant on a hundred degree summer day – she stepped close to me.

"You'd better mind your own business and keep your mouth shut as long as I work here," she said, "because you're next on my list. In fact, I will make you this promise: the next time I find something on you, I'm going to bring you down baby, and that's a promise, not a threat." She had more to say. "I want you to understand something. I've never liked Mr. Elijah Ray Anderson, and to say that I was happy that he was suspended is an understatement. The only thing that I am mad about is that he was not permanently let go. It makes my stomach turn every time I think that he will be returning sometime soon. You better remember what I said to you, because I am very committed to getting what I want." She slid away like some sort of serpent.

After that no good witch walked away I was so mad that it took just about everything in my power to not punch one of the school lockers nearby. I regained my composure and looked over to Mrs. Abigail Bailey. She had a look of disgust on her face.

"Thank you Jesus!" she cried.

"I can't believe that evil women got in my face with all that," I responded.

"Well, believe it honey," she said, "because I learned long ago that woman is bad news. You can't trust her. I am unfortunately speaking from experience. We used to talk when she first started working here, but she turned on me with an unholy vengeance that would reach beyond your comprehension or imagination. But that was ok, because when I prayed to my Jesus that hateful woman took ill for two weeks before returning back to work. When she did return I thanked Jesus, because she never bothered me again. In fact she stayed away from me like I was the black plague. So my advice to you Mr. Jeremiah Johnson is that being prayed up with Jesus is your best defense against her." Mrs. Abigail Bailey continued to speak with conviction. She said that she was fully aware of what had happened to Mr. Elijah Ray Anderson, and how she felt so bad for him – and that he wasn't really a bad man once you got to know him.

"Let me tell you something that I haven't told anyone else who works here concerning a conversation that Ms. Paula Gooden and I had long before Mr. Elijah Ray Anderson started working here. This conversation was so disturbing that I just kept it to myself and told not one soul. The only reason I am telling you now is because my spiritual voice said to do so. I know that you genuinely respect Mr. Elijah Ray Anderson, unlike the rest of his co-workers who are cruel to him on an almost daily basis. Anyway, that Ms. Paula Gooden is the head honcho around here, and is nearly always the first to instigate any cruelty at the start of the day." Mrs. Abigail Bailey went on to explain how Mr. Elijah Ray Anderson was basically set up in the beginning, when Ms. Paula Gooden purposely initiated a casual conversation with all of the janitorial staff about their high school years and all the fun they had during those years.

"They took turns talking about their high school experience, until they got to Mr. Elijah Ray Anderson. Two weeks after he'd started working here he made the mistake of telling everyone that he'd dropped out of school and had no story to tell. Everyone was silent, as if someone had died. At that point Mr. Jeremiah Johnson I felt so bad for him – because prior to this Ms. Paula Gooden had expressed to me how much she despised people who drop out of school. She said that they were a real menace to society, that they were dependent on welfare and had nothing of value to offer. In fact, she said they were no more than parasites and scabs, feeding off the rest of us. She said they should be peeled off and discarded. She even said that she took great pleasure in making a school dropout's life as miserable as possible whenever she came into contact with one. And Mr. Jeremiah Johnson, she said they have no excuse for their actions, and because they're on welfare leaching off the system that's not fair to us folks that work hard to get an education. I really couldn't believe what I was hearing, so I interrupted Ms. Paula Gooden and said to her that though I could somewhat understand were she was coming from, particularly in regards to those who dropped out of school by choice, what about those who might have been challenged with some sort of learning disorder, forced to drop out of school because the system couldn't work for them. Before I could say anything further, she angrily interrupted me. 'Like I said before,' she said, 'there is no good reason for anyone to drop out of school unless they are all retarded with a half of brain or something because learning disorders are just reasons that people use as an excuse in the place of laziness. It makes me very upset when I hear someone trying to use a learning disorder as an excuse for dropping out of school. And it won't be acceptable to me as long as I live,' she said. Anyway, by this time Mr. Johnson I'd simply had enough. With all that negative talk I decided to change the conversation to a lighter topic... But anyway, after that conversation, I found myself not wanting to talk to her anymore, and I began to avoid her at work. I just couldn't stomach her bigotry towards those who dropped out of school for whatever reason."

When Mrs. Abigail Bailey was finished talking, she once again spoke out the name of Jesus. "Enough talking about Ms. Paula Gooden," she continued, "let's get to work and focus on doing a good job today before the end of our shift comes."

"Ok!" I said, and we looked at one another and began to smile once again. Mrs. Abigail Bailey said a short prayer for both of us, which lifted our spirits while we proceeded to walk to our work area.

* * *

So Monday January 4th arrived, and Mr. Elijah Ray Anderson returned to work after his two week suspension. Of course, his return to work was keenly observed by his coworkers, who could feel that his anti-social attitude was at an all-time high. Anyway, things proceeded along like this, with a great deal of hostility in our workplace, for a few months. Things only started to change three months later, when Mrs. Abigail Bailey became very tired of all the negativity consuming Mr. Elijah Ray Anderson's mind, spirit and soul. Once again, Mrs. Abigail Bailey's spirituality spoke to her, suggesting that she perform another Christian duty for the sake of Mr. Elijah Ray Anderson's well-being. She went first to Jesus in prayer and asked that he give her strength and wisdom to help her to deliver Mr. Elijah Ray Anderson to him, to calm his spirit and heal his pain and suffering. She hoped that Mr. Elijah Ray Anderson would be able to forgive the people who had persecuted him unjustly. Armed with her divine motivation, she began to seek out Elijah at lunchtime. So one day, Mrs. Abigail Bailey walked to his table at the back of the room with a concerned look in her eyes. She asked if she could take the seat opposite him.

"It's a free country," he responded angrily, "do as you please!" He had that look on his face that would make a demon from hell back up. After she'd taken a seat and placed her lunch on the table, she began to bless her food with a prayer before eating. It didn't take long for his antisocial attitude to get the best of him. He looked at Mrs. Abigail Bailey.

"Why are you over here trying to sit with me? I really don't like people sitting that close to me."

"I am sorry if my presence disturbs you," she replied, "but to answer your question I was sent to you to perform a Christian duty. That's the gospel truth and the reason I'm sitting here with you. Do you have a problem with that Mr. Elijah Ray Anderson?"

"Not really," he responded.

"There you have it!" she said. "Some progress at last." Mrs. Bailey continued to speak with him, reminding him with her divine words that he was a good person, contrary to the opinion of those mean-spirited coworkers. "But," she said, "your anti-social attitude has made you blind to one of your coworkers; there is someone here who genuinely cares about you and went out on the limb to stand up for you. He was even threatened on more than one occasion as a result of it. In fact, to add insult to injury you've been acting much like your coworkers, insulting him and treating him with unnecessary disrespect. Anyway, the bottom line is, Jesus and I love you, and so does Mr. Jeremiah Johnson. He genuinely respects you, and he wants to help you whether you like it or not. I guess it's in his nature to stand up for what's right. Anyway," she said, looking away briefly, "my time is up. I'm just going to leave you with this divine message: a blessing from Jesus is coming your way. But if you don't change your ways, you're simply going to miss out on your blessing because your present behavior will cause you to become that which you hate so much. So wise up and be that good person that Jesus and I once knew." Mrs. Bailey got up from the table and walked away.

The following week I decided to speak once more to Mr. Elijah Ray Anderson. I passed him in the school hallway about 10:30 am on the Monday morning of April 1th. He was sweeping in his work area near the gymnasium. To my amazement, after months of relentless disrespect, Mr. Elijah Ray Anderson responded politely to me for the first time in a long time.

"How are you doing Mr. Elijah Ray Anderson?" I asked as I walked up to him.

"I am doing just fine. How are you doing this morning Mr. Jeremiah Johnson?" I tell you his unexpected response made my day. I had always believed that the man had good within him. At this point I thanked my Heavenly Father and Mrs. Abigail Bailey for her faith in Jesus and her courage in approaching a man with a wounded soul with love and kindness. I believe that these actions truly set him on the course of healing and finding the salvation he so desperately needed. I truly knew he would continue to receive salvation as long as he stayed on the right track: if he had a change of heart, all of the staff at the school would appreciate the change, along with his coworkers who (except me) were beginning to become afraid of him.

Over the next few days I came to believe that Mr. Elijah Ray Anderson was making great progress in trying to change his ways for the better. This was clearly evident in his attempts to be nicer to others. I had even begun to consider the possibility that he could one day become a friend of mine: during one conversation, out of the blue, we each learned that the other was also a parent. Although we weren't yet friends, we were beginning to be more friendly towards each other. It was a great start that I was more than satisfied with. But I will admit that I did initiate the conversation in the lunchroom first.

Our defining conversation occurred one day when I entered the lunchroom. I wanted to act much like Mrs. Abigail Bailey, invading Mr. Elijah Ray Anderson's personal space to try to break the ice. I was aware that I might be seen as a copycat, but I mustered up my courage and walked all the way into the lunchroom where Mr. Elijah Ray Anderson usually sat by himself. I'm not going to lie and say that I wasn't nervous or scared, because that is far from the truth. I walked towards Mr. Elijah Ray Anderson, ignoring all of the uncomfortable stares of my coworkers and the other staff in the lunchroom. To make a long story short, I accomplished my objective, much like Mrs. Abigail Bailey, except that my conversation with him was slightly longer than hers. At the beginning he was not very friendly. Indeed, he said very little except to say good afternoon while he continued to eat lunch. He simply looked at me, but he was courteous and he did listen to me for once (this may sound like a small issue, but he usually responded to any attempt to strike up a conversation by telling me to get out of his face or get away from him).

Anyway, at the start of the conversation I tried to think of something that I could talk to him about without him telling me to go take a flying leap off something very high. First I talked about the weather, but at this point he stopped eating his lunch and began to frown at both my small talk and me. So I changed the subject from small talk to something that mattered to me. I told him that I had a beautiful daughter in college, and that I missed her a lot. (She is still her daddy's little princess, no matter how old she gets or where she resides). I noticed that Mr. Elijah Ray Anderson had begun to take interest in my story, and so I took the chance to ask him whether he had any children. He simply nodded. Taking encouragement from this, I continued to tell him about my daughter and what she was like when she was a little girl. In an instant, it was as if he had come to life: he interrupted me to say he had two children and that he was raising them on his own. He then abruptly ceased talking and resumed eating his lunch. I had made a great deal of progress, and so I once again began to speak about my daughter and other topics until he rose from the lunchroom table. I politely asked him if he was leaving because I was talking too much.

"Ha!" He laughed. "I'm leaving simply because I'm done eating lunch!" I felt rather stupid, so I told him I was sorry that I wasn't paying attention and didn't realize he had finished eating his lunch.

"No problem Mr. Jeremiah Johnson" he said, before walking away from the lunchroom table, leaving me to finish eating my lunch alone. I called out, asking him if he wanted to tell me anything else about his children before leaving.

"No. Maybe some other time man," he called back simply as he walked off.

After the conversation I sat alone at that lunchroom table, a table that very few staff members would journey to during lunch time. It actually had a pretty good view and it was nice and quiet. Anyway, after lunch I met up with Mrs. Abigail Bailey. While we were walking to our work area we saw Ms. Paula Gooden in the hallway. We glanced at each other, hoping that she wouldn't notice us amongst the throng of people in the hallway. But as we soon discovered, hoping wasn't good enough, because that upright monster of a snake not only spotted us, but slithered over to deliver another one of her hateful messages. I remember thinking that surely she generated such speeches directly from a pile of hatefulness lying deep within the dark places of her soul, a soul I suspected she had loaned out to some demon. The particular message that she delivered maintained her hateful reputation. We asked her what she wanted. Her eyes lit up, and her mouth began to contort into a devilish smile. Her tongue then became a sharp knife, slicing the air with words designed to cut away at an individual's spirit and soul. Anyway, she began by telling me that she was unimpressed with what she saw in the lunchroom today when I walked over to Mr. Elijah Ray Anderson's table. She berated me, saying that she wasn't sure why I was trying so hard to get to know a loser bum like Mr. Elijah Ray Anderson, but she didn't care, because it wasn't going to stop her from making his life as miserable as possible while he continued to work at this school. She added that she would take pleasure in making the lives of two more losers (meaning us) as miserable as possible if we persisted in trying to be friends with him. Fairly quickly Mrs. Abigail Bailey and I tired of her tirade.

"Back up woman!" Mrs. Abigail Bailey said. "You need Jesus in your life. Go somewhere else with all that Satan talk. Thank you Jesus!" Mrs. Abigail Bailey added passionately as we began to walk away. Needless to say, Ms. Paula Gooden didn't like this speech, and she continued to stand there mumbling idle threats to herself while we walked away conversing, laughing and ignoring the woman that was simply up to no good.

The next day after our general office meeting, my buddy Mrs. Abigail Bailey and I were assigned to restock the janitorial utility closet with janitorial supply items and equipment. This task usually took all day. However, Mr. Elijah Ray Anderson had completed his assignment early that day and decided to help the two of us with our task. The assistance that he provided was much appreciated, because it meant we could finish the job much faster. In fact, the whole assignment turned out to be rather enjoyable, because Elijah was so pleasant and helpful. He even engaged in some small talk with us! During this conversation his articulate speech revealed clever and insightful thinking, and we noted his obvious intelligence. This was in spite of the fact that we were aware he was a school dropout, with all the negative connotations attached to that status. It made us all the more saddened by the way he was being persecuted by most of his coworkers.

As the weeks passed the drama continued in the janitorial maintenance office – but some things changed. Elijah appeared to be developing a totally different spirit, along with his sketch pad booklet. Furthermore, Ms. Paula Gooden was also becoming more hostile, angry and frustrated – she seemed to be all the more enraged by Elijah's newfound peace and ability to ignore her. I could see that she was desperately seeking new strategies to make this man's life miserable. Misery was clearly food to her hateful appetite, and she was particularly angered when she saw Elijah and myself working together on a task in peace and harmony, in a manner she could not interrupt or interfere with. She tried on many occasions to interfere with us, but the new joyful spirit that Elijah and I had created ensured that all of her hateful words and actions were simply ineffective. The result was a more pleasant workday for everyone.

Yet regardless of my own feelings, throughout this time I had to give Ms. Paula Gooden credit for her persistence! For instance, one day when Elijah and I were working together, picking up trash and placing it in a trash bag, Ms. Paula Gooden passed by saying derogatory things to us. However, she only became angrier with us when we used our conversation as a means to ignore her. On another occasion she decided to walk the long journey to the back of the lunchroom where Elijah and I where talking and laughing while eating our lunch in order to hear what we were talking about. It seemed she wanted to hear something that she might be able to use against us. Of course, we weren't going to be that stupid and simply ceased our conversation on her arrival. On other occasions we would just look at her and laugh, which made her extraordinarily angry, with fire in her eyes. It was clear that she had not given up her attempts at persecution.

A short time later, during a general office meeting, Ms. Paula Gooden once again attempted to incite conflict amongst the janitorial staff. At this meeting Ms. Cheryl Washington announced that she was assigning Mr. Elijah Ray Anderson and myself to work together as partners, based on how well we had been working together over the previous couple of weeks, and the high quality of our work.

"I hope," she jokingly added, "that this change will have the blessings of both Jesus and Mrs. Abigail Bailey!"

"Praise Jesus!" Mrs. Abigail Bailey responded. "My doctor has given me the ok to perform my work duties. And besides, at this point Mr. Jeremiah Johnson's training with those larger janitorial machines such as buffers will be best done by Elijah, so I'm more than satisfied with your decision Ms. Cheryl Washington. Thank you Jesus!" she concluded.

After Mrs. Abigail Bailey was finished speaking, Ms. Cheryl Washington began to speak once more, but she was politely interrupted by Mr. Elijah Ray Anderson. The entire office staff were obviously surprised, becoming quiet when Mr. Elijah Ray Anderson stood up, placed his sketch pad booklet on his seat, and began to use hand motions to indicate that he felt a strong need to speak. He explained how he had come to work everyday, not aiming to make friends or enemies, but to work in a collaborative and civil work environment. His priority was always to focus on getting the work done in a timely manner.

"But," he added, "I have now decided to come to work every day with the idea of trying to be a lot more friendly, because I have learned that it makes for a better workday."

After this speech Ms. Cheryl Washington dismissed us, and we all went to work for the day. A few days later I was surprised once more by Mr. Elijah Ray Anderson when he decided, for whatever reason, to begin a conversation with me about his children and what it takes to be a single parent. I admit that the personal nature of the conversation took me completely by surprise, but it was more than welcome.

Chapter 5

Children are our sweetest inspiration

Mr. Elijah Ray Anderson shared the following story with me.

"On the Saturday morning of December 29th last year, my seven-year-old daughter Kimberly approached me after she and her twelve year-old brother Isaiah had finished watching Saturday morning cartoons. With those big beautiful brown eyes that she knows I can't resist she asked whether I would take her and Isaiah outside to make a big snowman with the remaining snow from yesterday's winter storm. But before I could respond, she stared at me with a disturbed look on her face.

'What is that tear for?' She asked me. 'Why are you crying Daddy?'

'I didn't know I was crying baby girl,' I responded, and she in turn began to cry. She wailed.

'It's that job that's making you sad again daddy!' She began to cry a little louder. She told me how much it hurts her and Isaiah to see their daddy hurt and sad, especially before he goes to or comes home from work. I picked up my daughter and hugged her. Isaiah walked into the kitchen and found us; he had tears in his eyes as well, and he embraced the both of us.

"So Jeremiah I stood there hugging my children, staring out of the kitchen window. I was paralyzed with anger… I wanted to blame someone or something for the pain that had taken over my family. At this point my thoughts became irrational… I even began to blame those initial tears which started all of this by revealing themselves, and betraying me in the process by exposing the sadness and pain that I was trying to keep buried for my family's sake. But I guess that deceit wasn't working. All I could think of was the recent memory of my two week suspension that meant that my daughter's birthday on February 8th (when I was going to surprise her with the brand new pink bicycle she had been asking for all year) had to be canceled. The whole incident made me feel extraordinarily sad, sad that I couldn't deliver the longed-for present, especially as she had been such a good daughter all year. Jeremiah," he continued, "that suspension ruined my children's Christmas. I couldn't get Kimberly a new doll; I couldn't get Isaiah that new video game system.

"You know what? Those hatefulness coworkers of ours not only make my life a misery, but my children's lives as well. I've been feeling so angry about it! I don't know how I could ever forgive them. After the suspension I had to use the money I'd saved for Christmas to pay emergency rent (which my landlord had raised a week before Christmas) and utility bills. What change I had left over was all I had to buy presents. I had to shop at a dollar store for my children! I tell you Jeremiah, that hurt my pride deeply. I felt little, less than a man. But I couldn't ask for help, so I bought cheap, simple items for them, a coloring book with crayons and a baby doll for my daughter, and a chess and checker board for my son. But still Jeremiah, I was blessed on that Christmas morning, when I saw the happiness on my children's faces when they opened their Christmas gifts which they had retrieved from underneath our tiny artificial Christmas tree. They hugged me, and despite not getting the presents they really wanted, I think they were happy just spending time with me... And I'd been so worried about material Christmas presents. They told me that just having me home with them on Christmas day was a gift for them. I cried with happiness. You can't imagine how much I love my children.

"But you know what Jeremiah? Though my children are genuinely forgiving and understanding about our situation, I don't think I can feel the same. At important occasions like Christmas I'm always reminded of their mother – my ex-wife – and how she's just not there to support them morally, emotionally, psychologically, spiritually or financially. She abandoned us and our children, in favor of her career and her friends. Even while we were married she had cheated on me, telling me that I didn't make enough money as a janitor. It soured our marriage. Through all this she expressed no remorse or conscience whatsoever. To added insult to injury, in her twisted thinking she thinks she is justified in simply not being a mother to her children. Anyway, one day after an intense argument she told me about her inability to commit to her family, and that she didn't love me. She finally admitted to me that I was 'rebound material', and that she'd never loved me. Apparently she'd married me partly because I was a good man, but primarily because we'd had a child together. She even told me that she just felt sorry for me, and had never had any intention of marrying me until she'd become pregnant early in the relationship. She said that the idea of being stuck in a marriage with a person she didn't love made it very easy for her to cheat with other men. When she'd realized she didn't love me, it made it easier for her to be no more than a surrogate mother to our children. Eventually she outright abandoned her children, family and marriage with no regrets."

As Elijah told me his harrowing story he emphasized that one of the most disturbing aspects of his ex-wife's behavior was the way she was actually proud of being a deadbeat mother. She consistently showed little to no care for the welfare of her children, regardless of how terrible or traumatizing her actions were.

"The sad fact is that the children still have unconditional love for their mother, though she appears not to give a damn about them." Elijah was clearly very distressed by this, saying that he felt an overwhelming guilt for his role in them having a mother who had no intention of ever being a mother to them. He said he felt helpless, yet he also had an overwhelming responsibility to comfort his baby girl.

"All I could offer was an apology to my children. But the day came when they came to me, crying hysterically and asking why their mother doesn't love them."

I couldn't believe the tragic story I was hearing. But there was more to come, as Elijah continued to tell how thanks to his ex-wife, he and his children had become homeless after the divorce.

"I lost everything in the divorce. I lost my job at the same time. Once I became homeless," he continued, his eyes filling with tears, "my family became vulnerable to all sorts of negative influences. We wound up living the nightmare of staying in a homeless shelter for five agonizing months. We survived on welfare, on food stamps and Medicaid. Even the social service worker heaped degrading, insensitive abuse on me when she reluctantly assisted me with my welfare application. This social worker was nothing more than a demon snake wearing a skirt. She spoke through her sharp fangs whenever she felt a need to express her opinion as to why I was probably going to be denied benefits, apparently primarily because I wasn't a woman."

Elijah told me that the discrimination he had experienced from the social worker had made him highly upset.

"I'd tried to argue that although I wasn't a woman I was still a concerned single parent that needed help. But she didn't offer any help... She obviously hated men... She responded to me with the sexist and bigoted views she held towards all single fathers. In fact, she treated the whole thing as a joke, laughing and reminding me that now I must know how a single mother feels when she's left with the burden of having to raise a child when a no good man runs out on her! By the end of the interview I was fed up and angry, and I wanted to lash out at the social worker. I managed to mostly restrain myself, but I did raise my voice a bit. 'Two wrong don't make a right!' I yelled at her. 'My wife abandoned me and my children and she will be punished spiritually, just like all those irresponsible fathers who neglect their parental duty! Just do your damn job so that I can get some assistance for me and my children. I don't care to hear your opinions! If you're not going to help me then just tell me that, but don't waste my damn time.'

"After that outburst I walked to the front desk to initiate a complaint about the social worker. There was eventually a hearing, but it resolved nothing. I just felt insulted and assaulted all over again. Anyway, I decided that from that point on I would focus solely on the well-being of my children, ignoring the ongoing scrutiny and harsh treatment I would get from a range of sources. Sometimes such scrutiny would be subtle, other times it would be obvious. For instance, when I would take one of my children to the doctor, the doctor would often overlook me as if he was waiting for the child's mother to enter the room. But, in all fairness, Jeremiah, there were other times when I met a more positive response. Anyway, to cut a long story short, I landed this job and I was able to get off welfare and out of the homeless shelter. I thank God for that blessing... No one has any idea what I had to go through... I wouldn't wish my experience on my worst enemy."

After telling me all of this Elijah simply stopped talking. With a sad look in his eyes, he rose from the lunch table.

"I'm done with conversation for the day. We should go and get some work done."

* * *

The following day Elijah and I were assigned to sweep and mop the entire gymnasium. This task proved very difficult for me, even though Elijah chose to be considerate by allowing me to sweep the gymnasium while he mopped (because mopping is more strenuous than sweeping, he said). Once we were finished cleaning the large NBA regulation-size gymnasium floor I was tired and sweating. I immediately sat my exhausted butt down on the bleachers, and Elijah joined me. I was surprised when Elijah once again began to talk to me about his children. It was as if he had a desperate need to get something off his chest. I didn't mind listening to his story, as long as I could remain sitting and resting. So while I sat there he told me about the various heartaches and challenges he had faced in being a single father.

At a certain stage I interrupted Elijah. I figured because he was willing to talk so freely about his children, maybe he'd tell me why he dropped out of school. So I boldly asked him to tell me why he'd dropped out of school. After all, he appeared to be very intelligent, so I just couldn't understand why he would drop out of school. But it was quickly clear that he wasn't going to tell me. And the expression on his face clearly revealed that the topic was still very painful for him.

"Why can't you just accept it when our coworkers call me a stupid dropout? Just believe it and move on like I've done."

"I'm sorry Elijah," I responded as we sat there together on the bleachers, "but I just can't believe that you're simply some stupid school dropout." But he didn't want to talk about it, so I dropped the subject. "Well Elijah," I said, "I'm rested. How about you?"

"I'm rested as well, Jeremiah. Should we go and get started on the rest of our tasks for today and then go home for the day?"

"I agree – let's go," I replied.

We gathered up all our janitorial items and moved on to tackle our final tasks for the day.

Two days later, after arriving at work and ignoring the routine office drama that I no longer allowed to affect me, we were pleasantly interrupted by Ms. Cheryl Washington walking into the office. Her smile and lovely voice brought all of us to attention, allowing her to properly open her morning office meeting. During the meeting she informed us about the details of our spring cleaning agenda. She asked all of us to prepare for the spring clean, which would take place during the last week in March. Once the office meeting was over, she politely dismissed us and we left to our assigned work areas. Elijah and I were assigned to clean the gymnasium in the morning before lunch, so we dutifully left the office and walked to the gymnasium. Once there we both worked to the point of exhaustion until the cleaning was completed. We once again found ourselves collapsed on the gymnasium bleachers, tired out. However, while I was resting I noticed that Elijah wasn't as tired as I was. Indeed, he appeared unable to sit still, despite the fact that I was dead on exhausted. Anyway, after a while I told Elijah that I was done resting and that we should go to lunch. Elijah thought this was a great idea, telling me he was more starving than tired after all the work.

So pretty soon we were sitting down to lunch at what was now our favorite lunchroom table. I was still somewhat tired from the work that we had just done, but I was curious about what was bothering Elijah so much – he hadn't been his usual talkative self during the day, and this was only more obvious as we were sitting there at the lunchroom table. I didn't want to bother him with all my intrusive questions trying to find out what was bothering him, and so I decided for once to focus on minding my own business. I let Elijah eat his lunch in peace for once. While I ate my lunch I began to drift off in my own thoughts, thinking in particular how ridiculous it was to work this hard and not get the paycheck to match. I knew for certain that without my wife's income my wages alone would not support us. If my wife and I had to rely on my janitorial wages we would not be able to pay many of our bills. We would have to get used to bill collectors making phone calls to the house and talking to us as if we personally owed them money, with their arrogant and relentless threats which cause mental anguish and distress, exacerbating our financial crisis. I tell you, being a low wage earner in this country is not easy.

I remembered how when I was an auto plant worker, my wages used to be enough to support our entire household. I tell you, the shift to this janitorial job was a rude awakening, coming face to face with only being able to pay a few of my bills. This was not good for my self-esteem. However, I also learned a new perspective on life, developing a new appreciation and respect for low wage earners and the challenges they have to face. In light of my newfound wisdom, I was amazed and troubled by those individuals surviving on low incomes. I hoped that Elijah had another means to supplement his income, because I knew how depressing it was to try to support your family on such a low income. Pressures like that can become even more overwhelming when you are a single parent with a single low income. Such an income places an individual in the category of 'working poor', while those low wages can in fact ensure that person is denied all kinds of benefits from social services or government programs. The bottom line is that people have to accept that they are going to be left out in society to struggle alone, with no real relief in sight, despite being a faithful taxpayer.

At this point my thoughts and the silence at the lunchroom table were abruptly interrupted.

"Why do you want to know why I dropped out of school when so many others don't seem to give a damn? Why can't you just accept the common notion that school dropouts are just lazy losers, full of excuses?"

I tell you I was insulted by the question!

"First of all Elijah," I replied, "I care about my fellow man. Furthermore, my interest in wanting to know why you dropped out of school is based on my observation that most people, when asked, will tell you that it was an individual making a choice for whatever reason. However, your situation seems different. For one, you just don't seem to fit the stereotype of a school dropout. I feel in my spirit that your story has great value and should be shared with others, building a bridge of understanding. Knowledge from another person's perspective will prevent people simply lumping all of those that have dropped out of school into one category."

"I don't know what to say Jeremiah," said Elijah quietly. "No one ever cared enough about me to want to know what was going on with me, what's wrong with me." Elijah had a sad look on his face and his eyes were welling with tears. I realized that Elijah was trying to convince himself not to divulge his story, but his spirit was crying out for him to do so. This reluctance to discuss his story really seemed to me to again set him apart from those individuals that drop out of school with asinine excuses.

It soon became clear that Elijah had finished beating himself up, and had come to the decision that he would tell his story. It seems that this decision had been made after days of soul-searching, and had been driven in the main by a promise to a person he loved dearly. He told me that he would describe the entire situation to me, but he must first tell me where his source of inspiration and motivation comes from. He went on to explain that my desire to know why he dropped out of school was not the essential factor motivating his decision to share his story. He said I would better understand everything if I heard about the factors inspiring and motivating his disclosure. He also told me that he had never told his story to another soul before, and asked me to not share it with anyone. I reluctantly agreed, and sat there waiting with great anticipation to hear his words.

At this juncture Ms. Paula Gooden decided not only to journey to the lunchroom table we were sitting, but had the nerve to take a seat, wearing her devilish smile. We knew she was up to no good, and Elijah immediately stopped talking and we gave her an unwelcome look. She ignored our reaction, and greeted us rudely.

"How are *Stupid One* and *Stupid Two* doing? Why are you two dummies looking at me like that?" She continued. "This table doesn't belong to you two. If anyone wants to sit here they can and if you dummies don't like it, then you can move!" With a smug look on her face she looked around. "I'm actually starting to like this table now and I'm not moving." I took a look at Elijah – and I tell you, if looks could kill we would be attending this woman's funeral.

"Why are you over here bothering us?" I asked her. "With all the other lunchroom tables in here you can't tell me you couldn't find another table to sit at!"

"Bingo! You got that right!" she said gleefully. "I came over here specifically to give you two a reminder. I have not forgotten my promise to take you two down. It's no secret that I don't like you and you two don't like me."

She leaned back, obviously pleased with her revelation. She then began feeling around in her purse under the table in a suspicious manner, as if she was looking for something of great importance. This actually made Elijah and I feel very uncomfortable, because we didn't know if that no-good woman was going to pull some kind of weapon out of that purse. However, our suspicions soon subsided when her hand came up from under the lunchroom table with a stick of chewing gum clenched between her fingers and thumb. She placed the stick of chewing gum in her mouth and began to chew that gum like an old cow grazing in a grassy field. At this point, Elijah and I simply stared at her, wishing she would just leave. It wasn't long before our wish came true, but not before it did she opened her wide mouth again.

"You two have it coming, and it's just a matter of when and where. You can bet your bottom dollar that it's going to happen. Anyway, I'm tired of looking at your stupid ugly faces." She laboriously rose from the lunchroom table and began to walk away.

"Make like the criminal you are and flee, woman!" Elijah called out. We both began to laugh at that wildebeest as she walked away.

I saw Elijah breathe a sigh of relief when the visit was over.

"I'm glad that trifling cow is gone," he said with conviction. Once he was able to gather his confidence again, he began with great caution to resume the telling of his story, which he referred to as The Janitor's Secret. Elijah emphasized again how important it was that he be careful about who he shared his story with, because the consequences could be dire if the wrong person heard his story.

"Particularly," he emphasized, "a no-good person like Ms. Paula Gooden. You'll see what I'm talking about when you hear my story." He took a deep breath. "I guess I'm now ready to tell my story. I hope you're listening because I'm only going to tell it once."

Elijah carefully told his tale, beginning by describing the motivating triggers that made him first want to tell his story.

"In the second week of November last," Elijah began, "I was walking down a hallway here on my way to my assigned work area, when I noticed a great deal of noise just around the corner from the janitorial utility closet. I went to investigate the situation, only to find what appeared to be a group of about five six grader boys bullying another boy of the same age. The ringleader of the bullies had his victim pinned up against a locker, and had his fist drawn back for a punch clearly aimed at his face. The bully's face was snarling and angry, yet he was clearly enjoying the moment. I shouted at them, ordering the bully to stop. Although the boy hesitated at first, he eventually dropped his fist to his side and then turned with an angry look.

'What are you going to do if I keep on kicking his butt?' he asked me challengingly. 'Because you can't put your hands on me, or you'll have to deal with my parents! You're just a nobody loser janitor – why don't you go clean the crap out of a toilet somewhere and mind your own damn business!' The rest of his gang laughed appreciatively.

"I kept my composure, and I slowly and carefully told the child that he was obviously out of order and clearly hadn't been disciplined properly at home. But I also told him that his observation was somewhat correct.

'My present occupation comes with low wages,' I said, 'which means I don't have a lot to lose when I'm fired from this job after I whip your little butt like an Egyptian slave in the name of discipline and showing respect to your elders. I look forward to dealing with your parents afterwards, but in the meantime you're going to let that boy go now!' The bully complied, mumbling angry words under his breath. Anyway, I was pretty amused that my idle threats had such an effect – their eyes grew wide, the smiles were wiped from their faces, and the laughter quickly ceased. So I separated the victim from the bullies, standing next to him and shielding him from the rest. I then asked the ringleader what had happened and why he was beating the other child up. The response was chilling, and struck me to the bone.

'That dummy deserved to get his butt kicked because life is going to kick his butt in the future anyways, so I decided to get my licks in now. After he gets on welfare and my tax dollars support him while I work it will be too late for me to get my licks without going to jail.'

"I couldn't believe what I was hearing. How could this sixth-grader be saying this, without any sensitivity or remorse?

'Where is all this crazy talk coming from?' I asked. The origin of the tirade soon became clear – the bully's parents had told him repeatedly how they wanted to get rid of all the stupid, ignorant, uneducated people that drop out of school and end up on welfare. They had told him that these people expected hard-working taxpayers to take care of their lazy unworthy butts. They had even said, on more than one occasion, that if they could they would wipe all the worthless good-for-nothing stupid human beings off the face of this world. The bully seemed to think that all of this thinking was completely normal. I was sickened by what I was hearing, especially when I looked down into the face of the boy they had been victimizing. His eyes were overflowing with tears. The small child was clearly overcome with hopelessness and despair. I couldn't believe that the bully could be being taught such irresponsible values. Jeremiah," Elijah added, "I tell you his parents should not only be ashamed of themselves, but be held accountable for their irresponsible parenting." Elijah continued with the story.

"At this point I broke the group up, sending the bully and his followers back to their classroom, threatening to take them to the principal if they were seen in the hallways before the day was out. Once they were well out of sight, I walked the other child back to his classroom. While I walked, I asked him what his name was.

'Most people call me Little Joe.'

'Hello Little Joe!' I said, shaking his hand. 'My name is Mr. Anderson and I am going to walk you back to your classroom.' While we were walking I asked him what he had done to make the bullies pick on him.

'I don't know – I didn't do anything sir! Mr. Anderson, those boys have picked on me since I started going to this school. You see, they found out I had to use the resource classroom 'cause I have a learning disability.' The distressed child went on to explain how having a learning disability made him angry, and he didn't like the idea of feeling different or less than other people. He said he was constantly being told that he's not as smart as the other kids.

'Mr. Anderson,' Joe said, 'I think having a learning disability is not as bad as how I get treated every day. People are downright mean and unfair, just when they find out I have a learning disability. It makes me feel so bad that sometimes I wish I was dead or had never been born.' Poor Little Joe, his eyes once again filled with tears and his voice became incoherent with his grief."

Elijah turned to me. "I wanted so much to comfort Little Joe, but I didn't know what to do or say. I just told him that everything would be all right. Before I could say anything further, he began to speak again, revealing his desperately low self-esteem.

'I think the bully was right,' Little Joe said. 'There's no place in the world for a dummy like me! I'm not going to amount to anything in society, and my dreams will never come true. I'm just going to get bad, low-paying jobs and be a second-class citizen for the rest of my life.' It turns out that this is the kind of thing his parents would say when they thought he couldn't hear them, and each night he would cry into his pillow. It became clear this was the type of talk that Little Joe heard all day – doom and gloom about his future. His story was so mentally and spiritually draining I felt I couldn't listen any more. I had to return Joe to his classroom before I became depressed myself, because I knew there was an element of truth in what Joe was saying. I mean," Elijah continued, "just look at Ms. Paula Gooden's attitude towards those that have dropped out of school.   "Once we reached the door of Little Joe's classroom, I shook his hand and told him to take care of himself. I said that if he ever needed anything he would be able to find me in the school building."

* * *

"Little Joe's story wasn't the only one that motivated me. One week before Halloween last year I ran into Jolene Woodmere, the school's star player on the seventh-grade basketball team. Jolene is well known and well liked, and she usually exudes a larger-than-life popularity. But when I ran into her, she was very upset. Her teacher had persuaded her coach to not let her play in the next basketball game until she fully participated in a drawing contest, the Detroit Citywide Angel Night Poster Board competition. She felt it was a waste of her time because she was sure she had no drawing talent. She stormed out of the classroom, heading to the office in the hopes of having the issue resolved with the principal. On her way to the office she walked past me in the hallway – it was almost like she didn't even see me, she was so wrapped up in her anger. However, when she had got slightly further down the hallway she stopped and walked back to where I was mopping the hallway. I looked up at the sound of her voice.

'Excuse me sir,' she said, 'I don't mean to disturb you while you're working, but I have noticed you carry around a sketch pad all the time. Are you some kind of artist or are you just a janitor?'

'Hello, young lady!' I responded. 'Well I guess I'm an artist by birth and a janitor by occupation. Being a janitor is something I do, but being an artist is something I am. Is there anything I can help you with?'

'I hope you can,' she said, and then she went on to explain her predicament. Before she'd even finished her story, I'd sketched a rough picture in my sketch pad. I ripped out the page with the picture on it and handed it to her, asking if this picture was ok.

"She stared at the picture. She looked at me wide-eyed and open-mouthed – I'm not being boastful Jeremiah – amazed at how good the picture was and the speed at which I'd drawn it.

'I can definitely use this!' she Jolene. 'I see you're a great artist, so why are you wasting your time being a janitor when you could be out there making hundreds and thousands of dollars being an artist? I know that artists make way more than what you're making now as a toilet jockey – I'm sorry, I mean janitor!' I told her I wasn't offended, and then explained that the reason I couldn't use my art to make lots of money was due to a personal hindrance, which eventually prevented me from pursuing a career in art.

'I'm sorry to hear that,' Jolene said, and she had a sincere sadness in her voice. 'I hope someday soon all of your problems will be taken away so that you can become the artist that you were born to be. Don't give up on your dreams!'

'Ok!' I said. 'And thank you for your concern. I appreciate those words of wisdom from someone so young.' As Jolene walked away she called out once more.

'Thanks again sir! And you take care of yourself because I really have to be going now.' She left smiling and no longer upset, waving at me as she walked down the hallway. Once she was gone, I picked up my mop and got back to work."

* * *

"Well," Elijah said, "I guess there's one more story that motivated me to tell you why I dropped out of school." However, before he could begin to that story, our supervisor Ms. Cheryl Washington walked over to our lunch table. She told us that the buffer machine had broken down and that we had run short of the pads used for stripping the floors, so she said that we could stay on our lunch break until she needed us.

"Anyway," she added, "you guys really deserve an extra break, what with the way you've both been working above and beyond the call of duty lately. I'm really glad to have you both on staff."

"Thank you," we both said, quite pleased at her praise. She then left the lunchroom. Once Ms. Cheryl Washington had walked away, Elijah got back to telling me his final motivational story.

"Ok. One day my daughter came to talk to me. When she turned on the lights in my bedroom, she found me sitting on the edge of the bed with my head down and my eyes closed, rocking slowly back and forth.

'It's that job making you sad again, isn't it daddy!' she exclaimed. She told me that it made her upset to see me come home every day looking so depressed and exhausted. I remember feeling bad, seeing those tears on my daughter's face; I thought she was in more pain than I was at that moment.

'I'm sorry that you have to see your daddy in this state baby girl,' I said. 'But I need you to understand that daddy is beyond tired of going to a job were he is going to be paid low wages no matter how hard he works. The worst of it is that at work I am basically treated like crap, with no respect. They tell me all the time of my low position and status. To add insult to injury the people that I work for and the policies and procedures of the place appear to want to keep me down. All the rules and regulations bring out the worst in my coworkers. They're busy stepping on one another to get promotions, creating a hostile environment and all sorts of unprofessional business practices. My coworkers bring all sorts of personal issues into the workplace. I'm so sorry that I have to share this with you, but sometimes I wonder what would happen if everyone who is viewed as low status like your daddy in this country were to protest and simply stay home for a day... I wonder what impact that would have?'

"But at this point my daughter began to cry again, saying that she and Isaiah were hurt when they saw daddy constantly stressed out and down in the dumps about his life.

'We love you dearly daddy and we are scared that because of all the stress one day you will have a heart attack or a stroke!' She began to cry more intensely, telling me they she didn't want me to die and leave them all alone. It's true, Jeremiah" Elijah, continued. "I am all they have." He then told how this realization had brought tears to his eyes, which he had tried to hide from his daughter.

"I embraced her tightly. She continued to say that she felt her daddy was her only protector. She reminded me that I'd always told her that a person should practice what they preach – if they don't then that makes them a hypocrite. And so she began to speak tell me about a time when I'd told her not to allow things that hurt you to build up inside, because it will make you psychologically, spiritually and physically sick. I could well recall saying those things to her, and the way she'd smiled with her beautiful white teeth.

"In other words, Jeremiah," Elijah continued, "she made me make a promise that I would someday tell my story, getting all my internal feelings off my chest, so that I could be psychologically, spiritually and physically healthy again. Then I would be a better person and a better dad to my children who I love so much."

After this emotional tale, Elijah turned to me. "So this is it Jeremiah. I chose you to tell my story because of my daughter. She overheard me speaking to her grandmother about you, about the respectful way you have treated me here, which I particularly appreciate given the hateful coworkers we have. After hearing that conversation my daughter confronted me. Knowing I have no real friends, she told me I should at least talk with you.

'That Jeremiah person doesn't have to be your friend. As long as he is respectful and friendly to you, daddy, that's all that really matters.' Anyway, she made me promise that I would give it a chance. To tell the truth, once I had promised it made both of us feel better. In fact," Elijah continued, "her inspiration gave me the energy to leave some of this darkness behind. So after I'd made the promise to her, we walked into the kitchen and cooked dinner together while Isaiah set the small round table. We felt like a wonderful little family – and that is the reason I need to tell you my story," Elijah finished.

At this point our extended break was over, as Ms. Cheryl Washington returned to tell us she had located a working buffer machine and the pads needed for stripping as well. So we went back to work.

Chapter 6

Dyslexia is the real story

The first Saturday of February arrived, and my wife and I decided to get an early start on our spring cleaning for the year. We'd begun with the attic and had worked our way down to the basement, where we spent most of the morning cleaning. At one point Sophia took a break from the work and looked around.

"We've got enough boxes down here to build a three-story tall pyramid!" I told my wife that doing all this cleaning made me feel like I was at work performing one of my janitorial work duties, except that I didn't have my buddy Elijah to work with me.

"But I like working with you too because you are much prettier than Elijah sweetheart!" I grinned at her. "I know I shouldn't be talking to you about this, because I know you don't really like it when I talk about work at home, but the stories Elijah has been telling me have just blown my mind. He has told me about these inspiring children, including his own daughter. The conversations I've had with him have been going over and over again in my mind. Basically, he's turned completely around, and I can't figure out why. At first he'd been unwilling to tell me his story about dropping out of school, but then he'd become so eager to tell me about those inspirational children. I just hope he keeps talking to me, especially given the promise he made to his daughter. I hope he's not going to renege and compromise his integrity."

Sophia had been listening to me carefully. She always knows what I need to hear. "Well, Jeremiah," she said, "remember that Elijah does have the right to change his mind. And you have to be mindful that talking to you about these things could be very painful as well as being therapeutic for him. Jeremiah," she added, "you should be proud of yourself, because that man has made a lot of progress while you've been there, and it's only been a short period. So be more appreciative of that. You need to be very careful not to have Elijah move too fast by telling you a painful story that may result in him having a complete relapse. He could well go deeper into his shell, especially because you are not a psychiatrist or therapist. Please keep that in mind, sweetie." Sophia came to me and held my hand. "Jeremiah, I also want you to keep in mind that Elijah's stories of his inspirational children, which you shared with me, were heart-wrenching and extraordinarily disturbing to hear. Don't make the mistake of overlooking the significance in Elijah wanting to share his story with you. That in itself is extraordinary! It's obvious he wants to open up to someone, and that someone could be you. So just be patient because maybe one day he will choose to open up to you and tell you the story you want to hear. But at present you must ask yourself whether you are spiritually ready to hear this story, this Janitor's Secret. Remember, everything has to be in divine order, and maybe that's why you haven't heard his story yet. Now, are you just going to sit there on those boxes or are you going to give me a hand?" she smiled at me.

We cleaned all day, and it was soon dinnertime. We ate our dinner together at the dinner table, enjoying each other's company and conversation, light years away from workplace talk. Soon after dinner was over we attempted to watch a little television, but we were tired from the spring cleaning and went to bed early. The next day I left home for work, after giving my wife a hug and kiss in appreciation for another one of her delicious breakfasts. Once I arrived at work, my workday began with another routine janitorial office meeting. It didn't last as long as it usually did however, and I was glad because it allowed us to finish the early morning portion of our assigned work quickly.

The early finish of our work gave us the option of a most appreciated break just before lunch. However, because we both had strong work ethics we chose to use this time to properly prepare our work area with janitorial supplies and equipment for the assignment we had after lunch. As we did so I found myself taking close notice of Elijah. He was quiet and distanced today, as if he had a lot on his mind. I was in a good mood, and I chose to respectfully ignore my impulse to ask Elijah what was going on with him. As my wife had suggested, I just minded my own business and didn't bother him. However, I did try to pick up his spirits by telling corny jokes. These got no reaction whatsoever, so I decided to leave him alone. Once I had acknowledged his mood, I simply concentrated on enjoying my day.

So we went to lunch. As we walked to our table, Elijah suddenly stopped in his tracks with a blank stare on his face. He turned to look at me, suddenly looking confused. At this point I became a little nervous. I asked him if he was alright.

"No!" He replied loudly. He paused for a few seconds, and then he just blurted it out, in a low but clear voice not for all in the lunchroom to hear.

"I have dyslexia."

Without any hesitation I stepped away from him.

"You have what?"

"I have dyslexia, Jeremiah!"

I was lost for words. Elijah wasn't.

"Why are you stepping away from me as if I'm contagious? I'm not, Jeremiah."

"I'm sorry, man," I said. "I don't mean to be insensitive, but one can't be too careful in this day and age, with all these germs floating around. Excuse my ignorance, Elijah, are you taking medication for your dyslexia or is there a cure for what you have?"

"Well, Jeremiah," Elijah said slowly, "I guess I understand your ignorance. To answer your question, I have learned a little about dyslexia and I haven't found any kind of medication or a cure for the condition. But don't worry Jeremiah, I have learned that you can't catch dyslexia from touching someone with it, or from someone sneezing on you. Basically," Elijah paused, "from what I can tell dyslexia is a condition that causes a person to frequently view and write letters of the alphabet and numbers in reverse, amongst many other symptoms. It's what they call a neurological language disorder, and it's not contagious at all."

We stood in the middle of the lunchroom, looking at each other. I thought about what Elijah had just said, and realized that I trusted him and was reassured by his explanation. We resumed walking together, side by side together to our usual lunchroom table. We both sat down. Elijah was quiet once again, but although I could not yet say anything my mind was buzzing with questions. At one point during lunch I boldly turned to him and asked him how people become dyslexic. Elijah looked at me, still chewing on his ham and cheese sandwich. He took a careful sip of his orange juice and swallowed.

"Jeremiah," he said, "you don't become dyslexic, you are born dyslexic. Dyslexia is hereditary, so that means that you are given dyslexia from one of your parents or maybe both. "Elijah paused, and a look of great sadness came over his face."

"But this knowledge doesn't stop me from feeling heartbroken knowing that I gave my daughter dyslexia. When I felt she was mature enough I reluctantly told her that she had dyslexia, and I told her everything I know about it. I told her that I had given it to her, and I apologized. I was very proud and surprised at her level of maturity.

'Why are you apologizing daddy?' she responded. 'It's not your fault! I still love you. Besides, it makes us special now, doesn't it daddy? Like you always said, we're not going to let stuff that we can't control get us down.'

I told her she was right. 'We are going to deal with our dyslexia to the best of our ability.' But in the back of my mind I still didn't know whether I could thank God for being dyslexic, because it seemed to be only shortcomings and no benefits. Anyway Jeremiah," Elijah continued, "My son is not dyslexic. When I told him that his father and sister were dyslexic, he said of course he didn't care about that. He said he loved us no matter what."

While I was listening intently to Elijah his words triggered a memory, of my job interview when I ran across a dyslexic man called Melvin. A disgruntled office worker, who was obviously prejudiced towards people who had dropped out of school or suffered from a learning disability, had no sympathy for Melvin. She had tried to defend her bigotry by pointing out what she thought were the negative effects that people who drop out of school have on society. At the time I fell completely into her web of bigotry, when I chose to agree with much of what she was saying. But afterwards I felt ashamed of myself, especially after consulting with my wife, who had immediately set me straight in a loving way. At this point I considered it best to keep this embarrassing story to myself. I thought that my present situation with Elijah represented a chance to redeem myself.

I was about to become lost in my own thoughts, but Elijah soon put a stop to that.

"Are you still listening? Because I haven't finished speaking, Jeremiah."

"Yes, man I'm still listening," I said. "I was just distracted by an old memory."

Once Elijah had my attention again he took a bite of a pear, before checking that I was still looking at him. He asked for my word that I would not tell his story about why he had dropped out of school to anyone, because he had always planned to take his story to the grave! I thought to myself that it couldn't be that serious, until I saw the somber look in his eyes. So I agreed and gave him my word that I would not tell anyone what he was about to say. He smiled lightly, but with concern. He finished eating the pear and placed the remains back in his bag on the lunchroom table. Taking a well-deserved breath he looked down at his hands. Elijah then looked back up at me, and taking in my expression he asked whether I had any questions. I said I did but would wait until he had finished. He nodded.

Elijah's face became shadowed with sadness. He began to speak of the year he entered elementary school. He turned to me and told me that it was important that he go on record to say that he did not drop out of school, and I will understand this when I hear his story in its entirety. He also told me that he was looking forward to the day when the stigma of being labeled a school dropout, of any kind, will cease.

"The fact is," he said, "school dropouts are treated like felons serving a life time sentence of second-class citizenry." At this point his eyes could no longer hide the strain of his memories, which were clearly holding him in a psychological state of bondage. I felt in my spirit that the telling of his story (which I believed was well overdue) would free Elijah from much of the mental distress he had been feeling. As he began to talk again, I interrupted him with a question, forgetting my earlier promise. Calmly he reminded me that I said I was going to respectfully allow him to tell his story without any questions until he was done. I told him he was right and I apologized, feeling embarrassed. I told Elijah he could resume telling his story.

"Thank you, Jeremiah," he said.

Elijah commenced telling his story.

"It was a Wednesday in September, many years ago. My mother was getting me ready for my first day of kindergarten. I was five years old, but I can remember the day as if it was yesterday. I soon found myself standing in the doorway of a building, my hand partially opening a screen door. The building was part of a public housing community estate (which they used to call 'the projects'). I watched the pigeons, sparrows and squirrels going about their business, although I remember thinking that they looked as if they were playing most of the time. As I watched the animals I found myself in a state of quiet serenity. As one particular pigeon took flight I noticed the beautiful blue sunny sky was gone, replaced by strange light reddish-gray clouds, bringing the smell of a rainstorm on the way. The morning weather was still comfortably warm, and I could feel the warm morning breeze on my face. My curiosity sated, I turned to go back inside but bumped into my mother's knee and rolled to the ground. I was unhurt, and it became one of those memorable moments when my mother reached down to pick me up, but first she tickled me to the point I nearly couldn't breathe and almost wet my pants. We giggled and laughed together while she raised me from the floor as if I was her prized possession. She placed hugs and kisses all over my face, clearly showing her love for her baby boy. Then the moment was over and I was safely back on solid ground. My mother kneeled down so she was at my eye level. She told me I was her big boy now, and I was going to grow up to be a great man. She was adjusting and straightening my clothes, wiping my face clean with her thumb, so I would make a good impression on my first day of kindergarten.

"My mother took me by the hand and we walked down the few steps off the porch. I jumped off the last step onto the sidewalk. My mother and I began to walk along the path to my school. We enjoyed our journey, as my mother was singing to me and testing me as to how well I knew my colors and shapes. She had me recite the letters of the alphabet, and we both laughed when I tried to count to a hundred as I could barely count to ten. She chatted to the other parents walking their children to school for the first time alongside us. Our journey was over before I knew it. We stood together outside the front doors of the Elementary School along with the other parents and children. The school bell rang, signaling that it was now time for us to enter the school building. The doors of the school building were very large and heavy. I tried to open one, being a 'big boy' for my mother, but I could barely reach the door handle. My mother laughed a little and opened the door for us, so we would not hold up everyone else waiting outside. Once we were inside the school building my mother once again knelt down and gave me a hug and kiss on the cheek. Seeing the frustrated look in my eye and correctly connecting to the incident with the school door, she reassured me that one day I would be able to open the door. In the meantime, she told me, I was still her big boy and she loved me very much. Her words made me feel good and boosted my confidence.

"My mother stood up and took me by the hand. We walked down the school hallway and stepped into the school office, I'll never forget my excitement wrapped in nerves that I felt when I looked up to see the smile on my mother's face. With excitement in her voice she boldly and proudly said to the office secretarial staff 'Good morning! I am Mrs. Olivia Anderson.' The office secretarial staff politely responded in harmony with all their salutations as well. My mother continued on with her great enthusiasm, explaining the purpose of her visit. 'Today is my baby boy's first day of kindergarten.' Before she could speak any further she was approached from behind by the school principal with her smile and handshake, when to my own surprise I became shy and hid behind my mother's legs. The principal looked much like my mother but shorter. She looked down at me. 'Hello!' she said. 'How are you doing this morning down there little man?' 'I'm just fine ma'am,' I responded, peeking around my mother's legs. We left the office and as we walked further down the hallway I asked my mother dozens of questions. In answer to one of these, my mother told me we were on our way to my kindergarten classroom. My stomach was beginning to fill with butterflies. We reached my kindergarten classroom. My mother looked down at me with a smile and asked if I was excited to meet my kindergarten teacher and classmates. I was terrified, but I looked into my mother's eyes and nodded my head yes. After another reassuring hug and a kiss my mother took my hand, using her other hand to open the door.

"As we walked into the classroom the kindergarten teacher greeted us with a smile and kind words. She came towards us, and I resumed my hiding position behind my mother. I was full of fear. I looked around the classroom, seeing many small school desks (many of them were already occupied with children) and the teacher's large desk. I also saw a huge blackboard with the numbers and the letters of the alphabet written on it. The classroom had bright multicolored walls covered in pictures, and there was one large clock on one wall. The shelves were full of all sorts of toys, games, puzzles and a variety of blocks. My view was interrupted as my mother knelt down in front of me with misty eyes, giving me a hug and a kiss on the forehead. I returned the affection, wondering why she suddenly looked so sad. My fear rose to an even higher pitch when she said that I had to stay here in the classroom and be her big boy, because she was going to leave and pick me up later. I didn't want to be left in this strange place. I thought maybe my mother was trying to give me away – the feeling of abandonment was more than I could bear. My mother tried to leave the classroom, but I refused to let her go. She and the kindergarten teacher began to struggle with me, trying to pry my hands from around my mother's body. Eventually I was overpowered, but I continued to struggle to get back to the loving arms of my mother once again. The teacher held me, and instructed my mother in a commanding voice to please leave the classroom.

'He will be all right, really! Just come back at the usual pick up time.'

My mother backed out of the classroom, tears running down her face, as I cried out for dear life to her, frantically pleading.

'Please mommy don't leave me, don't leave me here!'

"After my mother had left I cried for another long while, my eyes swollen and puffy, my nose running, hyperventilating with anxiety. Finally I realized that all of my crying wasn't working – my mother wasn't returning. I vaguely understood that I just had to get used to the cruel reality of her absence. So I began the necessary process of calming myself down. Reluctantly I let my kindergarten teacher hug me. In a comforting voice she told me that everything would be alright.

'So please don't cry anymore,' she said, 'because it makes us sad to see you cry.'

I remembered my mother's request that I be a big boy after she left, so not to disappoint her I tried to stop crying and attempted to set my shyness aside so I could meet my classmates. My kindergarten teacher smiled, and in a soft voice told me her name was Mrs. Melinda Lawson.

'What is your name?' she asked.

I answered in a quavering voice. 'My name is Elijah Ray Anderson and I like to color and draw.'

After my introduction, she asked all of my classmates to introduce themselves. I was offered a box of crayons and a sheet of paper to color on, and in no time at all I was happily coloring up the page at one of the desks.

"The first real activity of the morning was reciting the letters of the alphabet and counting numbers up to ten. I was successful at this task and felt very proud. After the learning session was over my classmates and I were allowed to play with toys and games for a while. Then, our kindergarten teacher brought out a great big book from behind her desk. She told us it was the story of Pinocchio, a fairytale. We all wanted to know what a fairytale was. With her infectious smile and obvious enthusiasm she responded by not only telling us what a fairytale was, but by informing us that the story of Pinocchio was one of her favorites. She said it would be a pleasure to share the story with us. She read it out aloud to the whole class, and we all loved it, as we loved the many other stories she read to us throughout the year.

"That first day of kindergarten I was beginning to worry that my mother was taking too long to come to pick me up. However, before my eyes could tear up once more I looked up and saw my mother at the classroom door. I felt so happy I did not wait for the bell to ring but immediately got up from my little desk and ran as fast as I could into her arms. I was covered with hugs and kisses. Jeremiah, that moment stands out in my mind like it was yesterday; I was overwhelmed by the feeling of never wanting to let my mother go. My mother and I then left the school hand in hand, and on the way home I once again noticed the color of the sky, the same as in the morning. The rainstorm had never eventuated.

"As we were walking my mother asked her big boy how his first day of kindergarten was. I was still in turmoil from my feelings of abandonment in the morning, and stumblingly and rather incoherently tried to tell her all that had happened and how I had felt. I wanted some kind of apology from her, reassurance that she did care about me. Of course my mother immediately embraced me and told me how very sorry she was and how bad she felt leaving me in that manner. She looked me in the eye and told me it made her sad every time she thought about it. I saw how hard it must have been for her and so I put on a brave face. I stuck out my chest and told my mother that her big boy was doing alright. It had the desired effect, and her smile reappeared. I felt in my spirit that the morning ordeal had a profoundly negative affect on her as well. As we walked she told me that she never wanted to put us through anything like that ever again. This disturbed me a bit because I had actually enjoyed the rest of my first day. I realized I wanted to go back to school! I made a futile attempt to agree with what she was saying, until I spotted her smile.

'Are you sure you really want to go back and experience all that sadness of me leaving you again?' she asked slyly.

'No mommy! I mean yes mommy!' I cried confusedly. 'I want to go back to school tomorrow to show you that I can be your big boy.'

'Well,' my mother said, 'since you believe that Elijah, I will listen to you and take you back to school tomorrow morning as you ask.'

I tried not to show her how happy I was, but the way in which I jumped up and down gave me away.

"While walking home I began to reflect back on my day, and realized how much fun I had at school. I really enjoyed hearing the fairytale, and thought that if I didn't go back it might make my kindergarten teacher feel bad. I was excited to get home and tell my big brother and little sister all about my day (aside from the crying), and of course my father as soon as he decided to come home from the streets and visit his family. The following day I was so excited about going back to kindergarten I got up earlier than everyone else in the house. I managed to bathe all by myself and then I dressed myself in the school clothes laid out on the top of the dresser by my mother. Once I was dressed I went downstairs to watch my favorite morning cartoon show, until my mother called me into the kitchen to eat my breakfast with the rest of the family. I sat down at the round table and quickly poured milk in my bowl of cold cereal. I hurriedly ate my cereal, causing my mother to ask why I was in such a hurry. I explained that I didn't want to be late for kindergarten, trying to hide my growing excitement. All morning I asked my mother over and over again if it was time for us to leave for school.

'Not right now,' she would respond. 'In a minute Elijah sweetheart.' After those minutes, which felt like hours, I finally heard my mother call me from her bedroom upstairs to get ready for school. When she came downstairs we left the house and joined the path to school.

"My excitement was at an all-time high, and my mother had difficulty keeping up with me. Then I began to notice how fast my mother and I were arriving at school, and once I saw the school on the horizon my excitement fled in an instant. The feeling of shyness crept over me all over again, and all of the emotions of the day before began to resurface. I felt the urge to turn around and run home. But I reminded myself that a big boy must keep his word, especially to his mother, and I tried to fight all the negative emotions that were trying to prevent me from returning to school. Looking back I thank my Heavenly Father and my mother for providing me with the strength to recover the confidence I so desperately needed at that moment. With this help I was more than able to fight off most of those feelings, and as we reached the school doors much of my earlier excitement had returned. Again tightly holding my mother's hand we entered the building. As we walked through the hallway to the kindergarten classroom I felt victorious. Using my newfound confidence I let go of my mother's hand. She asked whether I would be all right. I smiled nervously and said I would be fine, yet I was struggling to keep the fountain of tears that threatened to burst in a flow under control. I gathered myself together and gave my mother a hug and a kiss on her cheek.

'I love you mom but you can leave now,' I said, 'because I will be alright.'

Her eyes grew wide with pride. She told me she loved me, and thanked me for being such a big boy for mommy.

'You're welcome mommy,' I said, as I turned to walk toward my assigned school desk. I told her mother I would see her later, when she came to pick me up at the end of the day.

'Ok,' she said, and she left with a tear in her eye but a smile on her face.

"I enjoyed my second day at school. First thing in the morning Mrs. Lawson asked the class to stand and raise our right hand to pledge allegiance to the flag. We took our seats and then commenced reciting the letters of the alphabet and their sounds. Afterwards she had us try to count up to fifty. There were other children there that could count up to one hundred! So far I was doing fine, and soon we were allowed to play with the classroom toys, games and blocks, which I very much enjoyed. I liked the blocks the best, and used them to construct castles and skyscrapers. Before I knew it, it was cleanup time, and then Mrs. Lawson turned back on the lights to read us a fairytale."

Elijah paused. "Jeremiah," he said, "that was my daily routine in kindergarten, although sometimes we had field trips to places like the Apple Orchard, City Zoo, Ice Capades and the Science Center. I will never forget those school plays. In one I reluctantly performed a dance and singing in a white bear costume made by my mother. I still remember the fun I had at our Halloween party with all that tasty candy, and the delicious food we ate at our Thanksgiving dinner. But what really stands out in my mind is the genuine love and respect I felt our teacher Mrs. Lawson had for all of the children, and her patience and kindness in the way she talked to us. She made us want to learn, with her talent and passion for teaching. Jeremiah, it was a great pleasure to have her as a teacher, and my formal schooling was clearly having the perfect start."

Here Elijah sighed, and a look of regret filled his eyes. "This is where my story changes. Some months later, after the summer vacation, I found myself sitting in the same school but in another classroom. My first day as a first grader was another Wednesday morning early in September." Elijah looked at me. "I've come to believe that it was this year that marked the beginning of all my academic failures. It was this year that so tainted the rest of my education and the rest of my life. During this year I was also confronted with the cruel reality that not all teachers are friendly; my first grade teacher introduced me to alienation and isolation in the classroom. I was six years old, and I learned about alienation and isolation about a week after becoming a first grader. I was playing in the designated play area at the back of the classroom, where all the toys and games were kept. My teacher hurried over to the area, and apprehended me much like a security guard would a common criminal. She began yelling at me, and grabbed me painfully by the hand. I had been holding a toy block, a cardboard item that resembled a house brick. She swiftly repossessed the toy, still verbally raging at me. I was frightened and confused. I didn't know what crime I could have committed to make my teacher respond to me in such a rough manner. She dragged me away from my partially built castle and the other children and dumped me back in my seat, reproaching me forcefully all the time. She continued berating me. Most of my classmates looked on in horror but some began to laugh at me. "From what I could discern through the dramatic shouting and the rain of spit and horrid breath that reeked of feces hot on my face, she was telling me that I was to stay seated and not to get up for anything until I had finished my class work or when my parents came to pick me up."

"After her tirade my teacher walked away from me, still mumbling a variety of angry, mean words. I sat at my desk with my head down, my face running with tears. I felt overwhelmed, humiliated and worthless. As a small child I could not conceive of anything that would cause anyone to act in such a matter. My mother had certainly never treated me like that for any reason." Elijah turned to me. "I guess it wouldn't surprise you to learn that the event had a damaging effect on me. My self-esteem dropped like a stone. I guess it would have been alright if my teacher had helped me with my class work, but in the weeks that followed I found myself ignored and overlooked. I found I was soon unable to keep up with my classmates academically. I wasn't able to finish my class work in time, and so I was always the last child struggling to complete any task. I had to hear the sounds of children playing in the background of the classroom, when all the children had finished their work and I was still sitting at my desk. This went on for weeks, as I sat at my desk, my mind numb with frustration as I tried as hard as I could to get the assignment done so that I could play as well. But no matter how hard I tried I seemed to always finish right at the end of the class."

Elijah shook his head, remembering. "That wasn't even the worst of it," he sighed. "When I was finally done with each assignment, after struggling through every step, I usually got everything wrong! So my teacher would tell me off in front of all my classmates. She told me over and over again that I just wasn't smart enough. I began to believe her – why shouldn't I? I had no evidence to the contrary. I was faced with the reality of not only being slow, but also an academic failure. I held this title right through the rest of first grade. I began to turn on myself, having all sorts of negative mental thoughts about my academic inferiority. I often wondered whether I was simply born with an inadequate brain, or whether it was because of the difficulty I had concentrating and remembering information. I worried that I was lazy or a daydreamer, as my teacher constantly told me I was. I was also frustrated, because I didn't know how to articulate to my teacher what was going on inside my head, without her dismissing whatever I said as simply an excuse for not finishing my assignments. As time went on I felt only more angry and sad. Usually, when thinking about the whole thing, I would conclude that my teacher was right in making me feel as if I was not as smart as my classmates, and so it was right that I should get treated in that way. After all, even at this young age I had learned that this world had no place for dummies like me, as she would say.

"Jeremiah, my teacher was an authority figure. How can a child argue against someone like that? Especially given that I was doing so poorly academically. My grades were so bad that the only time I saw an 'A' was when they wrote my name Anderson! Obtaining an 'A' grade seemed impossible, regardless of how much effort I put in. My teacher made all of this that much worse by encouraging a great many of my classmates to spy on me. Every time I decided to leave my desk with my class work unfinished to play in the play area these children would run up and tell her. She would reward these classroom spies with candy and other sweet treats, as well as classroom privileges such as passing out paper to the other classmates or washing off the blackboard. When I was caught in this way she would physically drag me back to my desk or make me stand in the corner, after paddling me on my backside if I was unlucky. So to avoid all that drama I learned to stay at my desk until I became bored out of my mind. My head would begin to drop while my eyes would slowly close as I started to doze off to sleep. This would lead to the same effect – the classroom spies would get rewarded and I would get paddled and have to stand in the corner of the classroom until my mother come to pick me up or I simply fell down with exhaustion.

"At that point, Jeremiah, I was fed up with everything concerning school and education. Furthermore, in spite of all that I was *not* learning, I did learn the painful lesson that I should not talk, trust or socialize with my classmates or teachers. Especially because I had come to view my teacher as no more than a prison warden, and my classmates her guards. Of course, all the ill-treatment I endured inevitably made my school life miserable. I thank my Heavenly Father for the fact that it did not take away my love of learning, but it did ensure I developed a hatred for school. I was so tired of being told how stupid I was. Once, early on in the year, my mother arrived to pick me up from school. I was so very mad and upset, but hid my tears because she looked so happy picking up her big boy from school, and I didn't want to spoil that moment for her. I remember I got up from my desk and walked over to her, but was soon standing appalled and incredulous as my horrible teacher chatted in an oh-so-friendly manner with my mother. Her previously angry face was masked with a smile as fake as a three dollar bill. She concluded her conversation with my mother by telling her to have a good evening, and then had the gall to turn her fake smile on me and tell me to also have a good evening too.

"I remember I just wanted to get away from my teacher and the school as soon as possible. All I could think of was the awful way she treated me, constantly telling me how stupid I was. How could a school hire someone like that to be a teacher? I was being made to feel dumb by a school system that I thought was supposed to be educating me. Each day after returning home I would concentrate on being strong in front of my mother, each time blowing the chance to tell her that I hated school and was not as smart as my classmates. I thought telling her these things would break her heart, so every time she would ask me what was wrong I would say, 'Nothing, mommy.' But after eating dinner and watching a little television, I would go to bed and cry myself to sleep.

"During that year I quickly learned that the only time I was ever going to get relief was when she was absent for the day, which happened all too rarely. When we had a substitute teacher I would immediately view it as an opportunity and use it to my advantage. You see, the substitute teacher wouldn't be aware of how my teacher ran her classroom. She or he wouldn't know that I was labeled the dumbest child in the classroom. If I was lucky they might even mistake me for being a smart child. As soon as class began on one of these days I would place a smile on my face and raise my hand for the substitute teacher to come to my desk and help me with the classroom work assignment. However, it was usually only a matter of minutes before the substitute teacher became even more frustrated than me. By this time they would realize I was the only child still sitting at my desk, and they would tell me to go and play with the rest of the children. I would especially like it when the substitute teacher would tell those children that tried to be spies to stop telling on folks and to mind their own business. Sometimes these spiteful children would confront me in the play area, whispering to me that they were going to tell the teacher on me when she came back. I would try to be defiant at the time, but would inevitably pay the price when she returned.

"Anyway Jeremiah, I was able to put a stop to those bedtime crying sessions. But I couldn't stop the sadness I felt growing inside me. I became a second grader on another Wednesday in September. I was seven years old. But once again I found myself in a school setting where my academic struggles were ignored. My second grade teacher's lack of interest in me and dedication to not ever teaching me soon sealed my fate. He even established a label for me, calling me a child 'slow in learning'. This crushed my spirit. Apparently I was impossible to teach. Anyway, he said he wasn't going to waste his valuable time on me, because he felt he needed to focus on all those deserving children who could learn faster than me. So that year I just took up space, much like one of the school desks in the classroom, and my grades suffered even more. You know Jeremiah I guess I should give my second-grade teacher some credit: he didn't feel a daily need like my first-grade teacher to remind me that I wasn't as smart as my classmates, that I was lazy and didn't want to learn. So my second-grade teacher didn't verbally attack me, but he didn't really say or do anything for me except ignore me. I didn't feel that was right, but I preferred that over the condescension that I had become used to encountering at any given moment.

"Anyway, at this point I began to realize what made me happy. I was bored out of my mind one day, sitting at that school desk, and I started daydreaming about being back in kindergarten, when I was happy drawing all those pictures and

I had a teacher that genuinely loved her children. She would encourage us to do our best, and you know what? We did, without the knowledge of one child being any smarter than any other. Once my daydream ended and the reality of the classroom began to return, I decided that since I was going to be in this classroom taking up space and serving no purpose, I might as well be doing something to occupy my time until it's time to go home. So I began to use my school pencil as a coping device: I began to draw, and this gave me a sense of purpose and happiness. Once I found that drawing made going to school more tolerable, I began to draw as often as I could in class, especially whenever I faced the teacher's 'expert opinion' that I was not smart and would never amount to anything in life.

"But I've got to say, that second grade teacher wasn't perfect. He did put me down due to my inability to keep up with him and the rest of my classmates. At one stage he was explaining a class assignment on the blackboard, and I just wasn't keeping up. This made him so angry and frustrated at me that he decided to have me stand up in class; he pointed me out as an example of what an academic failure looked like in the flesh. He was infuriated with me because I couldn't manage to get any of his classroom assignments right, which I guess was embarrassing for him. So after that I began to realize that I couldn't win. So I began to draw and daydream nearly all the time, withdrawing from what was going on in the classroom and making myself invisible to the teacher. I guess he got what he wanted, as he was able to teach who he thought were the more deserving children without me interfering. Meanwhile, I gave up on learning, except to the reality that I was dumb, which my teacher often insinuated and my bad report cards would show. Anyway, how could he, a professional teacher with a degree, be wrong in his assessment? I was just a child that was slow in learning that provided no value in the classroom. Except maybe as some physics demonstration – as that element that just takes up space.

"After second-grade ended I was so glad. I thought I was going to get a break in life for once, after my family and I moved to another public housing community. My mother said that this would better our lives. But yet again I was sadly disappointed in my new school. It was no better than the school I'd just left. I clearly remember a time when my homeroom teacher decided to have a surprise reading and math test a week after I found myself in the third grade. I failed the reading test and I failed the math test. I felt pretty bad about it because I had never learned to read, but it got worse. Right after my first attempt to read the next child gave a flawless and eloquent reading. It was so good that the third-grade teacher began to slowly close her eyes and move her head in a graceful side-to-side manner: as if her ears were being pleasantly served a delicious meal. This sat in my mind while I remembered her face while I'd tried to read. She had a disturbed look, as if she was about to call 911 to report a crime in progress. When this third-grade teacher was done with her praise for one child and putdown of another, she immediately created a system to classify her students, as trucks and cars. This not only allowed her to physically separate the good readers from the bad ones, but it also allowed her to make distinctions between the children. This seemed to make her happy. Anyway, this was a bitter-sweet situation for me, because after her initial separation process was over I was finally presented with an opportunity to meet the other children in the classroom who she considered not very smart. In her classification terms, those of us she deemed reading deficient were trucks, because we were slow and bouncy. The good readers were cars, because they were fast and smooth. It was bad enough that we had to deal with the teacher's labels – which did nothing to teach us to read – but it also made us the unfortunate targets of the other children. So we suffered at the hands of our peers as well. All that labeling created an environment that was so hostile for the children who were doing poorly academically; we all became victims of all sorts of attacks from our classmates.

"One day I just had enough of the children who were victimizing me with all their cruelty and the backing of the teacher. Anyway, soon after that day I was physically attacked outside the school when I was on my way home by a child who had been threatening me all day. He'd been telling me that he was going to beat up the dummy from the Projects, balling up his fist as he spoke. That afternoon he decided to follow through on all his threats. He knocked me down when I was walking, and he began to beat and kick me – until I took all my anger and frustration and placed it in my fists. Before I knew it, I'd managed to get off the ground and deliver one blow that knocked him out cold. His friends who'd been egging him on began to back up and step out of my way, while I tried to walk to my school bus. But at that point I was escorted to the school office by a parent who had witnessed the whole fight. It didn't matter that I'd been fighting in self-defense. The principal gave me a two week suspension. He disrespectfully pointed out that my behavior stemmed from my being an underachiever and having the misfortune of living in the Projects. He said this was the primary source of my anger and aggression. He was really bigoted towards the less fortunate. Even worse, he said all of this as if I wasn't there, talking to my mother and the boy's parents as we all sat in the school office. After he finished, he then reassured the boy's parents that their child would be safe in the school, as the school had a zero tolerance policy towards any violent behavior. He casually disregarded me; he wasn't interested in hearing my side of the story. He even ignored the other parent who had witnessed the other child attacking me first. With contempt on his face, he looked over to my mother and told her that she should thank these good people for them not asking that she pay their child's medical expenses and for them not pressing any charges with the police. When he spoke, I saw my mother's face become sad, and she dropped her head in shame. This made me extraordinarily angry at him and his school, with all its unfair policies and those no good teachers. All of it had made me so angry I wanted to commit a real crime right then and there; I wanted to hit him in the eye just like I hit that boy. But I restrained myself with all the strength from my Heavenly Father. At that moment I was so upset that I just wanted to leave or be anywhere other than the school office, because I didn't want to hear anything else from that principal and that boy's parents. Anyway, if nothing else at least one good thing did come from that afternoon, and that was the end of my being victimized by the other children. Word got out amongst them all that I would defend myself if they attacked me."

Elijah stopped talking for a moment. "I am sorry for the tone in my voice Jeremiah," he continued, "but it makes me so angry even thinking about that situation. I'd rather speak about something a lot more pleasant. At that school I got to know a few other children who were being punished for not being smart, who were viewed as underachievers much like myself. I was so glad that I'd met other children, for the first time in a long time, who I could possibly relate to and who could possibly relate to me. Up to that point I felt like the only child in the world who was suffering in the way I was. I've got to admit though that I did feel bad for those other children, and guilty that their presence gave me a sense of comfort. But at least I didn't feel so alone. But even when I was happy with those other children, I was rudely interrupted by that third grade teacher. I guess she sensed a small level of happiness within me, so she instructed me to stand in front of all my classmates as a display, showing the other children what a stupid dumb person looks like. But anyway, I was still able to thank my Heavenly Father for stopping that teacher's despicable behavior when I was saved by the school bell. The sound of that school bell for once represented an opportunity for me to get to know my new classmates outside of the confines of the classroom.

So I focused on trying to find the confidence and courage to say something to my new classmates while they walked past me as if I didn't exist. You know Jeremiah, when I stood there in fear and I allowed those children to walk by without even introducing myself, at that moment I finally figured out what being stupid and dumb was. I just stood there like a coward, afraid of rejection. I truly believed that no one would ever be my friend, and that included those other children, despite us all being in the same boat. But before I could allow myself to wallow in self-pity, I reminded myself of my sad daily reality. That gave me a big boost in courage, so I lifted my head in confidence. After taking in a large breath of cool fresh air under those gray skies, I walked over to the area of the playground where the others had gone. I could see one of them, a girl, clearly sitting middle ways up on the monkey bars with her hands in the pockets of her denim jacket. The two boys were standing near her like bodyguards. They were all chatting with each other. So I bravely walked up to them, and interrupted their conversation to ask them how they felt about what the teacher had done after the math and reading test, when we had been labeled as trucks and cars.

'I don't know about you,' I said, 'but I found it insulting. It annoyed me when the teacher told the girl passing out the classroom assignments to skip over us because we weren't smart enough to do the work. She said it made no sense to waste her precious paper on us!'

Anyway, before I could go on complaining, the children stopped me and said that they knew what was going on and that they did not like it one bit. But they also knew they were children with no real power to defend themselves from any adult attacks, especially from the teacher. They said that over time, they'd all learned that the best thing to do with a teacher like that was to simply stop showing any feelings or emotions.

They said that I should ignore any attacks, particularly from teachers. It was sad, you know Jeremiah? They said that the reality is that we are all slow learners, and how can we ever defend ourselves from a teacher when our family and friends are usually the first to jump on the bandwagon in announcing that we are slow learners. And you know? No one was going to do a single thing about it. We were all alone."

* * *

"Those children kept on talking to me.

'Why do you keep getting upset about your situation', one of them asked me, 'you know most people don't care about those of us that are LD.'

'What's LD?' I asked.

'It means Learning Disabled, I think,' the girl sitting on the monkey bars said, 'but I think some people just use it as a joke for people who aren't too smart. Anyway, getting upset doesn't solve anything, so stop wasting your energy on things you have no control of.'

I thought about what she'd said. Before I knew it, she was asking what my name was.

'My name is Elijah Ray Anderson,' I said.

'Well my name is Sherry Robinson,' she replied. 'My buddy over here is Russell McKinley, and this is Bruce Harrison.'

'How are you doing Elijah? It's nice to meet you!' Russell called out.

'What's up Elijah,' Bruce added, 'just hang in there, because everything will be alright as soon as you learn to not care about what people think or say about you!'

After Bruce's comments I decided to set aside my complaining for a moment – I reminded myself that I wanted to get to know these guys. I didn't want to mess things up, so I paused and began to talk.

'Hello guys,' I said, 'you have no idea how glad I am to meet every last one of you.' They all looked surprised, and then we all laughed. At that moment I found the joy of laughter for the first time in a long time. And you know what? I wasn't being laughed at for a change. Once we were done laughing, a question that had been burning in my mind suddenly surfaced.

'Hey guys,' I said, 'I want you to know that I'm not in anyway trying to be disrespectful at all and I hope that we can all be friends – but I've got a question. What do you guys think has caused us to be slow learners? What is preventing us from keeping up with everybody else in class?' The questions just tumbled out of me. 'Do you think it's something that happened at birth? Can it be fixed? I desperately need an answer to that question, because I'm so tired of being seen as a slow learner! I seem to exist in a constant state of frustration... But then maybe we are just supposed to be slow learners, maybe we do have inferior brains that are functioning out of whack, somehow allergic to words and numbers. I hope that's not the case, because I truly believe that if we don't find out what our problem is or how to treat it soon, it's going to cost us dearly. We'll be treated like second-class citizens all our lives, just for being slow learners. I believe that if the help we need comes after we grow up, chances are it might be too late because our lives could be in irreparable disrepair. So what do you guys think about that?' I asked.

'Well I don't really know how to respond to that Elijah,' Sherry laughed, 'because that's a lot to think about! But sometimes I do wonder if my problems have anything to do with the fact that I can't stay focused. I just can't seem to concentrate on all those letters and numbers. And that makes it hard to do any of the things the teachers want us to do. I don't know how normal this is, but whenever I try to read a book or a magazine, I find the letters on the pages begin to move like they are on a wave. It even makes me sick! Once in second grade my teacher at my old school had me stand up and try to read this long passage from a school textbook, and I literally passed out soon after I began to read. All those letters and words on the pages of that book began to move like they were made of water. I became sick to my stomach and dizzy in the head. I just lost my balance and fell to the floor – but not before hitting my face, hand and right arm on the desk. That scared the heck out of my classmates! Anyway, I ended up lying on the classroom floor in a puddle of my own puke. They told me later that my eyes had rolled to the back of my head while my body had been jerking and shaking all over the place. They even said I let out an ear-piercing scream as if I was being possessed by demonic forces. I woke up later in the hospital. I was still pretty sore, but I think I was more embarrassed. I felt so embarrassed and ashamed that I didn't tell my parents what had caused me to pass out. Well anyway, that ends my story,' Sherry finished, 'so have any of you ever experienced anything like that before?'

Russell spoke up. 'Yes,' he said, 'except that my experience was slightly different. Basically I can't use the letters of the alphabet or numbers to achieve any school assignment. I don't believe my brain functions abnormally like our teachers believe. I just think my brain is different, like it deals with things differently to the ways other kids' brains work. Anyway, let me move back to what I wanted to share with you guys, especially after hearing what Sherry told us. I've got to say, it made me glad hearing Sherry's story, because I don't feel so crazy now! I tell you guys, whenever I've tried to read a book all the letters on the page simply detach themselves from the page. But I did discover that if I kept the book as flat and still as possible, I could keep the letters and words from moving about so much. But then one day at school I had to stand and try to read much like Sherry did. I knew it would hurt, but the teacher didn't want to hear any of my excuses. So I began to open the book and get ready to read, but all the letters, words and numbers began to detach themselves, sliding off the pages of that book in a weird slow motion. They all fell to the floor, and then began breaking like fancy China dishes and disappear. Essentially I was standing there with a book of blank pages which I couldn't read. I don't ever remember becoming sick, but I do remember feeling very strange. So I just stood there until the teacher became frustrated enough to tell me to go and sit down.'

"When Russell was done telling his story, we paused for a little while and a sense of wonder fell upon us as we tried to collect ourselves after the stories we had just heard. Eventually, Bruce stood up after tying his shoes, and put his hands in the pockets of his black jacket, like it was his turn to speak. So after he turned his baseball cap backwards on his head, he then looked up at the sky and began to talk.

'I thought I would always keep this story to myself,' he began, 'but here goes nothing. I still remember this particular situation as if it was yesterday. So one day I found myself in the school office in trouble again, probably due to my hyper activities and attitude and personality to match – or probably due to the seizures I used to get. Whenever I tried to read or do anything academic, I used to get these headaches and nosebleeds, so I just couldn't sit still in the classroom. Or anywhere else for that matter. Anyway, that caused me all sorts of problems. Because I wasn't very good academically – or socially for that matter – the teachers and my parents had just about written me off. None of them know about the struggles I face every day just trying to sit still in the classroom – just trying to learn something. I just can't do it! And every time I try to read the letters or numbers on the page of a book, they all just seem to rise up off the page and move around. I'd get so confused and frustrated when that'd happen, and I wouldn't know how to deal with it. And you know what? I'd told my parents and other people about it, and no one would believe me, and they'd get all angry with me. My big brother in prison made me promise over the phone that I'd stay out of trouble. He wanted to help, but he couldn't do anything from where he was… But at least he did manage to make my struggle a lot easier, when I began to understand how much he identified with me. He told me about all the other people in jail, and how they'd all struggled with academic failure throughout their school years. Lots of them had some type of learning disability that for whatever reason went ignored or untreated while they were at school. So my brother pleaded with me to do whatever it takes to stay out of trouble, he didn't want me to wind up where he was, locked up like an animal due to the mistakes he'd made after dropping out of school. He told me that it was a cruel world out there for people who dropped out of school, and it's almost impossible to drag yourself up. Especially when you didn't drop out of school by choice, and you're still challenged with the learning disability with all its disadvantages. So my brother told me to keep my head up and to stay out of trouble. I've got to keep going with my education to follow my dreams. So I'm going to do that for my brother in prison.'

"Once Bruce was done speaking, I found myself overwhelmed by all the stories I had heard, and I knew it was time to tell my story. But I wasn't feeling that confident, because their stories were so spectacular and my story felt so mediocre in comparison. So I hesitated for a moment, and I looked down at the ground. Yet again I fell out of place. Eventually, Sherry took notice of my hesitation, and I guess she wanted to help me.

'Your story doesn't have to be spectacular or extreme to be important Elijah,' she said, 'so please tell your story, because we want to hear it!'

'Ok!' I said, and I began to tell them how I struggled every day with trying to stay focused. 'I want to stop daydreaming, I want to learn something in the classroom,' I said, 'but every day I wouldn't be able to control myself, and the teachers would attack me. All that would do is get me daydreaming again, because that usually cushioned their hostile treatment. Anyway, when I'd start daydreaming, I'd often wonder why

I was always treated like that, as if my brain was inferior or defective or just downright broken. That would make me very upset – like I feel I'm ok but everyone else thinks I'm broken! I hate to admit, but my mind feels like some sort of machine that's broken. I can't handle all the things they want us to learn, like they aren't meant for me.' I stopped for a bit and looked at the other children. 'I want to say something else to you guys. I hope you don't laugh, but I think I figured out why I can't do anything in the classroom. I don't like to tell folks about it because it's related to what might be going on in my head. I truly believe that my mind just wants to focus on being allowed to be creative and allowed to daydream. It just isn't interested in being limited or controlled by all the obstacles that the teachers put in our way. Anyway, that makes sense to me. Well guys, that's all there is to my story.'

"Just as I finished telling my story to the others our recess period ended. The school lunchroom monitors, a woman and a man, blew their whistles and instructed all of the children to line up in front of the school building. All of the children came running from the field and the playground areas. The four of us were pretty slow, as we all still wanted to talk! Russell and Bruce and I waited for Sherry to climb down from the monkey bars, and then we began to walk back to the school building. We eventually met up with the rest of the children, and we quickly took our places at the end of the line. When we were standing there in the line I just couldn't stop thinking about how proud I was in myself, how I had finally conquered a fear and might have gained three new friends! What a good day it was! Unfortunately, once we went back inside the school building and back into the classroom my new found feeling of accomplishment was met with the all too familiar negative treatment and hostile environment created by the teacher. Yet now I was able to withstand this treatment a lot longer after that day's victory. Eventually however, I got just as tired of the constant humiliation and jokes as I always got. With all the jokes and sarcasm thrown at me, I slowly put my head down on my desk, trying to hide my face in my arms. When I raised my head, I pulled a sheet of paper out of my book bag sitting underneath my desk. I put the sheet of paper on the top of my school desk, and brought out a freshly sharpened number two pencil from that same book bag underneath my desk. I put the lead point of that pencil onto the surface of the paper, and I began to draw. "As soon as I was drawing, something very special came over me- like some kind of hypnotic state- which seemed to automatically drown out all that classroom negativity." I felt like I had escaped into a very quiet cloudy haze; everything was peaceful. I essentially found solitude, a serene calm within me. In that state, I felt like I was having an out of body experience – I simply wasn't in the classroom anymore! I found myself in a weird state of consciousness, with my spirit floating on some kind of journey where all evidence of time was gone. Yet the peace I was experiencing in my journey was soon interrupted by an invading memory; a dark memory that was normally tucked safely away in that storage place in my mind were drama and trauma exist – a place which I never plan to visit, but which occasionally visits its grim wares on me. That invading memory was strange and disturbing, and I couldn't really distinguish whether it was a dream or vision.

"Anyway, in the vision I saw my mother walking swiftly with me through a rainstorm. She was carrying a large black umbrella that she was using to shield us from most of the heavy downpour (it had a bit of a leak), but it certainly didn't block out the thunder and lighting and wind. But regardless of all that commotion, it still wasn't enough – as she dutifully explained to me as we walked through the front entrance of the school building – to stop my mother from getting to my school for the Parent-Teacher Conference and to pick up my report card.

"Once inside, we looked at each other and than began to laugh for no good reason.. My mother closed up the large umbrella and gave it a few shakes while we wiped off our shoes on the mat provided near the front door.

"We walked to a classroom to visit the teachers for the Parent-Teacher Conference. As my mother picked up my report card and talked with my teachers, I began to notice the other teachers and parents and children in the school hallways. Some of the children had long sad faces, and quite a few of them were crying, I can tell you. Many of their parents were also quite obviously upset with their report cards, they weren't looking happy at all.

"I thank God for sparing me from that drama, because my mother didn't fuss at me for whatever reason. But still, her face was full of a sadness that she couldn't hide – all due to my report card. And I tell you, that made me feel very bad, as I really wanted to get good grades as well.

"'Thank goodness, we've finally arrived at the classroom for the last teacher visit,' I said out loud. My mother responded with a look of tiredness, as if all this had taken a toll on her. She mustered up a little more strength and took a deep breath, and we walked into the last classroom for the day.

"Once inside the classroom, we passed by a large blackboard and a few school desks until we arrived at a large oak desk. On top of the glossy desk were some assorted papers, a few books and a name plate. Behind it stood a well-groomed teacher I was most familiar with. After welcoming us with a firm handshake he announced his name in that low monotone of his, and then began to speak to my mother.

"'Thank you for coming today,' he began, 'how are you doing, what with all this rain?' My mother responded politely. 'I'm doing just fine sir, thanks for asking.' The teacher then politely asked us to take a seat next to his desk. As we sat down, he continued to speak in a friendly way with my mother, and she smiled and laughed a little with him. I figured everything was OK so I turned to look outside the classroom window and watch the dark storm clouds rolling in from the west, with the sound of thunder and lightning streaking across the gray skies.

"I slowly began to daydream, but I was soon interrupted when I began to listen to the well-groomed teacher with his monotone voice. He was speaking to my mother about my poor academic performance, saying that her child had failed once again. He went on and on with all his opinions, and he didn't seem to care if I was there or not."

"Wow! That must had been terrible for you guys to sit there and listen to all that."

"Yes it was Jeremiah. In fact it was humiliating, but there's more. Since I didn't like what was being said, I slowly turned to look at my mother to see how she was doing. She was sitting there calmly and slowly nodding her head up and down as she listened intently to every word he said. He never really made eye contact with my mother, but he did become very animated, making a lot of hand gestures. In fact he looked a bit nervous.

"I was a little concerned about my mother having to listen to all that negative talk, but then I realized she's a good person, and she never seems to get upset about anything. So once again I turned to look out the classroom window to try to ignore all that was being said about me.

"But I was pretty uncomfortable, I can tell you. I began to listen again as the conversation got worse. Once again I turned to check on my mother and immediately took notice of her calm demeanor and beautiful face – but though she looked calm, I could tell that she was severely distressed, disgusted, angry and frustrated as the teacher went on and on, telling my mother her child was an underachiever. I think that it broke my mother's heart to hear all that, I could see it in her eyes as they began to water up with tears. And to make matters worse he continued to talk, showing not a scrap of professionalism or sensitivity.

"'I feel so disappointed and betrayed,' my mother finally said. As she began to speak, her calmness dissipated and her body began to shake. Her left foot began to tap against the classroom vinyl floor, and she began to become more animated, much like the teacher was earlier. She was clearly angry hearing this teacher talk. As she spoke I became sad and anxious to leave. It hurt me, watching my mother who I love so dearly become so emotional.

"'Why do you wait to the last report card to inform me of all this? You've been making promises to me, gaining my trust, telling me everything was going to be all right. You said you were going to do all you could to help my son. Don't you remember how you always stressed the importance of parent involvement? I've been involved the whole time! What I want to know is what ever happened to teacher involvement and responsibility?' My mother asked angrily.

"The teacher looked a bit frustrated and angry at the question. But my mother wasn't done yet. 'How do you justify letting a well-behaved child just sit in your classroom and fail academically? You like the fact that he is not a troublemaker, so instead of assisting him academically you decide to sacrifice him as if it's no big deal when he falls through the cracks. I guess you feel you're not going to be held accountable anyway. Maybe you think you can pass on your responsibility, insinuating that I'm to blame, or that 'you just feel you can't save them all.' Well that's ridiculous. This is his future we're talking about!"

"My mother slowly shook her head in disgust. 'It's a shame,' she continued. 'But I want to thank you for teaching me a real lesson today – that bad teachers and bad school systems are allowed to exist, which basically means good committed teachers and good effective school systems are doomed and will take a backseat and suffer along with our children's educational futures.. And another thing,' my mother went on to say, 'just because a parent doesn't have a high school diploma and is deemed uneducated doesn't mean they're less smart or less valuable than those with all sorts of educational degrees. And don't you forget that sir!'

"'So what is your real motivation,' my mother continued, "because if it's money, I strongly believe a mediocre school teacher should collect a mediocre pay check, much like those many children that will grow up and become adults practically forced to receive minimum wages or mediocre pay due to their not having a decent education.'

"Before the teacher could say anything else, my mother frowned and looked straight into his eyes. 'I sat patient and quiet and listened to all you had to say, and now you're going to listen to me. I hope you learn something today sir, so listen very carefully to a parent for a change. I can't speak for all parents,' she continued, 'but I need to say this. It's very disappointing and unfortunate when good parents are discouraged from trying to help out in their child's school, when they're ignored or simply dismissed. It seems so many teachers and principals treat most parents as if they are the enemy when they respectfully challenge the operation of their child's school. Parents are simply excluded and alienated from the system. It's like a dictatorship. And I'm sorry to say sir, that's not how I operate. I don't believe real progress will come until teachers and parents learn to respect each other and work together in the best interest of the children! If a teacher is not self-motivated and committed to teaching, why do they expect the children to be self- motivated and committed to learning in return?'

"The teacher then began to speak. 'I'm sorry you feel that way. I did all I could to help your child, but would you please lower your voice?' After that command, he then began to lecture my mother, telling her that a parent-teacher conference was not the place for parents to take out their frustration and anger against the teacher and school, simply because a parent doesn't like any bad news the teacher might be giving.

"At that point I believe something snapped in my mother, I think the insult was too much. She launched into a big verbal conflict with the teacher – until in all his arrogance and rudeness he bellowed at my mother 'I'm sorry for your state of denial but in all due respect it's not the teacher's fault or the fault of the school system that your child is an underachiever and a slow learner and not all that smart. The only mistake I've made is making a promise I couldn't keep. The fact of the matter is that your child simply lacks the ability to learn and there's really no hope for him. I hate to say it, but he's a lost cause! He can't even learn the basics! So stop the whining and wasting my time and face reality.' He stood up, and then my mother and I stood up as well. I stood beside my mother, hoping that all the arguing would stop. I covered my ears with my hands, trying to drown out all that noise. It seemed like that argument was never going to end.

"Eventually it did end, as my mother, with a look of sadness in her eyes, said in a steely voice 'Excuse me sir! What did you just say to me?'

'I made myself perfectly clear,' he responded unpleasantly. Before I knew it my fear was quickly replaced with amazement, when I saw my mother's open right hand launched at tremendous speed towards his face. It stopped in mid-air only a few inches short. His eyes grew wide and we all stood there in silence, shocked at what had just happened.

"As soon as my mother calmed herself, she lowered her hand, much like a weapon being placed back into its holster. Anyway, Jeremiah, I was still kind of scared and shaken by the whole ordeal that had just unfolded. My mother turned to look me directly in the eyes, while her eyes streamed with tears. She sobbed, but got the words out eventually. 'Ok Elijah,' she said in a strong voice that I'd never heard before, 'let's go.'

"The teacher was now standing there dazed and quiet, staring intently out of his classroom window. A small crowd had also gathered at his classroom door. But they quickly stepped aside when my mother and I began to walk out of that classroom into the hallway. I was so glad to be leaving, but my mother wasn't quite done yet. Once we were in the hallway she just stopped in mid-stride - 'Oh!' She said. 'God please protect our children against such awful teachers!'

"She then turned slowly to look at all the people who had come to see what all the commotion was about. At this point my mother just ignored all that unwanted attention and turned her attention back to me. With a very stern and demanding voice much like a military officer she said to me 'I'm sorry you had to witness all this craziness, but I want you to promise me son, that you won't ever as long as you live accept anyone telling you that you're not smart enough and can't learn! Do you hear me Elijah?' 'Yes ma'am' I replied.

"I proceeded with great caution at that moment. I'd never seen my mother like that. She was usually in good spirits! But as we continued to walk I soon begin to feel proud, imagining my mother to be a great hero or a soldier, leaving a great battlefield wounded but not defeated. Once we finally made it through the school doors – into what was now a sunny day – I felt a great deal of relief. The vision began to fad away as my soul and spirit once again turned to a more serene place. Eventually, I heard the soft spoken voice of a woman, saying to me 'I see you like to draw.' I slowly raised my head to respond to her.

* * *

"Anyway Mr. Johnson, the fact of the matter is that the rest of my education seems like a painful blur when I think back on it now. I can tell you more stories, but the point is that school simply ruined my life beyond repair. Year after year I received bad report cards and failures. I endured years of living in the shadows, feeling embarrassed, being ashamed at failing the first grade once, the third grade twice and the seventh grade five times! But my pathetic educational story doesn't stop there. Most of it is a dismal blur, but the fourth grade stands out in my mind due to an encounter with a substitute math teacher.

She humiliated me to the highest degree in front of all my classmates. It was my turn to answer her question about what I wanted to be when I grew up. I told her that I wanted to be an artist, and she responded by laughing hysterically at me. She said I should focus on getting a real job like working in an auto plant or some other type of factory. Boy, she just wanted to crush my dreams, with her narrow mind and negative views. She said that I would just be a poor starving artist. If that wasn't bad enough, she closed her discouraging and depressing speech with more condescending laughter, telling me that real artists only become rich and famous long after they die. I heard that and I was deeply hurt, as if my world had been forever crushed.

"But I should tell you more about the woman with the soft-spoken voice. I looked up at her, and she asked what my name was. I told her my name was Elijah Ray Anderson. She told me her name, Ms. Rita Wilson. I was now in the seventh grade, and I had already failed it four times. You might not believe it, but I was eighteen years of age and I was taking the seventh grade for the fifth time. I was sitting at the back of the math classroom. So I finally stopped drawing and looked at the woman who was standing at the side of my desk. I looked up into her beautiful face, and saw that she was wearing a smile that you could feel was illuminated by her extraordinary spirit within. I tell you, it took my breath away. I couldn't remember the last time I'd been in the company of a teacher that genuinely cared about their students. I felt so special when she asked me if I liked to draw.

'No,' I said, 'I love to draw!' I handed her one of my pencil drawings.

'I love it!' She replied. As soon as she said that, I couldn't stop talking. I told Ms. Rita Wilson that I couldn't wait for this math class to end, so that I could go to my next class which was art. She laughed a little, and then with a smile told me that she was not only going to be my substitute teacher for math, but she was also going to be my substitute teacher for my next class. So shortly after our conversation the school bell rang and Ms. Rita Wilson had us all line up. She marched us down the school hallway to the art room, where I felt at home. Anyway, I continued to talk with Ms. Rita Wilson. I soon learned that she wasn't just a substitute teacher, but that she was actually an art teacher. That made it much easier for me to talk to her – and talk to her I did! I talked to her to the point where she allowed me to work in collaboration with other inspired art students in the classroom. For once it was a pleasure to actually go to school, despite the fact that I was eighteen years of age in the seventh grade, with absolutely no commonality with my classmates. I was six years their senior and getting about as old as the teaching staff! Anyway, Ms. Wilson became concerned about my future when we had a conversation about my educational background. I told her everything, and it made her burning mad. It kind of scared me, because I'd never really seen anyone care or get upset about my education, and now she wanted to help me. At this point in time Jeremiah, I just didn't know what she could possibly do to help my education. I'd already just about given up on getting an education; I'd pretty much accepted my fate for what it was. But saying that, I also wasn't going to stop her if she wanted to help me. In fact, I thank her for just wanting to help. But on the other hand I felt sad for her, because I hated to think that she was just wasting her time on me. Anyway, at one stage she asked me to provide her with a pencil drawing for the classroom. Two weeks later I completed a poster sized pencil drawing and brought it to class. Everyone just fell in love with the drawing. At the end of the day, after I had already gone home, Ms. Wilson decided to hang the drawing over the art room door outside the classroom, because she was so impressed with it that she just wanted to share it with everyone. So the next day when I returned to school, as I was walking to the art room, I discovered a frightening scene: a large noisy crowd of students had assembled at the art room door! I just stopped dead in my tracks, until I saw a couple of students looking and pointing up towards my drawing, which I realized was hanging over the art room door. It was weird –

I'd never experienced that level of positive energy directed towards me, not for anything I'd ever done in my life. I wasn't prepared for what came next, when the crowd of students admiring my drawing began to compliment the drawing. One girl said she thought that the picture was painted, while someone else in the crowd said no, it was done in pencil. Soon after that, the crowd then wanted to know who had drawn the picture. I was standing right there in the crowd, and I decided that they weren't about to find out from me! I slowly began to move out of the crowd, before taking off down the school hallway.

"When I think about it now, I think I responded that way because I was shy. When the crowd cleared, I went back to the art room to find my teacher so excited about the crowd that had gathered in front of her art room door, all because of my picture. She looked at me and smiled.

'Here,' she said, 'this is for you, to reward you for your drawing.' She handed me a brand new Art Portfolio! I was so happy, someone actually took an interest in me! But her generosity towards me didn't stop there. She revealed to me that she had managed to have the school place me in the eighth grade, on a second chance opportunity. She said I would start the next day. At that point her excitement soon dissipated. She looked at me and noticed that my response wasn't favorable.

'What's the problem?' she asked me. I said nothing. But my conscience wouldn't let me rest with that.

'Wait a minute Ms. Wilson,' I said, 'I do have a problem with the whole idea of being placed in the eighth grade. I don't think it's going to make a big difference in solving anything at this time, unless you have a time machine as part of your solution. I just don't see how being placed in the eighth grade is going to fix anything substantially. Ms. Wilson, I thank my Heavenly Father that you're here now, but unfortunately you just came too late in my life, and you can't by yourself fix my education. I am eighteen years of age in the seventh grade, and still in terrible academic shape.' Once I had finished talking, I found myself having to pause. I tried to hold back all my tears and collect myself.

'Ms. Wilson,' I said, 'I know without a doubt that when I leave this school it will be minus a formal education.'

* * *

"The following day, I arrived at my middle school. With no real expectations, I had decided the previous night that I would set aside my negative ideas and meet Ms. Wilson at least halfway, so I allowed her to escort me to my first hour homeroom teacher's classroom, where our arrival and my first day went off without a hitch. But, like so many times before, after two weeks had passed I again found myself frustrated, struggling academically and putting up with new teachers who downright refused to have anything to do with teaching a struggling student. So at that point my patience began to wear thin, dealing everyday with mean-spirited teachers, who simply shouldn't be teaching children at all. Perhaps one day soon, with a better screening process, they won't. Anyway, I found myself becoming angrier and angrier, enduring all sorts of condescending treatment. At least by that time I had learned how to hide my emotions out of respect for all that my art teacher Ms. Wilson had done for me. In fact, she even continued to take time out of her busy day to come and check on me in my eighth grade class. I really appreciated those visits. Anyway, she checked on me regularly, until one day she came with a sad expression on her face. She told me that she was leaving my school because the art teacher she had replaced was returning to school. I struggled to hold back the tears. She gave me a quick hug and a brief motivational speech, and then she walked out of the classroom. This was a shock to me. In a daze, I looked out of the classroom windows to watch her leave the building and get into her car and drive away. I didn't ever see her again.

"Well anyway Jeremiah, though it took me sometime to come to grips with the fact that Ms. Rita Wilson had left, I gathered up some strength from my Heavenly Father and did my best. But honestly, I don't think I'll ever forget the unconditional love and support that she gave me. I still miss it. In fact, the sad reality is that I never got any support like that from anyone else, not even from my family. And nothing from my teachers and the overall school system. And they claim to be in the business of educating children. I know they failed me – eighteen years of age and still in middle school, facing chronic academic failure. Even worse, my failures were continuously overlooked. Not one red flag was raised or one eyebrow lifted. I wasn't a class clown – I was routinely awarded good citizenship certificates. But they did absolutely nothing to help my situation, except to make me believe that the school system's efforts to teach simply didn't extend to those of us who apparently had the misfortune of being slow learners. All of this meant that our educational needs simply went untreated. Our education was denied. As some people put it, we just fell through the cracks. And do you know what that means Jeremiah? That parents, teachers and the entire school system are not responsible for any child's educational failures, despite the fact that they may have caused them. Meanwhile, those children that do fall through the cracks are left to a life time with the stigma of being a school dropout. In fact, they'll probably be held entirely responsible for their educational demise and that's a sad state of affairs."

We both looked up, slightly dazed after our long conversation. Ms. Cheryl Washington was walking towards us at the lunchroom table.

"I want to share one last thing with you about Ms. Rita Wilson," Elijah said, "just as soon as we find out what Ms. Washington wants". Ms. Washington arrived at our table with a smile on her face. It seemed like she was in a particularly good mood, because she said that she needed us to sweep and mop the music classroom, but once we were done, we could take the rest of the day off for being such good dependable workers. "I just can't say how glad I am to have workers on my staff who I can really count on," she said. We both thanked her, and with that she turned and walked away, her infectious smile disappearing in the lunchroom crowd of people. At that point we were both kind of surprised – we hadn't expected the afternoon off! So we just looked at one another for a moment, before Elijah began to pack up his lunch.

"Let's get that job done immediately!" He began. "I'm keen to go home and spend some time with my family – but I will finish the rest of my story before we leave."

"Come on Elijah, let's go!" I said, but he was leaving me behind with his rapid walk. It was no surprise that we arrived at our work area quickly. As we walked, everything seemed to be going just fine – until we saw Ms. Paula Gooden walking out of our assigned classroom, looking just as suspicious as normal. She surprised us when she became startled by our presence, but that didn't last long, as she immediately began to tell us that Ms. Cheryl Washington was looking for us, as if we were in deep trouble. I looked over to Elijah, and to say that he appeared irritated would be an understatement. So I immediately announced to Ms. Paula Gooden that we'd already spoken to Ms. Cheryl Washington, and we were fully aware of the work she had assigned us. I asked if there was anything else she needed to tell us before we began our work. Of course, it would be too much for this woman to just walk away, so she ignored my question and instead warned us that serious disciplinary action would take place if we wasted that much time in the lunch room again just talking about nothing. She even said she would make it her duty to make sure that we were properly dealt with, and she would go over the supervisor's head to report us! Before I could say anything back to her, Elijah looked at her and spoke.

"Ms. Gooden, I heard that hell's fire starter's been reported missing – and they need you back."

"What did you say you good for nothing dummy?!" She snapped back. Before the argument got out of hand, I quickly stepped in, and asked Ms. Gooden if there was anything else she needed to tell us before we got to work.

"No!" She replied angrily, and as she walked away she mumbled something under her breath about how we were going to pay for messing with her. She kept mumbling as she walked away, something about "it won't be pretty" and "you just wait."

"Whatever you say," we both called after her. "We walked into the music classroom and instantly got to work. We were working so fast that I accidentally mopped the wrong half of the floor! not allowing us to exit the classroom with out stepping on a wet floor, blocking off our exit! When I realized what I had done, I thought Elijah would be ferocious, but he wasn't. He just laughed a little bit, and began to speak.

"I guess this must be the time – I should tell you the rest of my story while we wait for the floor to dry. So anyway... where was I?" He asked. "Actually Jeremiah," he continued, "I remember now. I was going to speak about the positive affects a substitute art teacher named Ms. Rita Wilson had on me, long after she'd left my school. So let me concentrate for a moment. Oh!" He cried. "I know exactly what it was I wanted to share with you – that my art teacher Ms. Rita Wilson was an undeniably decent human being, who remained in my mind even when she left. In fact, she left me with a small but powerful feeling of hope, because I knew that I wasn't written off by everyone. When she would say or do nice things she would really show she cared about me, I guess in the hopes that I would eventually catch on and begin to start caring about myself. I know that she understood my low self-esteem, and how it was negatively impacting on my entire being. In spite of that knowledge, she still persisted in trying to encourage me as often as she could, especially when she would talk to me about being eighteen years old and still in middle school.

She also made me think more seriously about my future. I learned to appreciate her conversation, because at that time no one else bothered to talk to me, just about everyone viewed me as not going to amount to anything in life. Everyone except "Ms. Wilson and my mother thought otherwise, but to everyone else I was invisible." Anyway, she was different because she happened to view me as a person and a decent human being, as more than just an educational failure. She also did something that was very important to me: she didn't treat me like a child; she managed to respect the fact that I was an eighteen year old, no longer thinking with the mind of a child. Unfortunately, she was the only person in that middle school who acknowledged that I was practically an adult that needed to start concerning myself with adult issues, with adult concerns and responsibilities. Anyway, she left me with these inspiring words: she told me never to forget that some people, with special attributes much like my own, will have to take other routes in life to achieve success: there is more than one path in life, and when you need to take another path do so! I know that these words of wisdom profoundly changed my life for the better, and they allowed me to focus on other things, and not just my educational failures. They allowed me to start thinking about the paths that would allow me to carve out a respectable and productive future for myself.

"The prospect of having a future excited me enormously, and I went immediately to the school guidance counselor to get some information. But once again, I couldn't get her to provide me with any help. In fact, she was no help at all, especially when she reminded me how my educational situation was a great deficit to me. Because of my education, she just couldn't find any programs or opportunities that she could suggest I get involved in. She closed our discussion with a sincere apology, which didn't mean a whole lot to me at that particular moment. Anyway, once I left the guidance counselor's office feeling nothing but discouraged, defeated and dissatisfied, I found myself going to just about anyone who I thought might be able to help me. But there was no one to be found… until one day my mother placed a small torn piece of paper in my hand. The piece of paper had a telephone number written on it, taken from some television commercial she'd seen that day. She said that the commercial had advertised a vocational school with all sorts of training, including an alternative form of education where they paid you while you learned. I thanked my mother for the information – I was really surprised when my mother just came out of the blue and did that for me. She'd spent years trying to get me educated, and it had nearly destroyed her, especially when she fought all those agonizing years alone without support of her husband. In the end, she wound up not really knowing what to do about my situation, so I guess out of fear and helplessness she just stopped trying. But that's not her fault, because trying to find a viable solution for her son had made her feel helpless. I don't blame her one bit. My situation was more than one single parent could deal with, especially when my mother also faced negative stigma and treatment from having to live in a public housing community. Anyway, soon after my mother provided me with that information, I stood up from the sofa in the living room where I was watching television and gave her a hug and a kiss on the cheek. She returned to her bed room. That's where she would spend most of her time now, sitting on the edge of her bed watching television all day as if her zest for life had just been zapped away with all those years of disappointment and struggle. She's had no real happiness in her life for years, and that makes me feel very sad. She deserves a better life.

"Anyway, I called the number my mother had given me immediately, because I had no other plans that afternoon. After making that call and speaking to one of their administrative personnel, I soon learned that I met all the necessary requirements it took to enroll as a student at the school. I hung up the phone with a smile on my face, pleased with my small victory – I had obtained an appointment for eight o'clock the following morning to fill out the necessary application paperwork! Though I was told I had better be quick – the school filled up with students quite rapidly – I was pretty excited. In fact, I was so excited by the idea of a new school that the rest of the day seemed to take forever!

"The next morning I lined up at the Warren, Cross Town bus stop to get the bus to what I hoped would be my new school. Usually the bus would take forever to arrive, but that day I thanked God because it was on time. I got on to that crowded bus, packed with all those schoolchildren going to school and adults to their jobs, but I still got a seat next to a window. I stared out of the window and began to daydream as the bus drove along, drowning out the conversations, noises (and strange smells) filling the bus. Eventually I transferred to the Woodward bus and then again to the Jefferson bus before I reached my final destination. I pulled the cord to alert the bus driver to stop the bus. Getting out of the bus, I soon spotted the school across the street from where I stood. I was still so excited that I jogged swiftly across the main street, nearly getting hit by some of the early morning rush- hour traffic. Out of one old ragged rust bucket of a car a driver leaned his arm and yelled at me to "get out of the street you damn fool". I ran on. I was a bit like a football player trying to score a touchdown. Anyway, soon after that near-death experience, I walked safely into the Job Center Academy with the goal of becoming a proud student of that school, keen to grab any opportunities with both hands. Once I was inside the building I found myself walking amongst an ocean of other applicants. They were all there for the same reasons as me. Eventually one of the school staff escorted me into the school office, where we were all asked to fill out the registration paperwork. I knew this was coming, so with my deplorable spelling and reading skills I had prepared earlier by getting my mother to write down the relevant information onto a sheet of paper that I would later transfer to the registration form – I was a bit like a student unprepared trying to cram all that information into an exam.

"In fact, I should tell you now Jeremiah about the other techniques I'm ashamed to have used to get through things like that mind numbing registration process, what with my terrible reading and spelling abilities. Basically, whenever I find myself confronted with needing to read or write, I ask people around me how to spell a word, and then I put on an act as if I'd just forgotten how to spell that word. They often join in explaining how they have a difficult time spelling those small words, while I think to myself how I always have a difficult time spelling any word, large or small. I should say, however, that after years of deliberately watching children's television shows like Sesame Street during my teenage years, I've learned to read simple words enough for me to just about get by. It's still difficult though. Anyway, in the end I managed to make it through the registration process. And it paid off – I learned soon afterwards that I would become a student of the school, starting the following September. I was so surprised and happy when they told me that the shock of the announcement didn't wear off until I was back on the city bus heading home. Once I arrived home at about four o'clock I ran over to my mother and gave her a hug and a kiss. She was sitting on a milk crate on our porch smoking a cigarette. I told her right away that I would be a student at the Job Center Academy this coming September. She congratulated me and smiled.

"After we'd celebrated, I went inside our apartment to take a nap – I was so tired after the registration process and the long bus ride home. But when I woke up it was the next day! It didn't really matter, because before I knew it it was the last day of school, and my summer vacation was about to start. I remember sitting there in the school classroom, excitedly watching the clock and waiting impatiently for the school bell to ring for the last time. I was looking forward to that coming September, when I would no longer be an eighteen year old middle school student just taking up space, drawing pictures just to pass the time. When the school bell finally rang, it was like everything began to move in slow motion, even my heart felt like it was slowing down. I slowly stood up from my school desk for the very last time, and then walked toward and through the door way of the classroom for the very last time. I walked down the school hallway and towards the front doors, before finally exiting my middle school feeling like a prisoner ending a twelve year sentence. Once I did manage to make it outside (after maneuvering through all the other students who were headed in the same direction), I found myself standing in front of the school building.

"Jeremiah, I stood there and took a deep breath. I looked up and down that school building. I took it all in, remembering how glad I was to be leaving that school, how for so many years I had felt like a prisoner held captive. I thought about that final moment of freedom that came with the ringing of the school bell. Well, I said to myself at the time, I guess I've been standing here long enough. I had tears in my eyes as I turned away. At that point I heard a female student call out my name somewhere behind me. In amongst the crowd of students I immediately recognized my buddy Sherry, standing alongside Bruce and Russell.

'Where did you guys come from?' I asked them.

'We've been standing behind you the whole time,' Sherry said, 'just trying to get your attention. You were in some kind of trance!' I apologized to them, and we all began to chat with each other with smiles on our faces, as if we had just met for the first time. Eventually our conversation turned serious. They asked me if I was glad to be finally joining them at high school in the fall.

'I won't be going to high school,' I said. 'The school administrative body rescinded my transfer there, so basically I'm failing once again. But happily things are different this year, because I won't be returning back to this school in the fall.'

Before I could continue to explain, my buddies interrupted with concern. They asked me if I was dropping out of school, because that just wasn't cool with them. I can understand where they were coming from – hey, I felt the same way about dropping out of school! I reassured them that I wasn't dropping out of school. I told them that I had applied some weeks ago to another school, and that they had accepted me. I told them I was starting this coming September, and that I was really excited about what the new school could offer me.

'Where is this school and what's its name?' Sherry asked.

'It's called the Job Center Academy, and it's located near the downtown area of the city,' I said. Before I could tell her more, she began to jump up and down with excitement.

'I've seen that school on a television commercial,' she said, 'and I've heard about it as well. Everyone says it has a great reputation, and it's really hard to get into! So congratulations!' I thanked them for their support, and they smiled. Sherry gave me a hug, and I could see that she was trying to hold back the tears. Bruce and Russell also stepped up and gave me a man hug, and I told them to take care of themselves.

'Promise to keep in touch guys,' I said. We exchanged telephone numbers. I was fighting back my own tears, and I felt compelled to say one more thing to Bruce.

'Stay out of trouble man!'

'For you Elijah I will try. But you stay smooth man. We will see you around!' Once I was done saying my final goodbye to my buddies, they began to walk towards the school buses. They got on their bus and it drove off. I watched them wave goodbye from the window. I got on my bus and it drove off as well.

"So I finally arrived home, tired after an emotional day at school. I decided to relax by eating a sandwich and drinking a pop while sitting on the sofa watching television. After a while I fell asleep. It seemed like only a couple of minutes later when I was woken up by my mother, who was telling me to get up because it was time for me to go to work. I remembered all of a sudden! I'd applied for a summer job some months ago, before I'd registered for my new school. As I got up I realized that I'd actually slept through the night again! So I took a shower, got dressed and ate a quick breakfast; the early morning sun was breaking through the clouds. I thought about that sun and thought that this was the birth of a new day – when I'm ready for my first day of work. Or at least that's what I thought, until I found myself with fifty other teenagers performing ground maintenance around the city's expressways, alleyways, parks and fields, using only manual equipment and tools! Boy it was hot working in that long summer, we worked five hours a day every day from Monday to Friday. We worked all summer long as if we were in a chain gang, and the only thing that kept us going was the little paycheck we received at the end of each week. It was hard work, but I tell you I was so glad to have that summer job, because it made it possible for me to buy nice things, including clothes and school supplies. I will admit that I was happy when the summer was over and the job ended, but we did have some fun times. In all honesty, it was an experience I will never forget – it was when I received my very first paycheck. Eventually September arrived, and with it my first day at the Job Center Academy.

"So there I was, sitting in my new school on my first day. I was ready to learn! Unfortunately, I found myself once again facing the fact that my brain was not cooperating with me. No matter how hard I had tried in the past to achieve academic success, I had met only academic failure. And I was worried. I was starting a new school, and I knew that if I didn't get some good grades I could be kicked out. So I decided I would go to the school library every chance I got… But even that didn't help very much, as I continued to find it very difficult to read. Again, my academic goals seemed out of reach! In the end, I ended up just going to the library to relax and draw all sorts of pictures…

"One day in the library I saw this beautiful young lady. I was concentrating on my drawing, but I paused for a minute, and when I did I saw her take a seat at the table next to mine. She had a whole pile of books in her hands and more under her arms – so she didn't really notice my presence. But I tell you Jeremiah, she was beautiful! I wanted to get to know her immediately. I truly believed I had fallen in love at first sight. I always thought that was ridiculous, but that's what you get. Anyway, I wanted to walk over to her table to introduce myself, but I really felt unworthy, what with my lack of education. Nerves and butterflies filled my stomach and kept me anchored to my seat for a while, but eventually I managed to gather up enough confidence to move. I got up from my chair and walked over to her table, hoping to get her attention from all those books.

'Hello!' I said, hoping a simple greeting would work. 'My name is Elijah – and if you don't mind, I would like to get to know you – if that's possible.' She slowly looked up, and giggled slightly. I was ready to run for the hills! But then she began to speak. She said her name was Melanie Hopkins – and then she said no I don't mind and yes it's possible! After our introduction we both began to smile. Then we quietly chatted for more than an hour, until it was time for us to go back to class. We exchanged telephone numbers before we left the library.

"Anyway Jeremiah, I won't go into the details, but in the days after that we met quite regularly... and we gradually became a loving couple. We had lots of fun times together, going to the movies, taking long walks through the park holding hands and laughing. We'd talk about all our hopes and dreams, about what we wanted to do in the future. But what really sticks in my mind are the times when we would go to a fast food restaurant and sit in the lobby area and act as if we were in a five-star restaurant. She didn't know it, but I wanted that for us, I wanted to provide her with all the fine things that life had to offer. Anyway, with that desire in my heart, I knew then that it was even more important that I graduate from that school. I became so motivated by my long term goals that I knew I would do whatever it took to graduate. So I initiated a plan of action. I set my insecurities aside, and I began to talk about my academic struggles with my girlfriend. I didn't tell her about all of my failures, because I didn't want to risk losing her, as she was my only real source of happiness at the time. When I did tell her about my academic struggles, she raised an eyebrow for a quick moment, but that was soon replaced with a look of concern. She then told me that she was going to do all she could to help me with my academic problem. After that we began to work long hours together in the library. Melanie would get frustrated sometimes trying to help me, but I learned very quickly to distract her with jokes when this happened. But in the end I became frustrated, because I was trying so hard to better my academic shortcomings, but even with the help of my girlfriend I was getting nowhere. I still found myself doing poorly.

"I eventually decided that in order to keep my spirits up, I would focus on living in the moment. I didn't want my academic problems to further interfere with my social life. So anyway, after a while, my girlfriend and I decided to raise our relationship to another level. We decided (after we had gathered up enough courage and confidence!) to meet each other's families. I brought her over to meet my family first – I was so happy when everybody welcomed her with open arms! My mother gave her a hug and then introduced herself, as did my brother and sister. So everything was going just fine – until I picked up a whole different vibe when I met her family. I don't know if Melanie's mother was just having a bad day when I met her, but she wasn't nice and friendly towards me at all. She was even a bit disrespectful, speaking to me through the screen door of her house! When Melanie told her where I lived, she practically closed the door in my face. Melanie got really upset at that. She tried to excuse her mother's behavior to me, and then she went back into the house to talk to her mother. I sat patiently on the front porch. A minute later I could hear them arguing... a little while later Melanie stepped back outside, and politely told me it would be best if I left. She gave me a kiss and told me she would call me later. So I just walked back to the bus stop. Although I was very happy with the kiss, I was pretty disturbed by the treatment I had just encountered. Red flags were popping up everywhere in my mind, I didn't know what was going on between Melanie and her mother. But I was at least able to lower some of those red flags when I thought about the respectful treatment I received from her two older brothers – at least I had managed to make some sort of positive impression with her family. But I was still worried. I didn't want Melanie's mother's behavior to cause problems in our relationship. Anyway, I knew deep down that my love for Melanie could help me to put up with any mean-spirited behavior from her mother. So the bottom line is Jeremiah, that despite her mother's hateful ways our relationship continued.

"Life was wonderful, until January the following year. It was a bitter blow Jeremiah, because my academic difficulties continued, and at the end of the month I was kicked out of the school. I felt awful. My worst nightmare had come true – I had attained the title of school dropout, with all of its negative implications. I didn't know how to tell Melanie; I was sure she wasn't going to take it well. I thought about it for hours, debating everything within myself. Eventually I just couldn't take it anymore, and I decided to tell her. She was shocked, but I think she took it ok. About a week later we had a heart to heart talk about my situation: she wanted to know what I was going to do. I told her that I was sick and tired of the educational system in the city of Detroit, and that I wasn't getting any younger. I was going to start seeking employment, and in the meantime I would apply for General Assistance – the G.A. The G.A. at the time provided a monthly cash benefit of $30.00 for people who were unemployed but were living with someone who had an income or was already on the system. She looked at me after I'd told her this, and I could see that my overall situation was beginning to bother her – that this would put a great deal of stress on our relationship.

"Despite my situation, we still believed that love would conquer all. With that philosophy in mind we decided to get married. Not long after we were married we had a beautiful baby boy, who we named Isaiah. At this point I became even more desperate to land a job, so I made a last ditch effort to obtain an education. I enrolled in night school. Yet once again, after six months my inferior academic ability interfered with my progress. I found myself unable to keep up with the academic demands of night school, no matter how hard I tried. I eventually stopped going, because I wasn't really accomplishing anything – except raising my blood pressure and stress levels. I'd had enough. I couldn't take any more academic failure, so I redirected all of my energy into trying to get a job, so that I could properly take care of my wife and child. But you know what Jeremiah? Looking for a job with no education was just as difficult as all my years of academic failure."

* * *

Elijah looked up, before continuing to talk. "At that point in my life I didn't know what to do anymore. All I faced was the reality of failure. So I stepped up my pounding of the pavement. I traveled all over the city and beyond, filling out applications, going to countless job interviews and visiting hundreds of unemployment agencies. But in the end, I just felt defeated. It wasn't long before I figured out the reason I wasn't getting a job. I mean, I was doing everything that was asked of me, filling out lots of job applications and returning phone calls to check on applications I'd lodged. I was always on time at my job interviews, and I was welled groomed and neatly dressed, shaking as many hands as possible while wearing a great big old smile. But I was always disappointed. And I tell you, all that failure and rejection began to wear on me psychologically, particularly when I would make a phone call to check on an application I had filled out and submitted more than two weeks ago, only to be met with a rude receptionist on the other end of the line telling me that I didn't fit their criteria. I would sincerely ask that she be more specific, and then she would get upset with me, as if I wasn't being genuine. Then she would just hang up on me. On plenty of other occasions – when I wasn't being out right turned down – employers would tell me that the position was filled, or make excuses like 'we're no longer taking applications', and 'you're not qualified for the position'. I became so discouraged by all that rejection, I began to truly believe that I would never successfully find employment. By this time my wife had already completed her training at the Job Center Academy and had landed a job in no time – all thanks to her graduating from that school and obtaining a diploma and a couple of certificates in the process. So I began to ask myself, what is the problem? Why can't I get a job? The answer was revealed to me one day after I'd spent more than eight hours in an unemployment office line. When I was finally called by the staff, I was sent to the back area of the facility, where I saw what looked like hundreds of cubicles filled with office workers, ringing with the sounds of typewriters, telephones and voices. I was taken to one of those cubicles and asked to take a seat and fill out a job application form and some other paperwork. Once I was done filling out all that paperwork, one of the intake office personnel pulled my application off the top of the stack of paperwork.

'Why did you fill out the educational background section of your job application with the line 'not applicable'?' She asked. I tried to answer her question, but I was rudely interrupted.

'Never mind sir!' She said. 'You're done here, you can leave now.'

I stood up and shook her hand, and began to walk away. Then I stopped in my tracks, because I had one more question to ask her – but as I turned around, to my surprise I saw that she had already balled up my job application, and I watched as she tossed it into the trash can. My question vanished. I now had a statement to make to her. I glared at her and told her that she should at least have let me leave her cubicle before doing something like that. So anyway, I walked out of that building feeling furious." Elijah stopped talking.

"It's funny that you should mention that," I replied, "because I bear witness of a similar situation that happened to a person that I met named Melvin. It happened while I was trying to get this job. I don't think he was aware that his application was thrown away, but I know how rude some people can be. But anyway, you go on and finish your story."

"Ok man," Elijah said, shaking his head at Melvin's story. "Well, as I was saying, I left that unemployment office feeling unimaginably upset. I went and waited for the bus. As I stood there waiting I was able to calm down, but the treatment I had just received made me feel downright worthless. It also allowed me to see the type of punishment and the prejudice and discrimination that I would be subjected to for not having a formal education. But I will admit that it did teach me a valuable lesson in the dos and don'ts of filling out a job application, particularly in regards to my educational information. Basically, I learned not to put any kind of information on a job application that would work against me, and that includes the truth. Particularly when it comes to my educational background. I truly believe that my educational background was seriously impacting on my job search, preventing me from getting any type of employment. But Jeremiah, even though it sounds simple enough to look at your job applications like that, it wasn't – particularly when you're a person of integrity. To purposely tamper with things like that just hurts to the core of your being. Anyway, from that day forward I learned to put vague insinuating information on my job application regarding my educational background, because at the time no one was asking for any proof in the form of an official diploma or anything. So I took advantage of the situation. I developed a strategy. And you know what? I finally got a job. I got a job in a small plastic fabricating company. It wasn't glamorous, but it was better than being unemployed. I was paid $3.35 an hour working forty hours a week. But it was a great accomplishment for me, and made me feel kind of good about myself, particularly after I got off the General Assistance welfare. But it was sad though Jeremiah, because unfortunately it turned out to be a big disappointment to my wife. I wasn't making enough money for her. I began to feel very bad and insecure about our financial situation, but what made it even worse was that my wife who I dearly loved began to put me down. She talked down to me just about every day, as often as she could. It just broke my heart. I don't think I've ever really recovered from the pain and the disappointing lack of support that came from my wife. I ended up not wanting to share anything with her ever again.

"So the pain in my heart and soul coming from my marriage gave me new motivation to once again pursue my education. I enrolled in an adult educational program to obtain a GED and create better employment opportunities. I wound up attending those Adult Ed classes without the support of my wife. And that made me sad, because I really wanted to share this information with my wife as a surprise. "But then she surprised me with a pregnancy! We had a new baby daughter. We called her Kimberly." But you know what really surprised me? Two weeks before she was born I learned that I was dyslexic. I didn't know anything about dyslexia or any learning disabilities, but my Adult Ed teacher became very concerned about my consistently poor academic performance in her classroom. She became suspicious when she noticed all the hard work I would do in class but still get everything wrong. Anyway, at that point she just came out and told me that I could be suffering from a learning disability. So she suggested I get tested, and after a month the results revealed that I was dyslexic.

"I tell you Jeremiah, that information was bittersweet. On the one hand at least I knew that I wasn't dumb, despite what I had been told all those years. But on the other hand I was then in my thirties. What a waste all my time at school had been! It should have been discovered that I was dyslexic when I was a child, but it simply wasn't! Anyway, I had to live with the consequences. I tried to tell my wife about my dyslexia, but she became very negative and insensitive. She said she wasn't buying all that dyslexia crap, and that I was sinking to a new low with all my excuses as to why I couldn't get a better paying job. She would go on for days with all her insults, as if I wasn't feeling bad enough. In the beginning I tolerated all her insults, because I pretty much agreed with her. In fact, she didn't know it but I was harder on myself than she could ever be. But she couldn't know that, because we were hardly communicating. Our marriage was deteriorating. She began to take comfort in her coworkers at her job and other outside influences, or ignore her family and watch all those soap operas on television. But the relationship was finally destroyed when she cheated on me with one of her coworkers. She married him later, abandoning her family and children. She tried to blame it all on me not making enough money to support us. Anyway, you would think everything was bad enough before that Jeremiah. I confronted her one day, suspicious that I was being cheated on. She responded by trying to justify herself. She told me that in the beginning she wasn't cheating on me, because she always used a condom when she was engaged in sexual activities outside our marriage. Like it was no big deal! We divorced soon afterwards, and I lost everything.

"I was looking after the family on my own, and I was no longer able to attend my Adult Ed classes. The possibility of ever obtaining my GED certificate seemed to slip away. Anyway, things seemed to just get worse. Two months after the divorce I had managed to provide some sense of stability for my children, but we were served with an eviction notice. We had nowhere to go. I soon learned that there were no homeless shelters in the City of Detroit equipped to accommodate a single father and his children. Anyway, we had nowhere to go, so the eviction had to be physically enforced. All my furniture and other personal items were set out on the curb. We couldn't do anything but stand there. My children were looking on with tears in their eyes, while the movers shifted our belongings on to the street under the protection of law enforcement officers. At this point all we had was a functioning used car that I had managed to buy after months of saving every little nickel and dime I could get before my divorce. That car saved us Jeremiah, it became our temporary shelter. At first we spent those cold nights sleeping in the car on Grand River Avenue's side streets, in a housing community littered with more than a few abandoned and boarded up properties,nearly got broken into one time... so we began to park in police station parking lots all around Detroit. It was safer there. Anyway, we kept on as best we could. But I got so tired and hungry... Eventually I set aside my pride and asked my mother if I could come and stay with her for a few days. She said yes and I thanked her and my Heavenly Father.

"I knew we couldn't stay too long, as I didn't want to jeopardize my mother's residency. I think having all of us there violated something in her rental assistance Section Eight Program. The program was monitored by inspection, so I knew that if we were still there at the end of the month we would be putting my mother at risk. If she was denied the financial benefits she was receiving I don't think she would have been able to pay the rent. I wasn't going to allow that to happen, but

I didn't know what else to do. I did know that I had to leave my mother's house as soon as possible, whether I had somewhere to go or not.

"All I could do was pace back and forth, thinking about my lack of options and our fast approaching homelessness. When my mother asked what I was going to do, I stopped pacing for a moment and turned to look her in the eyes.

'I really don't know what to do,' I said, 'and if there was a stress chart I wouldn't be able to use it, because my level of stress wouldn't be on it.' I was working a dead end job with pay that kept me at the poverty line, I had no education that I could use to better myself and my wife had left me because I wasn't making enough money. The only thing I seemed to be good at was failing."

* * *

"The bottom line is that I was just so sick and tired of feeling like an unfit parent, so sick and tired of feeling like someone who just kept falling short for his children and family. When I was talking to my mother I couldn't hold back my emotions and tears.

'I know what I have to do,' I said. She looked at me with a concerned look on her face, and I told her what I was about to do. She cried out, and pleaded with me not to. I told her that I felt like I had no other alternatives. I had an unimaginable dark pain in my defeated and dying spirit and soul. I grabbed the telephone off my mother's table and called the Child Protective Services. I cried out in agony as I told them to come and get my children because I just couldn't take care of them anymore. I spoke over the phone but my words became a stream.

'I've caused them to become homeless... I no longer have a home for my children and we live in a car... their mother ran out on me because I'm a loser and not a good provider... I hope that you can find them a better home with better parents that can take care of them because they deserve a better life than I can provide... please come and get them.' I hung up the telephone and told my mother that the Child Protective Services agent was on her way. All sorts of emotions began to materialize within me. I dropped to my knees and began to cry uncontrollably with my mother.

"After we'd managed to get control of our emotions, we heard the closing of a car door and a knock on the door. Reluctant to answer the door, I asked who it was. A lady called out from the other side.

'Good morning sir, I'm from the Child Protective Services.'

I let her in and she pleasantly introduced herself. She then asked me where the children were. I told her that the children were at school. She asked for directions to the school. I called the school to let their teachers know that a Child Protective Services officer would be arriving soon. After she'd gathered up all the information she needed from us, the Child Protective Services officer let us know that she would return after her evaluation, and then left for the school. My mother broke down again immediately, but at that point I was so numb and exhausted from all the emotional turmoil that I chose to maintain my composure.

"Two and a half hours later there was another knock on the door. The lady from the Child Protective Services had returned to deliver her findings.

'I met with your children,' she said, 'and I found no form of child abuse. In fact they were in good spirits. They were clean and nicely dressed, and showed no signs of neglect. When I mentioned you their beautiful faces just lit up. Indeed, Mr. Anderson, I believe it would be a tragedy to take them away from you, despite your situation and all that you are going through. You must be doing something right, because those are normal healthy children who would probably be damaged if I was to carry out your request. I am not going to take these children into protective care. But, I will say this; I know things are not going right for you at this time, but things will get better for you one day. Things will get better as long as you continue to take care of your children. They truly are blessings to you, and the fact that you're a man trying to take care of his children alone is commendable in itself. You will be rewarded for all your hard work some day by divine intervention.'

I felt a bit better, but her complements didn't take away all my insecure feelings; that I wasn't a good father or a good provider for my children. In fact, I still didn't know what would make me feel otherwise. I said this to her, but she interrupted me.

'One thing I want you to know,' she said, 'is that bad parents don't call Child Protective Services on themselves. It'd be nice if they did – that'd make my job easier – but we all know that's not reality. Elijah,' she said to me, 'I can plainly see that you have integrity, that you are a good person and a good father. I have no doubt in my mind that you will continue to take care of your children.'

She shook my hand and gave my mother a hug for comfort, and then walked out of my mother's house and into her small burgundy department issue car. I looked at the Child Protective Services State seal on the side door of her car as she drove off, never to be seen again.

"Soon after the Child Protective Services lady left it was time to pick up my children from school. I went off in a hurry, and when I met them I gave them a hug like never before. Once they were in the car and I was driving back to their grandmother's house, my little girl looked at me through the rearview mirror and asked me why I had a tear rolling down my face. I told her that it was a tear of happiness in thanking God for having blessed me with you two beautiful angels. Later that night I lay on the living room floor in my mother's house, with my children curled up beside me. They were sound asleep, unaware of all the pain their father was enduring over the terrible decision he'd made earlier that day. I tell you Jeremiah, I promised my Heavenly Father that I would never do anything like that again, no matter how bad thing got. I cried silently, trying not to wake up the children.

"The next morning after I'd dropped my children at school I got on the telephone at my mother's house in the hopes of finding a shelter somewhere that could take in a father and his two children. I found one, but it was outside the city of Detroit. This would make traveling back and forth to my children's school and my job a big old inconvenience to say the least. But anyway, the people at the shelter told me over the telephone that I needed to be there by 6 p.m., or that my space would be taken. So an hour after I'd picked up my children from school we left my mother's house to move into the shelter. As we arrived, I told my children what was happening, and that we wouldn't be staying there long. I remember how sad and devastated I was when the staff processed us. Anyway, things got worse. After we'd been at the shelter for a week I found myself not only challenged with trying to find a place to live but with unemployment. I was laid off from my job at the plastics factory. I felt terrible. We had to endure all these mind numbing rules and regulations at the shelter, and I tell you that took its toll as well. I felt like we didn't matter to society anymore: I was homeless and unemployed, on the fringes of society. We were invisible.

"Despite the pain it caused us, we survived in that homeless shelter for about five months. Eventually I met someone there who was able to help me to find a job and a place for us to live. He was a teacher who'd simply burned out – he'd lost his job and his home and his family. Anyway, he told me about a janitorial position at the school where he'd worked. I didn't move quickly, because I was concerned about how shamefully janitors are sometimes treated, as if they are invisible mindless slaves. But despite this concern I signed up. I became a janitor, and I'm still a janitor today. Things started to look up. I lost my car in an accident one day, so we had to use the bus all the time… and I've nearly lost my job because of that… but I still thank my Heavenly Father for the job. After a while we also found a place to live. It was within walking distance of my children's school. I'd walk my children to school down that sidewalk no matter what the weather was. The neighborhood was kind of rough, but it was all I could afford at the time. Anyway, it was a whole lot better than being homeless and living in a shelter. Actually, despite its reputation our new neighborhood actually helped me to rediscover that there are good people in the world.

"One winter school day not too long ago a neighbor of mine approached me. I didn't know her name, but we would speak briefly just about every day when walking our children to school. Anyway, on this one particular day when it was time to pick up our children she approached me in a dignified manner carrying some large shopping bags as if she'd just come from the shopping mall. She introduced herself by telling me that her name was Ms. Grace Carmichael. With a concerned look on her face, she said that she had in her bag a coat for me, because she felt bad for me and she was tired of seeing that old raggedy winter coat that I'd been wearing for the last two winters. I never thought much about the condition of my winter coat – as long as I was able to provide for my children any warmth was enough for me at that time. But Jeremiah, it was a breath of fresh air to have someone show that they cared about me. At that time, after living in the homeless shelter I was just about ready to believe that there were no good people on the whole planet. I looked at her and smiled, and I accepted the coat. I thanked her warmly, and we began to talk. From that day on we became close friends. I guess it was at that point that I began to feel a whole lot better about my situation. I was able to provide a real sense of security and stability for my children, and that meant a lot to me. I was so glad that my children were doing alright. So once it was apparent that my children were settled, I decided that I would again try to pursue my education. I enrolled myself again in an adult education program in order to work towards a GED. But to my surprise I was hit with a very low blow then, one that made me give up on ever getting an education. All of my 218 GED point grades that I'd earned over the previous ten years were wiped away in an instant. The GED test was revived and updated – with no real warning, as far as I could tell from what receptionist at the testing center told me when I spoke to her over the phone about the issue.

"Before I go any further Jeremiah, let me explain the GED points system so that we can be on the same page. In order to obtain a GED diploma you must pass with a 225 point grade after taking five tests on five separate subject matters. These five tests include a Writing Skills Test, a Social Studies Test, a Science Test, an Interpreting Literature Test and a Mathematics Test. It'd take more than one day to take all those tests, especially if you're testing for the very first time. Anyway, you have to earn at least 40 points on each test, and if you fail to do so then you must retake that test until you reach the passing point grade score of 225. Even if it takes many years to do so. So, all my years of taking that test, all those years of blood, sweat and tears building up 218 point grades were flushed away as if it was all just one big waste of time. I came to the conclusion that there was no sense in me continuing to beat that dead horse. After all those years of failure, I decided that it was time that I just learned to accept reality for what it was, whether I liked it or not. I had to move on and focus on taking care of my children. But I tell you, I felt desperately sad letting go of the idea of ever obtaining an education. But my sanity and peace of mind were more important and precious than an education.

"Anyway, I focused on my job. Mainly because of the way I had to obtain the job… Basically Jeremiah I'm going to tell you what I was going to tell you in the beginning… I guess I've told you just about everything about myself anyway! I'm going to explain to you what I call my janitor's secret. The janitor's secret? It's basically a term I kind of made up in the face of all the frustrations I faced in my life to describe the fact that I've had to become an impostor to obtain employment – or for that matter anything else that's desirable in life that requires an education. Basically, I've had to use deception to obtain this position; I've had to lie about having credentials that I don't have. And I hate it. This janitor's secret isn't easy to have, particularly as I think of myself as a person of integrity. It feels to me like a little piece of me is dying every day while I'm employed in a deceptive manner. You don't know the constant fear and stress that I have to deal with, hoping that my deception is never found out. Because if someone like me is found out, nine times out of ten they'll be fired immediately, probably ruining their life. In fact even if you've been twenty years on the job you can bet your bottom dollar that you'd be fired for your deception with no excuses to save you.

"Anyway Jeremiah, that is one of the main reasons why I didn't want to tell you my story, and why I have to ask that you don't tell my story to anyone. If you do, chances are the consequences will be devastating for both me and my children, and I am going to do all that I can to guard against that to protect my family." Elijah paused. "Well Jeremiah that's the end of my story, thank God! But look – your side of the floor is dry now, and I am more than ready to get out of here to go home to be with my children. So I'm going to quickly mop the other half of the room – but if you've got any more questions, I'll answer them now if you want. Once I'm done mopping I will also be done answering questions, so ask away!"

"Ok Elijah," I said. I paused for a bit, thinking about my questions. "What ever happened to your three buddies, Sherry, Bruce and Russell?"

Before he answered the question Elijah paused for a minute, with a strange expression on his face, as if he wasn't going to answer the question. It made me feel a bit uncomfortable, like I shouldn't have asked him that. But he kept his word and told me. "Sherry's parents eventually took her out of public school and placed her in private school, where their consistent support eventually paid off – she graduated high school and then went on to college, where she earned all sorts of degrees. She's got a professional job and she's happily married now, and she's got a little kid. She's doing just fine in her life. I spoke with her a couple of months ago." Elijah paused for a bit, and then continued. "Unfortunately, Bruce and Russell weren't so lucky. They didn't get any educational help from their parents or the school system. They both eventually dropped out of high school, and without a high school diploma they found it very difficult to find good jobs. They've both spent long periods unemployed, unable to provide for their families. They've told me they feel like less than men on a daily basis. Eventually they grew tired of feeling like failures, tired of being rejected by society's dislike for high school dropouts. So they ended up with nothing to look forward to, and they began to live for the moment. They got involved in selling drugs and other illegal activities, and were sent to jail a number of times. When they weren't incarcerated, they would live a temporary, instant gratification life – full of brand-name clothes, fancy cars, jewelry and a whole host of other things their hearts desired with no concern for the consequences and for how those things were acquired. Basically they were living it up, partying almost every day.

"Anyway, that kept going on until one summer evening. That evening I passed Russell's mother's house, and it looked like some chaotic event had just taken place. I saw Russell, so I stopped to asked him what had happened . Apparently Russell held a barbecue there at 6:00pm, while his mother's was at work." Soon after, Bruce and a crew of his other friends with a few ladies had come around to visit. Anyway, they raised the level from a simple back yard barbecue into a full-fledged party. They were blasting out gangsta rap music and eating ribs, hot dogs and potato salad and everything else, while they were dancing, smoking illegal substances and drinking plenty of beer and liquor. In layman's terms, the party was on! Anyway, two hours into the party the festivities were brought to a tragic end, when two strange guys unfamiliar to Russell entered the backyard where the barbecue was taking place. As soon as these two guys spotted Bruce and his boys standing, they pulled out pistols and just started firing. Everybody except Bruce and his boys ran for cover; Bruce and his boys drew their weapons and returned fire. That gun battle seemed like it went on for an eternity, but it was probably only a few minutes long. After the smoke cleared, a terrible stink of burnt gun powder lingered in the air, and the terrible scar of senseless violence once again ripped through our community , Bruce pushed Russell out of the way and then fell to the ground. As he fell he shot one of the other boys ending the immediate threat, but as he landed there was a horrible wound on the side of his head. At that point, Russell said, everything just kind of stood still. Nothing felt real. He held Bruce in his arms and cried out loud. He was screaming at the top of his lungs for Jesus' mercy. He was covered in blood, rocking Bruce's limp body back and forth like a mother would with her newborn baby. Eventually the police, ambulance and coroner arrived.

"Anyway Jeremiah, some days later Russell, Sherry and I attended Bruce's funeral. Alone with his grief, Russell announced to us that he had made a decision to change his life for the better: he'd reenrolled in school so that he could get his GED certificate and then work towards a real career. Well he worked at that for a while, but six months after he'd retuned to Adult Ed School, he discontinued once again, discouraged by his poor academic achievements. So with all those bad feelings of being a failure and the sadness surrounding Bruce's death, Russell went over the edge and back into his old self-destructive ways. In fact, he was in an even worse position than before. He stopped selling drugs and became a drug addict. He attempted suicide once, putting a gun to his head. Luckily the mechanism jammed when he pulled the trigger. Anyway, his life spiraled out of control, until eventually he hit rock bottom. Four years after becoming a drug addict, Russell checked himself into a drug rehab clinic – he's still there now, trying to get his life together. Last time I visited him he was doing a lot better, dealing with his drug addiction and Bruce's death. I think it helped him when we took a trip to the cemetery to put some flowers on Bruce's grave. When we put those flowers on Bruce's grave, it felt strange Jeremiah – we were silent for a brief moment, just standing there looking and thinking while a cool breeze brushed gently against my face, soothing that deep pain which lay beneath my soul and spirit. Eventually, we both broke the silence to reminisce about the fun times we used to have, especially when we were children at school. After about an hour, we left the cemetery. Anyway, that was about a year ago – that's the last time I've seen or heard from Russell."

"I am so sorry to hear about your friends," I offered. "If you don't feel like talking anymore, I understand."

"It's ok Jeremiah. I'm going to keep my word, if you have any other questions."

I paused for a bit. "I would like to know a bit more about dyslexia. Does it affect only one ethnic group?"

"No!" Elijah responded. "What I've learned so far about dyslexia is that no one ethnic group is immune."

"How do you know you're dyslexic?"

"Well that's a big part of the problem. On the most part you don't, unless you're tested for it. You might have suspicions when you're a child that something isn't right, particularly when you find yourself consistently unable to keep up with your classmates no matter what you do! I mean it struck me as weird that I was constantly told I was lazy, slow and not trying hard enough, despite the fact that I knew I was trying really hard. It seemed like my efforts would just go unnoticed by parents and teachers."

"Man, that sounds hard," I replied. "If someone is properly tested and they have dyslexia, is there any medication they can take for it?"

"Well first of all, whenever possible testing should take place during childhood. But if not, you can still be tested as an adult… even though that means there will have been many wasted years while your dyslexia has gone untreated. Anyway, to prevent that, parents should closely monitor their children's academic performance – while being very careful not to be too quick in punishing a child who's not doing very well. That child could possibly be challenged by a learning disability and may need help… and they're also probably feeling punished enough by the world already. So anyway, if you're monitoring your child's report card and have spoken to the teacher, you'll discover that your child is having real problems in their academic work. The next course of action should be to request that your child be tested at his or her school to see if they are eligible for access to specialist help, such as a resource room with a teacher specializing in helping children with special education needs, or an Individualized Education Program. A parent could also contact their state dyslexia foundation or go online for further resources. State dyslexia foundations can usually help with locating an authorized testing facitity that will be able to identify more accurately what learning disabilitiy your child might be challenged with. Basically, school tests might reveal evidence of a learning disability in a couple of hours, but they might not be able to pin down exactly what learning disability is affecting your child. When you go to a testing facility recommended by a dyslexia foundation, it can take about three days to test. They're expensive, but the cost is well worth paying if your child's educational future is important to you. If you're an adult and you want to be tested for a learning disability, then you're best off getting in contact with a national or state dyslexia foundation. You can call information or go online and you'll find them."

Elijah paused for a minute. "But to answer the other part of your question, I'm not aware of any medications that you can take for dyslexia or any other learning disabilities. For whatever this is worth Jeremiah, I do recall, that the process of being tested for a learning disability was pretty painless. "I'm pretty sure that at present a learning disability can't be detected in the blood, so a blood test isn't needed. There weren't any needles or surgery or electric shock treatment involved in my testing process. But I will admit that the testing process was mentally exhausting to say the least, largely due to the psychological endurance testing over a three days period."

"So does that mean…" I faltered for a second, before continuing the question, "that you're ultimately doomed once you've discovered that you have dyslexia or another learning disability?"

"Not really Jeremiah. As long as you're provided with the necessary support and opportunities by your family, friends, teachers and the school system, you'll be able to cope. Dyslexia is with you for life, or at least that's what I've learned. But I have heard of quite a few famous people who are very successful in their lives despite having learning disabilities or dyslexia. But the key thing is that their lives would probably have been a lot different – more like mine – if they weren't given the support they needed when they were growing up."

"OK," I said, "here is another question for you. Are there any other serious consequences of learning disabilities, other than the obvious negative treatment that you've already pointed out?"

"Yes! There most definitely is," Elijah responded. "In fact, I can give you an awful example of the consequences of not being able to read very well – or not being able to read at all – right away. I almost poisoned my own daughter with some over-the-counter medication once. I got her the medication because she had a cold, but I couldn't read the label, and it turned out it wasn't the right medication. Anyway, I was about to give her the medication but I was stopped in time by my son... I was so thankful for his ability to read properly, but I tell you, I was deeply disturbed by what had happened. I thanked my son for his assistance, and after I got over the initial shock, I made sure that such a situation could never happen again." Unfortunately, my success in dealing with that situation and the many others is usually short-lived after I am overcome with all those emotions of feeling angry, alienated, isolated, powerless and top it off with hopelessness to name a few which does nothing but, creates within me an unimaginable emergence of sadness and depression that will take ahold of me and won't let me go for days sometimes. When that psychological parasite loosens its grip and let me go from that dark painful place where its leaves me emotionally and physically exhausted.Sometimes I'm very much afraid that I may not have the strength to recover from such a dreadful journey that I prefer to take alone. So in the meantime I thank God for my children because they give me that extra strength I desperately need to fight daily against all the negative affects depression has to offer. "Don't worry Jeremiah I am doing just fine at the moment."

"Ok Elijah," I said. "I've just got one last question, and it's based on what you've told me you've been through. If you were given an opportunity to give some advice to parents concerned about their children's education, what would you say?"

"Well I guess the first thing I would say would be that every parent is the first line of defense in their child's education – it is up to them to ensure that their child's right to an education is not violated. Parents should also never turn their children over to any educational institution without being one hundred per cent involved – especially if their child is challenged by a learning disability. Parents should be particularly aware during the first, second and third grades, as that is when learning disabilities usually reveal themselves. It's also worth remembering that your child's teacher may not be well-equipped to recognize or handle children with learning disabilities. Most of them have not had training that can help them to recognize or deal with children with learning disabilities, so parents have to stay on top of things." Elijah looked over the floor. "Well Jeremiah," he continued, "I'm glad that was your last question, because I've finished mopping – it's time for us to get out of here!"

* * *

On my drive home all I could think about were the stories Elijah had told me – I was overwhelmed! One thing that I truly realized was that I didn't have it as bad as I thought I did. I'd been laid off, but I didn't have to deal with even half of what Elijah had to go through. I thought about his story. There were probably people all over the place living their janitor's secret… without any real hope of getting an outlet for their talents, with their intellectual capabilities being ignored and their creativity going to waste. All because they are exceptions to the rule. They have to hide and allow themselves to be ignored. I tell you it made me angry – so many talented people never getting the opportunity to fulfill their role in society. Such a waste! But it left me with this question – how can any decent society allow such precious resources to be simply sacrificed and ignored?

Chapter 7

The high cost of storytelling

After Elijah had told me his story, the changes that took place were amazing. For a start, it seemed like every one at work, including the teachers and the administrative staff, began to notice that Elijah was a more pleasant person to be around. It was like Elijah had a brand new attitude – he always wore a smile on his face, and just about everyone received it like a rare jewel. But, like the old saying goes, you can't please everyone. It seemed that the more Elijah would smile, the more Ms. Paula Gooden would frown and get upset. I don't know what was driving her, but later that March Ms. Paula Gooden became so consumed by anger that she literally got sick – to the point where she had to take a day or two off to recover. On one occasion she was actually hospitalized, after an ambulance was called to her home to pick her up and rush her to a hospital. But anyway, the rest of us were all enjoying the new Elijah and all the pleasantries he was bringing to the workplace. That is, until Ms. Paula Gooden's health started to return and she set in place an ill guided plan to cause more misery for Elijah.

On the morning of that day Elijah and I had cleaned the music room together. After that, I went to put our equipment away, while Elijah went straight back to the janitorial maintenance office. I wandered back to the office slowly. I walked through the door exactly as Elijah came storming out. He pushed me roughly aside, knocking me to the floor. I stayed down for a bit on my hands and knees, and watched him march down the hall while I tried to catch my breath. I tell you, he was angry, mumbling something about never trusting anyone ever again. That caught me off guard, but I had no idea what the hell he was talking about. I hadn't shared his story with anyone. Without knowing why he had lashed out at me in such a manner, I got up off the floor and started to chase him. But after a little bit I decided against it, thinking that it probably wouldn't have been a good idea while he was in that state of mind. So I went into the janitorial maintenance office instead, and saw Ms. Cheryl Washington standing at her desk with her head down in distress. I didn't care about her distress. I just wanted answers. My anger was deflated as soon as Ms. Washington explained to me that Elijah had just been fired because someone had reported to management downtown that Elijah had put fraudulent information on his job application.

"He pleaded his case with me," she said, "but I had to tell him that I couldn't do anything because the person that had revealed this information had gone over my head in doing so. He was frustrated, and he didn't want to hear anything else from me, so he stormed out. He did say as he was leaving that he did have some idea who might have snitched on him. You came in not long afterwards."

I felt awful for Elijah. He'd taken a horrible blow in being fired, and he also felt betrayed. The way he'd roughly treated me seemed insignificant in comparison. Anyway, once I knew why Elijah had treated me so roughly I had a change of heart, because with that information I was able to change my anger to concern. I asked Ms. Cheryl Washington for Elijah's phone number and home address. I wanted to be there for him during this terrible time. She responded by telling me that she couldn't give me that type of information, but before I could say I understood, she had already looked me in the eye and slid a piece of paper across the desk to me. It had all of Elijah's contact details written on it. I thanked Ms. Washington, and then left the office.

I worked anxiously up until lunchtime. When lunchtime arrived I used the school pay phone to try and call Elijah, but the telephone phone number Ms. Washington had given me was no longer in service. At the end of the day I called my wife to tell her what was going on, and that I would be a little late coming home. She told me to be careful. So I left the school and drove for about 45 minutes to the address written on the slip of paper. When I got there I put my head down on the steering wheel in frustration – the house was all boarded up. Elijah mustn't have updated his information with the janitorial office. This was probably the last place he'd lived with his children before they became homeless.

I drove home angry, feeling helpless and hopeless. I arrived home in an unpleasant mood, but I found myself once again reminded how precious my wife is. She knew I didn't want to talk and didn't take it personally; she didn't get upset when I went to bed soon after dinner. She gave me the space she knew I needed to handle the situation, but she did tell me that she would be there for me whenever I need her.

The next day I arrived at work and waited anxiously for Ms. Cheryl Washington to hand out all our work assignments. After everyone else had left, I told her about my lack of success in tracking down Elijah. I asked if she had any other information that I could use to find Elijah, but she simply told me that she had no other information she could share with me that would help my cause. I thanked her and went to work, with the additional intention of finding someone who could help me to find Elijah.

With that agenda on my mind, I commenced asking just about all the staff in and around the school – or indeed anyone I could think of – if they knew where Elijah lived. I asked just about everyone. But I got nowhere for quite sometime.

Eventually I had a profound breakthrough, some two months after Elijah had been fired. Anyway, one day the star of the girl's basketball team approached me while I was sweeping the floor of the gymnasium. She told me that she was aware of my search for Elijah.

"A friend of mine," she began, "said once that she lived on the block next to the one where Mr. Elijah Ray Anderson the school janitor lives. She doesn't go to this school anymore, but I still try to see her… Well I guess it's been a couple of weeks since I've talked to her now… Which is part of the reason why it took me so long to tell you this. Anyway, I just want to help out Mr. Anderson, 'cause I'm sad that he was fired from his job. He was more than just a janitor. He was a positive force and mentor to a lot of the children in this school." She looked at me for a bit. "In fact, he helped me out personally one day with his drawing ability, when I was being treated unfairly. A teacher basically tried to sabotage my participation one day, on the school's basketball team by making me do a drawing assignment. That teacher made me so angry!" She said. "Anyway, this might be Mr. Anderson's address." She passed me a piece of paper with an address written on it. I tell you the whole thing caught me off guard! I was surprised by the information she gave me, it was the first time I'd heard something like that. But she had something even more surprising to add. "I also heard this rumor that Ms. Gooden was responsible for Mr. Anderson being fired, after she used an electronic listening device that she planted in the classroom Mr. Anderson was last cleaning. After she'd listened to him talk, she immediately reported back to the school administration office downtown, where they took action against Mr. Anderson. The rest is history. Anyway Mr. Johnson," she said, "I don't care what anyone says, no one can convince me that what happened is just a rumor. Everyone knows that Ms. Gooden is not a very nice person, to say the least." She smiled at me, and then wished me good luck in finding Elijah. She walked out of the gymnasium to go to her next class.

Once she'd left, I found myself standing in the gymnasium alone, shocked – but not surprised – by what I'd just heard.

I tell you, Ms. Paula Gooden had such a reputation. When the shock of what I'd heard wore off at the end of my shift, I got motivated to act on the address immediately. I wanted to find Elijah even more now that I'd heard the rest of the story. I wanted to tell him that I hadn't told anyone anything about his story. When I finally found the address written on the slip of paper my heart was pounding – my nerves nearly got the best of me. I sat out in the front of his house in my car, trying to gather up the courage to go in and face Elijah. I still didn't know how mad at me he might be, since he thought I had told his story. Eventually I gathered up my courage and got out of my car and walked down the sidewalk towards his house. I walked up onto the porch, and knocked on the door. After knocking a few times I realized that no one was there, so I turned to walk away – but as I got back to the sidewalk, a next-door neighbor called out.

"Are you a friend of the man who used to live in that house with his two children?"

I was puzzled, but it was a bit of a lead. "Used to live there?" I called back. "When did he move?"

The neighbor responded with a strange look on his face.

"He didn't move sir. Uh… He committed suicide about a week ago. He put a gun to his head and pulled the trigger."

My head spun. I couldn't hear anymore. Elijah's neighbor kept talking… but I just couldn't hear it. I walked away in a daze, stumbling back to my car with Elijah's neighbor's voice ringing in my head. I got in the car… and I sobbed. I cried hard and long, clenching my fists to pound the steering wheel in anger. After half an hour or so I wiped my eyes, getting them clear enough for me to drive. I got control of my emotions and drove home.

When I arrived home my wife sensed that something was drastically wrong. She immediately got up from the sofa in the living room and hugged me tightly. It made me feel so secure that I soon began to cry again. I had a flashback about what

I'd just learned about my buddy Elijah. While crying I began to tell my wife what had happened. When I finished telling her, I was emotionally exhausted. I had no appetite. I skipped dinner and went to bed early. Just before getting in bed, I told my wife how angry I was with Ms. Paula Gooden, after I had learned about her possible role in helping Elijah's demise. My wife knows it: I don't easily get angry at people, I don't hate anyone… but, in that woman's case I felt compelled to make an exception. As I put my head on the pillow, I made a promise to myself – to never take any more of her foolishness.

Chapter 8

Tyrants make for bad business

The next day was no better. I felt down, and I didn't want to go to work. But I made it anyway. In fact, I made it to work earlier than I anticipated. I used the extra time to inform Ms. Cheryl Washington of Elijah's death. Moments later she announced the news to the rest of the janitorial staff. After telling everyone, she passionately asked for a moment of silence. We sat there silently. The thought of Elijah's children just kept going through my mind – who was going to take care of them? Who was going to love them the way he had? My thoughts were soon interrupted by Ms. Cheryl Washington with another announcement. At that point I didn't think things could get any worse, but boy was I wrong – Ms. Cheryl Washington informed us that following Mr. Nathan Jones' retirement last month, Ms. Paula Gooden would now be the assistant janitorial supervisor. At that point a couple of people spoke up, offering their congratulations to her. A couple of other people clapped. But I just couldn't. I couldn't celebrate her new job; it was just more bad news. And I wasn't trying to be pessimistic, but I just didn't think any good was going to come from giving her a leadership position.

Anyway, after about a week my concerns were realized. Newly armed in leadership, Ms. Paula Gooden quickly turned herself into a dictator, a tyrant on the rampage. The sad reality was that even when she learned of her tyrannical reputation she responded with an 'I don't care' attitude. She even let it be known that she was more than proud to wear her reputation as a badge of honor. She continued to use her leadership as a means of making the lives of everyone around her as miserable as possible. The result of her misuse of power was an unimaginably hostile environment in the work place; she would reprimand people,and even though she had limited authority even tried to suspend people for just about anything and morale was at an all time low. Of course, I was included in this. But you know what took the cake? When Ms. Paula Gooden had our supervisor Ms. Cheryl Washington written up – no one was safe in her presence. In fact, she allowed her tyranny to stretch far outside of the janitorial staff; she even started going after teachers and other school administrative staff – even students were not immune! Just about everyone found themselves reprimanded for all sorts of infractions.

Fate eventually stepped in and literally stopped her in her tracks, after she fell ill while one day at work and was rushed to the hospital by an ambulance. She was diagnosed then with full blown breast cancer. They might have been able to treat it, but she made the fatal mistake of sacrificing her health in favor of her power and status at work; work was her whole life. Anyway, about a year later Ms. Paula Gooden lost her agonizing fight with breast cancer. I tell you, when I heard that I wanted to thank Jesus, what with the terror and tyranny she had caused. But of course my conscience and common decency for my fellow human being wouldn't allow me to be that cruel! But anyway: this is all jumping ahead in the story.

With her new power, Ms. Paula Gooden sought to make my life a misery almost everyday. I'm sure – probably because I was close to Elijah – that I was at the top of her do not like list. One day over dinner I told my wife Sophia about the treatment I was receiving from Ms. Paula Gooden in the workplace. I probably didn't mean it, but I became so emotional in my explanation that I began a loud disturbing tirade; I went on to explain to Sophia how I would deal with Ms. Paula Gooden the next time she got in my face with her condescending words.

But luckily, before I could continue with my blood pressure raising tirade Sophia stopped me and suggested I calm down and lower my voice.

"Jeremiah, I really think you should be very careful in how you handle any situation with Ms. Paula Gooden. You wouldn't want to become what you despise. But at this point that's where you're headed – you have to stay positive and take the high road when dealing with her. Anyway, you should also understand that a lot of people function from a place of deep pain. What I'm trying to say to you is that if you respond to such a person with negativity, they will simply feed on it. Being positive would be more effective in such encounters. I really think that a large degree of anger and hatred with no compassion is very contaminating, and will consume any host that utilizes its energies on any level. And that's all I have to say, except that you're going to wash the dishes when we are done eating. You can work off all that unhealthy aggression that you are obviously harboring within yourself."

Despite Sophia's warning, the next day at work I found myself feeling uncontrollable anger towards Ms. Paula Gooden; I blamed her for all the negative feelings that were living within me. I found myself more than ready to respond to Ms. Paula Gooden like a predator pouncing on prey. My short wick was lit, and I was ready for anything Ms. Paula Gooden would try to subject me to. The bottom line was that she better watch out! I was not to be fooled with. In fact, I decided not to wait around and become a passive victim; I planned to confront her during her routine check of my work area and give her a piece of my mind.

So anyway, after I left the janitorial office meeting on this particular day I walked to my assigned work area anticipating one of Ms. Paula Gooden's attacks. When I got there and started cleaning, I rehearsed in my mind a whole bag of retaliations, a slew of ways to get her back. I thought of the best things to say to her, things to make her back down. She soon arrived.

The hairs on the back of my neck stood up in fear as I saw her walking towards me like the high ranking commander of some army. She was pretty small, but her intimidating presence more than made up for this. Every step she took in my direction made my heart race; it was pounding so loud in my chest that I could no longer think of any of the clever retaliations I had conjured up. She arrived. In a mean tone, she immediately started talking.

"Mr. Johnson," she said, "you better be done cleaning. It's time for me to inspect your area. If anything is out of place..." She smirked, and then her eyes darted to a cobweb I had missed in the corner of the classroom. "I will be writing you up for that!" She smiled at me, showing all her pearly whites! But she had more to say. "Hopefully," she said, "you will continue to provide me with mistakes that I can write you up for, so that at some point you will meet the same fate as your buddy Elijah." Ms. Paula Gooden laughed in my face, provoking me like you would not believe. Soon her laughter stopped and she got serious, looking me in the eyes.

"I can see that you want to do something to me Mr. Johnson, and if that's the case, bring it on! Because if you do anything to me, I will personally make sure you never work in the janitorial profession again." I stood there dumbfounded, feeling defeated. I thought to myself how lucky she was that I would never hit a woman for any reason. Might I say though, if it had been a man causing me all that grief, it would have been a different story! But I still didn't know what to do or say. But then something weird happened. I closed my eyes for a brief moment to try to regain my composure, and I began counting to ten – and then all of a sudden I felt a strange but wonderful feeling: I pictured myself in my mind's eye and I didn't like the negative image I was seeing. My wife's warning came back to me. Something in me changed, and I decided to change my strategy and become as positive as I could be in the face of all that negativity. Without any hesitation I immediately began to implement my new plan of action. I smiled and lowered my voice. This reaction seemed to take Ms. Paula Gooden off guard.

"What kind of game are you playing," she asked me, "changing from that tough guy to a wimp with no heart?" I responded to her again with more positivity – and that brought about some sort of a breakthrough!

"Why do you feel the need to be so hateful towards other people, especially those that have dropped out of school?" I asked her, with a concerned look on my face. She raised an eyebrow and then stepped back, putting her hands on her hips. Her face changed, and she began to look confused – as if she wanted to say 'why the hell are you asking me such question?'. Before I could continue, she caught me off guard – out of the blue she began to speak about how she came from a well educated family, until her oldest brother Calvin said he was bored with school in the twelfth grade, and decided to drop out despite being at the top of his class. There was a bit of anger in her voice as she explained this to me.

"It was such a stupid decision!" she cried. "It hurt me dearly, I looked up to him. And it hurt the rest of the family. It was a shameful act, embarrassing us to the highest degree. And if that wasn't bad enough, he sank to a whole new low, marrying a high school dropout with eight children. Neither of them have a job and they're all on welfare, leeching off society and hard working taxpayers. Much like your buddy Elijah." She continued to talk. "His decision set a bad precedent for other family members and relatives and some of his own friends, they all chose the same loser path. How can you respect people like that? How can you respect people that simply don't want to do anything for themselves, except rely on scraps and hand-outs from others?" She was angry. "I soon learned, Mr. Johnson, to have nothing to do with school dropouts like my brother or anyone else. Their reasons don't matter to me."

I tried to cut in, to explain to her that sometimes we have to step back and respectfully allow family and friends to make their own decisions, no matter if we like them or not. "If we do that," I offered, "we show them the love we have for them, and that's what is really important." Anyway, what I said just didn't go over very well with her. In fact, I think it triggered something deep inside her, and she instantly became the Ms. Paula Gooden that I was most familiar with once again. She gave me a hostile look. "I don't know how you managed to trick me into telling you any of my business. But that's over with now! I am still writing you up for that cobweb, and don't you forget my promise that I'll write you up every chance I get." She turned around and took her hands off her hips, and then began to slowly walk away, back on the same path she came in on. The only difference was that now she was wearing a facial expression of surprise and confusion, instead of her usual frown.

A week after our encounter she was avoiding me like the bubonic plague. In fact, she eventually stopped her pursuit of me. But her desire to make other people's lives miserable didn't disappear; she sought out other victims in the workplace until her eventual death. When we gathered in the janitorial maintenance office after her funeral to offer her a moment of silence, I realized something important. The real tragedy for Ms. Paula Gooden was not her death, but the way she chose to live her life. She lived her life in bondage, tied up with toxic hatred and anger. I really think that was the ultimate cause of her death. All she had to do was change her mind and her ways, and I truly believe her life would have changed for the better. But her death arrived first, and robbed her of that precious opportunity.

Chapter 9

Moving on is sometimes necessary

After Elijah's death and all the problems at work, my wife became a little concerned about my mental health. So on a beautiful sunny day she decided to surprise me by taking me downtown to a jazz concert and taste festival that was taking place on the river front. I tell you, I got there and I forgot about all my troubles. We were having the time of our lives, like children at play. We tried to eat everything in sight at the taste festival. There was food galore, but I particularly liked the fish and chips! Anyway, after eating so much of the delicious food, we sat down for a bit of a rest, waiting for the jazz concert which would begin in a couple of hours. It was really wonderful having that precious time together, being able to escape the problems of our everyday lives for just a moment. After sitting down for a while we noticed that the crowds of people were starting to make their way towards the outdoor stage where the jazz concert was going to be held. So about half an hour before the concert was scheduled to start we joined the crowd, hoping to get a good spot to watch the concert. Once we found a nice grassy spot near the riverfront stage we erected our portable chairs. While the musicians and the stage hands were setting things up and testing the sound system, I decided to make another trip back to the nearest concession stand to get some more fish and chips and a can of pop. I asked my wife if she wanted anything.

"Yes," she replied, "please bring me back a diet pop!"

"I sure will," I replied.

Ten minutes later I returned to our spot, but our chairs empty and my wife was nowhere to be seen. I looked around for a bit, but I couldn't see her. Eventually I looked down at a psychedelically colored blanket stretched out on the grass next to our chairs. In the middle of the blanket sat a beautiful lady reading a book, while three children were playing around her while. I politely got her attention and said to her that the lady who'd been sitting in one of the chairs next to her was my wife.

"Did you see were she went?" I asked.

"Not really," she apologized with a glance to her book, "but your wife did ask me to watch her chairs for a moment, as she just had to run off. She said she would be right back. But I don't know which direction she went off in sorry! I was reading my book when she walked off." I thanked her, and then took a seat. I thought my wife had probably just gone to the restroom, so I didn't panic. Anyway, I was at ease about where my wife had gone for a little while, until I heard my name being called out by her over the loudspeakers! She was asking me to come to the stage because it was urgent. I tell you, at this point my heart was racing and I was a bundle of nerves. I damn near ran to the stage in fear that something bad had happened to my wife. I was thinking that the afternoon had been going too good to be true. When I finally reached the stage I saw my wife, and she had the strangest look on her face — as if she'd seen a ghost or something. Before I could ask her what the problem was, I felt a tapping on my left shoulder from behind. I thought it was one of the jazz musicians that I had passed on my way to see what the problem was with my wife. Anyway, I turned around to see who it was, and my heart skipped a whole rhythm of beats. I tell you I nearly lost consciousness: I became overwhelmed by the sight of the individual now standing in my presence. My next impulse was to grab the individual and hug them, tears flowing down my face with not a care in the world.

"How are you doing Mr. Jeremiah Johnson, it's been a long time since I saw you last," Mr. Elijah Ray Anderson said. I found it very hard to speak. Eventually I got some words out.

"You're right," I was choked with emotions, "it has been a long time since I last saw you Elijah." I thank Jesus again for this special reunion. "I was told that you had committed suicide. Mrs. Abigail Bailey and I were both heart broken by the news of your death."

"Well Jeremiah I'm sorry to hear that… but, as you can see I didn't commit suicide! Though I will admit it did cross my mind on more than one occasion. In fact, only the love for my children stopped me from going through with it… Anyway, the story probably got confused – my oldest brother Daniel, who I loved so much and will miss intensely, did commit suicide. My whole family was devastated, particularly my mother. I've always been told that I look a lot like my brother, so I can understand the mistake."

"Oh… that makes sense Elijah," I said, "I had been led to believe you committed suicide after speaking with your neighbor."

"I'm really sorry that you got the wrong information Jeremiah. All I can say is that I used to visit my brother a lot at the house where he eventually committed suicide. But anyway Jeremiah," he paused, "enough of rehashing the ills of the past, let's move on! And firstly, let's get off this stage." So we thanked the musicians for the use of their stage, and my wife and Elijah and I headed back to our blankets and chairs. While walking back, my wife and Elijah began to explain to me how they had met shortly after I had gone to the refreshment stand. My wife told me that a couple with three children had sat down on a psychedelic blanket just near our chairs.

"When they had settled in," my wife continued, "the couple both smiled at me and said hello. Since they seemed to be friendly enough, I spoke back to them – and before I knew it we were all engaged in conversation – until the conversation took a strange turn and we properly introduced ourselves by name. When he said his name was Elijah all I could think of was this couldn't be the person I think it is. But my suspicions were soon confirmed. I asked him if he'd ever met a man by the name of Mr. Jeremiah Johnson." My wife nodded at Elijah. "He raised an eyebrow and smiled slightly, and said 'yes!'. As soon as he said yes, Elijah then asked me if I was Jeremiah's wife. I said I was, and he got up from his blanket and gave me a hug, and told me how my husband was a very good man, a decent human being." My wife smiled at me. "Elijah told me that you would stand up for him at that janitorial job when no one else would. He said he soon learned how genuine you were, particularly when you would not take his bad attitude personally, when you understood all the meanness and cruelty he had to put up with, and the unfair deals he got from incompetent supervisors. But before Elijah could tell me more of his story," Sophia continued, "I politely stopped him and told him that you would be more than happy to see him again. Anyway, at that point Jeremiah I came up with a plan to surprise you – Elijah agreed with the plan, and the rest is history!"

So anyway, my exciting day didn't stop there, because after we made our way back to our blankets and chairs, I felt more than privileged to be introduced to Elijah's new wife and their three children. His beautiful new wife already had a child before she had married Elijah.

* * *

Elijah shared his story with us while his children played in the background. He started his story by pointing out his beautiful daughter and smiled.

"Well it seems my beautiful little girl just got tired of not having a mother around – or some nice lady that would make her father happy. So she decided to take matters into her own hands. About five months after I was fired from my job, when I was primarily surviving on nothing but welfare checks, I decided to take my children to the Art museum downtown just to get out of the house. I think it was a Saturday afternoon; it was beautiful and warm and sunny. My children and I were enjoying all the wonderful Art museum exhibits and paintings, until my little girl just out of the blue began to pressure her father into having her brother take her to this one particular pencil drawing that was hanging on the back wall of the Art museum. A beautiful lady was looking at the drawing. I didn't have a problem with my daughter's request, but I don't think I can say the same for my son, because he resisted her request until I told him it would be alright as long as he stayed within eye sight – and where his sister wanted to go was well within my range of sight. Anyway, once they had permission, my little Kimberly practically dragged her big brother Isaiah over to the pencil drawing where the beautiful woman stood. When they arrived at the pencil drawing, she deliberately stood right by this woman's side, and put her little plan into action. She put on a beautiful ear to ear cool aide smile, and with her lovely brown eyes and soft voice began to interview the beautiful lady.

'Hello, Ms. Lady! How are you doing today?' She began.

'I am doing just fine little lady,' the beautiful lady replied, 'and how about you?'

'I am doing just find too,' Kimberly replied.

'So what is your name little princess?'

'Kimberly!' My daughter replied. 'What's your name Ms. Lady?'

'Well my name's Ms. Kathleen Tensely. So what brings you over to this pencil drawing little Kimberly?'

'I like art Ms. Tensely! Do you?'

'No Kimberly – I *love* art! I happen to be an artist myself! I paint, but I also find drawings and illustrators fascinating – and that's why I'm here viewing this drawing.'

My daughter then asked this beautiful lady if she liked children!

'Yes, indeed!' Ms. Tensely replied. 'In fact I have a little daughter named Colise, she's just about your age.'

'So why isn't she here with you now?'

'Well Kimberly she just didn't feel well today, so I decided before coming here that it would be best if I dropped her off at her grandmother's house where she could get some rest and eventually get well. But if she'd been well, she would have been here with me today!'

'OK, Ms. Tensely...' Kimberly smiled cheekily, 'so why is a beautiful lady who likes children, such as yourself, not married?'

'How do you know that I am not married Kimberly?'

'Well Ms. Tinsley I don't see a wedding ring on any of your fingers.'

'Well your observation is correct Kimberly. I am not married, I'm waiting for that good man to come – and wouldn't it be nice if his arrival was soon! But until then I'm just happy to wait patiently.'

'That makes sense to me Ms. Tinsley. While you're waiting for that good man to come, would you mind if I introduced you to someone now?'

Ms. Tinsley smiled. 'I don't mind at all Kimberly!' After she said yes, my daughter practically dragged her over to where I was standing, looking intently at a magnificent painting. Eventually I heard my daughter call out for me – asking me to meet someone she had just met. When I turned around I saw a woman so beautiful that no art work in the museum could possibly match her. She became even more beautiful after we properly introduced ourselves to each other and began to chat. I tell you Jeremiah, I found the beauty of her personality refreshing, particularly as it matched her exterior beauty as well. After a while our pleasant conversation was interrupted when she answered her cell phone, and told me that she had to leave to be with her daughter. We exchanged telephone numbers before she hurried off. So... well, we kept in touch. We became close friends, and then we formed a loving relationship. Eventually we got married."

Before Elijah could say anything else, his wife politely interrupted him to talk to me.

"My husband respects you so much Mr. Johnson, and speaks highly about you as often as he can!" She blushed. "He often talks about the positive impact you had on his life. So on that note, I am glad that I have finally been blessed with the opportunity of meeting you Mr. Johnson and your wife as well."

"That's right," Elijah added, "not only do I respect you and thank you for being there for me at that crazy job, but I also want to take this time to apologize for knocking you down out of anger on the day I was fired. I did think that you were to blame – at least until later that week, when I found out who had actually snitched on me. It makes me feel bad, because I should have come back and apologized to you… but I was held back by my pride, and I just didn't want to return to that school. My never look back attitude just got the best of me."

"I understand Elijah," I said. "I'm not mad at you at all, and I accept your apology for knocking me down that day. I appreciate all the nice things that you and your wife have said about me… Anyway, I'm looking forward to new beginning, I'm not looking back on the ills of the past; they can take a backseat in our reunited friendship." Before I could say anything further, the jazz band standing on the stage began to play. Their music hyped up the crowd and silenced our conversation. I tell you, that music was therapeutic, washing over spirits, souls and minds. As the musicians played, Elijah and his wife and their children danced to the rhythm, absorbing the energy of the music. Once the first performance was over and the sun was starting to set over the riverfront I started to feel like my wife might have another surprise up her sleeve. She began to convince me that it was time for us to go – I wasn't quite ready to go, but I sensed a bit of urgency in her voice.

"Ok sweetheart," I said, "let's go home."

"Ok," she smiled, "but you are sure you don't want to stay?"

"I am sure honey, we've had a long day and I'm kind of tired – it's probably good that we leave now." So we got up from our portable chairs and began to pack up our things. I looked over to say goodbye to Elijah and his family. Elijah looked up.

"Are you leaving?" He asked.

"Yes," I replied.

"Ok, but before you go I'd like to speak with you for a minute."

"Sure," I said, and we took a couple of steps away from our wives for a little privacy. When we had established that distance Elijah turned to me.

"Jeremiah, I have to say how truly blessed I am to have this wonderful woman in my life. She supports me and respects me as a man – and she didn't run for the hills when I told her that I was unemployed and that I'd never really made a lot of money. I told her that my problems stemmed from not having a good educational background due to being challenged by a learning disorder called dyslexia. When I told her this she smiled. 'It's not about money all the time,' she said, 'because you are already rich in ways that money can't buy. You're a committed father and you've taught your children integrity, honor, honesty, morals and decency. In fact,' she said to me, 'you can't buy happiness. The qualities you do possess are more valuable than any amount of money.' She also pointed out that my short comings did not dehumanize or devalue me, because she saw that my overall value as a person was larger and more substantial than my shortcomings.

"But here's a happy thing Jeremiah – soon after our conversation I sold my first pencil drawing for $2500.00! It seems like my art can sell! I put my pride aside and allowed my wife to help me out, since she worked as a curator at the museum where we first meet. With her help, my pencil drawings now sit on display at a local art gallery for the whole world to see. My wife also surprised me when she told me that she used to teach children with special education needs, much like the one's I am challenged with. I think that background is what motivated her to support me when I was able to let my guard down. She helped me immensely, and I eventually passed my GED! I've set my sights on going to college in the fall, where I want to pursue an art degree." Elijah had one last thing to say. "Before you go, we have to exchange telephone numbers so that we can keep in touch. Oh…" he looked a little nervously at me. "Also, my wife is pregnant. Would you and your wife consider becoming Godparents to the new child?"

"Elijah, that is an amazing honor. I must speak to my wife first, but I'm sure that she will be more than honored to take on such a role."

"I understand," Elijah replied. "Well that's it, Jeremiah I'm done." We shook hands firmly, and without goodbyes he returned to his wife and children, and my wife walked over to me and we began to walk back to our car. We held hands like loving couples do. As we walked away, I took a moment to look back. I smiled when I saw Elijah cuddling his wife, and then she pulled out his familiar sketch pad from a book bag and began to sketch a picture. It looked like she was sketching their children at play with that beautiful sunset on the horizon over the river. And that's the mental picture I'll always remember of my buddy Elijah. I turned my head back with a smile and gave my wife a kiss on her cheek. We walked off, trying not to step on anyone.

When we finally reached our car we drove off with our windows down, so that we could continue to listen to the jazz music as we drove off. While my wife drove us home I decided to thank her for this beautiful day, and for the spiritual reunion I'd had with Elijah.

"Thank you!" She replied. "But you need to thank God for the reunion with Elijah, because I had nothing to do with that divine arrangement. In fact, I was as surprised as you were!" We both laughed out loud. Before I knew it my exhaustion got the best of me, and I fell asleep while my wife drove us home. Once we arrived at our house my wife woke me up. It was now completely night time. I just wanted to go straight to bed, despite the fact that it was only about 9:30 p.m. But when I walked inside my house and turned on the nearest lamp in the living room I almost had a heart attack – it seemed like hundreds of voices were shouting "Congratulations Jeremiah!" all in unison. I stood there dumbfounded, not knowing what was going on. I looked around, and saw all my family and friends rallying around. I saw my buddy Jerome, and I immediately asked him what was going on.

"You'll see," he replied, smiling cheekily. He just looked like the cat that swallowed the canary. At this point I just wanted to know what was going on! So I began to make verbal demands. I was confused, I tell you. But no one would tell me what was going on, despite me making idle threats such as telling everyone that I was going to put them out if they didn't provide me with an answer soon. So I guess my wife had enough of my frustration and turmoil, and she walked over to a small bookcase in our living room and retrieved her Bible. Once she had her Bible in her hand she then proceeded to remove an envelope from between its pages. She walked back over to me and placed the envelope in my hand, and asked that I open it now and read it out loud, or to myself if I preferred. I decided I would read it to myself, since no one would tell me what was going on in the beginning. I kept my eyes on everyone while I tore open the envelope. Once I had the envelope open, I took a letter out from the inside and unfolded it. Once I began to read the letter it took only a few seconds for my raised eyebrows and the confused expression on my face to gradually change into a broad smile, and then a flood of emotion. I abruptly shouted out with joy! With my excitement I soon informed my wife and everyone else in the living room of the contents of the letter – it was a reinstatement letter, telling me that I'd got my old job back! I was to report to work at the auto-plant this coming Monday morning. I thanked

God and then my wife – and then the living room came to life with music. The party was on!

Before I knew it, I was performing one of those crazy solo dances that football players do after a touchdown. I had my eyes closed and I was just enjoying the moment. After that I wanted to dance with my wife – but when I opened my eyes she was nowhere in sight. I started to maneuver my way through the crowd of guests to look for her. I soon found her in the kitchen at the sink preparing a large refreshment tray of fruit, vegetables and assorted meats and cheeses to be served to our guests. Soon after I spotted her I walked up behind her and put my arms around her waist and then hugged her tightly.

"Why didn't you let me know about the letter?" I asked.

"Well, a couple of days back your buddy Jerome called to alert you that people were being rehired in order of seniority, and that he knew you'd be getting a letter soon. But you weren't there to receive the call, so at that point I asked Jerome to keep this information to himself, because we could congratulate him with a surprise party when he did get the letter. We both knew how much you'd suffered since your layoff. Soon after Jerome ended the phone call, I immediately began to pray, and I seriously believe I prayed hard enough because the letter came the next day. I thanked God for answering that prayer, and I began to plan this party!"

"Well Sophia, I can't be mad at you – you had my best interests at heart. All I can really say is wow! It's so nice of you to do something like this for me. It's so nice and wonderful to know that someone loves you and cares about you." I paused. "But I would like to know sweetheart, did I pass my spiritual test?"

"I am sorry Jeremiah, I can't answer that question… but what do you believe?"

"I do believe that something divine took place today. In fact the more I think about it, the more I realize how profoundly today's events have affected me: a man that I supposed was dead isn't, and I learned to be more compassionate for my fellow human beings. I've really learned to be more respectful of disabilities, particularly those that don't come with obvious signs like wheelchairs, crutches or other medical devices. Dyslexia and other learning disabilities may not stand out or appear to be life-threatening, but they still have the ability to completely devastate a person's life, much like any other disability or chronic disorder… especially when they are ignored or they go untreated in the name of ignorance. It really is sad that those who are dyslexic or challenged by learning disabilities are punished by society for having that learning disability, for having the nerve to look deceptively normal. So after learning all that, I now truly believe I have passed my spiritual test. I know that there will be many more spiritual tests in my life; I welcome them as priceless blessings."

Before I could utter another word, my wife placed the large tray of food she was preparing for our guests on the kitchen counter top and turned her whole body around to face me. She placed a finger to her lips.

"No more conversation."

She seductively took my hand and walked me into the dining room area, and put her arms around me. I followed her lead and we began to slow dance; the few people in the dining room became spectators. But we ignored them, and the sweet music of our love for one another drowned out the world around us. I could only feel the beautiful rhythms of our two hearts beating as we held close to each other; it took my breath away, and that's no secret.

Chapter 10

Accomplishments are never easy

Some accomplishments are never easy. The pursuit of an education can seem almost impossible when you are challenged, like Elijah was challenged in *The Janitor's Secret*, with dyslexia or other learning disabilities. Yet as bad as a learning disability can be, it can seem that the actual experience of a learning disability is not as devastating as the negative treatment that goes with it. In today's society, those with learning disabilities must endure an almost constant barrage of negativity; any attempt to share personal information about a learning disability with others is usually met with a lack of compassion, with ignorance or with hostility. Society in general is rife with bigotry, prejudice, discrimination and condescension against those with learning disabilities. Perhaps this is because those with such disabilities seem, on the outside, to be normal – it is certainly true that people believe that learning disabilities are merely excuses for poor performance.

The characters of *The Janitor's Secret* are fictional in nature, but they represent what I believe is the devastating truth about the challenges of learning disabilities. It is true that the learning problems associated with dyslexia and other learning disabilities are compounded with social stigma and with poor social skills. Consider Elijah, an eighteen year old man-child stuck in elementary school and cut off from his peers. Sadly, the damage inflicted on a person's social skills at school doesn't stop years later. In fact, many of those suffering from learning disabilities find themselves existing in the unfair and unfortunate shadow cast by being a high school dropout. It seems that few people are interested in accepting the fact that some individuals did not drop out of school, but that the school system *failed them*. The loss in self worth and self-esteem that comes with being forced out of the school system amounts simply to a belief that you will never amount to anything in life. It is no surprise that many with learning disabilities can see no further than the ground beneath their feet. The simple fact is that being exposed to a kinder and friendlier school system, able to cater to the diverse needs of students, could make a profound difference to many.

* * *

The overall content of this book is based on my personal experience of living with dyslexia. Over the years I have sought information and resources that might have been able to help with the condition, but my searches and pleas have largely fallen on deaf ears – I have often faced the sad prospect that I may never get the help I need. With this in mind, I have decided to share with you some information to ground and demonstrate the overall point of this book. Basically, I want to raise awareness so that others are saved the pain I have experienced due to my dyslexia. So before I vanish out of sight down the proverbial cracks in society where all the rejects go, I would like you to know my reason for placing explanatory documentation in the back pages of this book – my reason for living with my own janitor's secret throughout my adult life. Hopefully, armed with better knowledge you will be able to avoid what I have had to live through. I hope that the story I've told in the book – and the documentation I am supplying now – will at least give parents, teachers and the overall school system a better awareness of the terrible problems caused by dyslexia and other learning disabilities. My additional reason for adding this documentation is to make available a visual for parents, teachers and the overall school system to understand what it actually looks like after a child has been failed by parents, teachers and the school system. What the documentation contain in the pages that follow demonstrates is the sad fact that once a school transcript has reached such a critical condition, with years of academic failure, it might perhaps be too late: you just can't turn back the hands of time. Yet if parents, teachers and the school system properly use this documentation as a preventive tool, I hope they will be alert to the dangers when they can still be avoided. It would truly be a tragedy if a school transcript like the one shown on the page that follow is ever generated again. In essence, in my view such an educational failure is a crime; such negligence should be held accountable. Yet once a child grows up without an education, it is they who are penalized, denied opportunities and employment and considered a second class citizen. Many good minds and productive people are lost in this process.

I hope that the following documentation – my educational record – will generate in you a better understanding of the need for diligent, compassionate and intelligent education that can help those who sit outside societal norms.

Appendix A

Documentation

1. School Transcript Documentation
2. Alternative Education Documentation
3. GED Documentation
4. The Administrative Handbook
5. Dos & Don'ts

I ask that you seek permission before using any of this documentation for any purpose other than noted above.

Cornell Ray Amerson

School Transcript Documentation

I include first a copy of my school transcript revealing my academic failures caused by the lack of adequate support during my formative school years. I have circled a number of important points, providing further information where necessary.

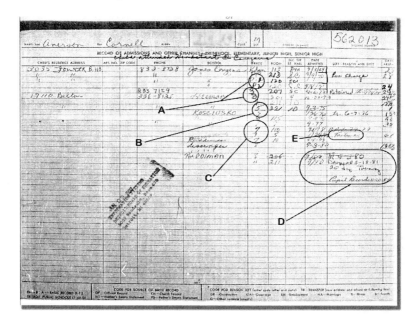

A. Despite a number of warning signs being evident in my early school grades, nothing was done about it by my parents, my teachers or the school system. This failure contributed directly to my ongoing academic difficulties.

B. Alongside the neglect of my education, my self-esteem suffered significantly with the labeling and treatment that came with being an academic failure.

C. At this point my right to an education was totally destroyed, along with my self-esteem and my ability to socialize with my peers. I found myself eighteen years old and still in the seventh grade, despite the eighth grade being recorded on my school transcript as a means to pass me on from grade to grade. This was a common practice.

D. At this point I was dropped from the public school system, with all the humiliation that entailed. I hope that no one else has to suffer such a failing of the school system.

E. The word failure is extraordinarily offensive, insulting and disrespectful. It is an unfair label that I must continue to deal with to this present-day. But the truth of the matter is that I was failed by those around me during my formative school years. No one stepped in, despite all the red flags that should have been raised and responded to. No tutoring interventions or alternative educational opportunities occurred. I wasn't a classroom clown or disturbing others; I sat in quiet distress. But, in the end I am expected to wear the badge of failure, and the school system has never taken responsibility for this.

Parents: you must accept the task of being the first-line of defense in your child's education. My school transcript shows you must take on a proactive role in making sure you are on top of things, you must find time to attend parent-teacher conferences, and you must monitor your child's report cards. The simple fact is that it is only through diligence that you will be able to respond in a timely manner to any problems; your child's future depends on your support. So please – don't let your children down by making the mistake of surrendering your parental responsibility to teachers or the school system. As my transcript and *The Janitor's Secret* shows, the potential consequences of doing this can be devastating.

I hope that my school transcript will at some point serve as an aide to encourage greater accountability and responsibility on behalf of parents, teachers and the school system, and as a reminder of what it looks like when a child is ultimately failed by a lack of commitment and support by parents, teachers and the school system. I truly believe that any 'failure' is not solely the fault of the child.

Alternative Education Documentation

My experience in the mainstream school system left me feeling somewhat defeated and sore, but my efforts to attain a formal education did not stop there. Despite my circumstances, in 1983 I decided to seek alternative forms of education, as shown in the documentation presented below. What I want to stress is that though many people assume those who drop out of school are defeated and will discontinue their education, many will work diligently to seek out any educational opportunity, never giving up! To this stage I remained unaware that I suffered from dyslexia, though I had some suspicions.

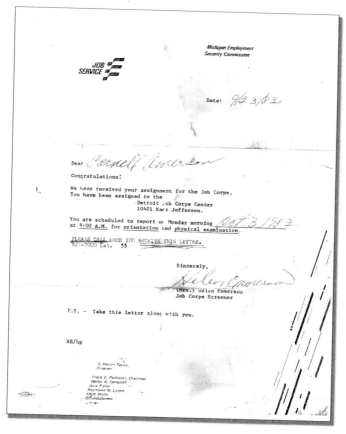

GED Documentation

This document is a copy of my GED scores for a test taken in 1987. It shows that I was beginning, at this stage, to experience some academic success; I was attending an adult educational program and had two excellent teachers. Indeed, one in particular appeared to realize that I might have been suffering from a learning disability. I believe she drew this insight from her own circumstances of being challenged with a sight impairment.

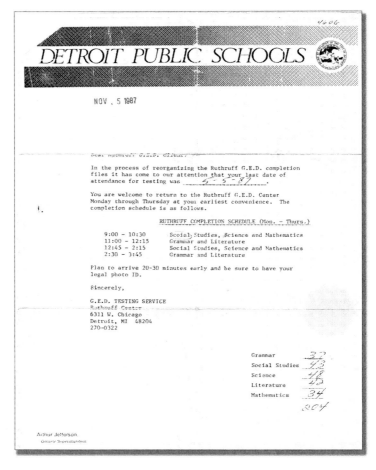

But her ability to teach was not impaired by her seeing difficulties by any stretch of the imagination. In fact, I found her teaching to be phenomenal. The other teacher that worked along side her was also exceptional, as you can see from my GED test scores – my first attempt at the test. Yet my academic achievements were short lived; my two excellent teachers were replaced by others not nearly as understanding. My academic failures resumed once more.

GED Documentation

I made a final attempt to pass the GED test in December 1997. The documentation presented below shows my scores for this test. Soon after this period my scores were simply wiped away in an administrative change at the testing center. I was diagnosed with dyslexia in the early part of 2002.

```
 1/07/98                DETROIT BOARD OF EDUCATION              15:17:33
                            ADULT EDUCATION
                          GED HIGH TEST SCORES

 STUDENT SS#  ██████████   NAME   AMERSON CORNELL
     GED=  N      DATE OF BIRTH              SEX  M       ETHNIC  B
 -------------------------------------------------------------------------
         FIRST TESTED   1/20/19             LAST TESTED  12/01/97
                        (MM/DD/YY)                       (MM/DD/YY)
                                                         LAST FORM USED  AT
                        TEST DATE    FORM    STANDARD     %ILE
                                               SCORE      RANK
  (I)    ENGLISH        12/01/97     AT         40         17
  (II)   HISTORY        5/20/96      AQ         52         58
  (III)  SCIENCE        5/05/87      MY         48         43
  (IV)   LITERATURE     5/04/87      MY         42         21
  (V)    MATHEMATICS    12/05/95     AP         36         08
  (VI)   ESSAY                                             00
                                          TOTAL  =    218
                                          AVERAGE =    43.6

               ENTER X TO EXIT
 F3=Exit     F6=Student View
```

GED documentation

The document on this page shows the basic format for how GED testing scores are established and distributed to those who take a GED test.

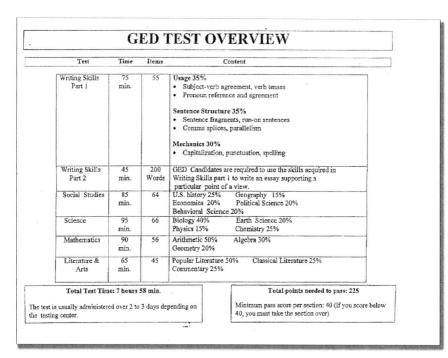

GED TEST OVERVIEW

Test	Time	Items	Content
Writing Skills Part 1	75 min.	55	**Usage 35%** • Subject-verb agreement, verb tenses • Pronoun reference and agreement **Sentence Structure 35%** • Sentence fragments, run-on sentences • Comma splices, parallelism **Mechanics 30%** • Capitalization, punctuation, spelling
Writing Skills Part 2	45 min.	200 Words	GED Candidates are required to use the skills acquired in Writing Skills part 1 to write an essay supporting a particular point of a view.
Social Studies	85 min.	64	U.S. history 25% Geography 15% Economics 20% Political Science 20% Behavioral Science 20%
Science	95 min.	66	Biology 40% Earth Science 20% Physics 15% Chemistry 25%
Mathematics	90 min.	56	Arithmetic 50% Algebra 30% Geometry 20%
Literature & Arts	65 min.	45	Popular Literature 50% Classical Literature 25% Commentary 25%

Total Test Time: 7 hours 58 min. The test is usually administered over 2 to 3 days depending on the testing center.	Total points needed to pass: 225 Minimum pass score per section: 40 (If you score below 40, you must take the section over)

I would like to reiterate that I was unaware of my dyslexia until 2002; I was unaware of the disorder throughout my years of academic failure in school, alternative schooling and GED testing. I was tested for dyslexia in 2002, soon after I learned that adults could still be tested for a learning disability late in life. Of course, the best time to be tested is early in life when you're a child. Despite the negative connotations that often come with being challenged or labeled as having a learning disability, it doesn't mean you're stupid or dumb; indeed, that is often the first obstacle you must face and overcome in your educational life. I believe, however, that much can be achieved by redefining the meaning of the learning disability label in your life, by viewing yourself as a person who happens to learn in ways different from other people – and that there is nothing wrong with that.

The Administrative Handbook

The next few pages provide some information on a booklet named the Administrative Handbook for Detroit Public Schools; the booklet contains vital information which could have provided a solution to my academic problems. In essence, the booklet details the responsibilities and obligations of teachers, principals and the overall school system to parents and children.

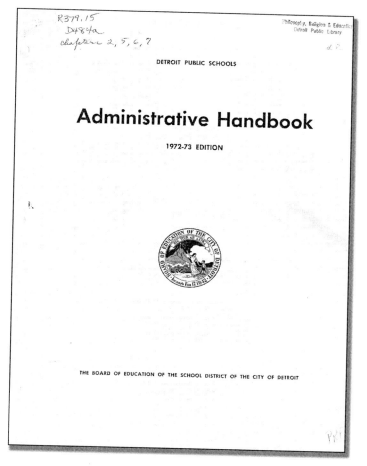

What I strongly advise is that parents concerned about their children's education pick up a copy of this booklet and the student code of conduct handbook to allow them to become adequately informed before any problem occurs. Unfortunately this was not the case for me, and absolutely nothing was done to stop me from falling through the proverbial cracks of society.

The Administrative Handbook

This page from the Administrative Handbook describes each child's right to an education. However, due to a lack of intervention during my academic troubles in school, my educational right was denied; I continue to pay the penalties for this.

II-H

Student Rights and Responsibilities

(Statement adopted by the Central Board of Education, September 7, 1971.*
See also II-JD.)

HA. RIGHT TO AN EDUCATION

a. Students have a right to participate in the approved, planned, balanced educational courses and programs described and outlined in the curriculum guides and courses of study of the Detroit Public Schools.

b. No student shall be denied the opportunity to participate in any program offered by the Detroit Public Schools, because of race, creed, color, or country of national origin.

c. Every member of the school community, including students, parents, and the school staff has the responsibility to promote a school climate free of fear, harassment, violence, or disruption; regular attendance at school; orderly conduct and behavior; as well as to provide maximum opportunities for effective teaching on the part of staff and effective learning on the part of the student.

HB. STUDENT DRESS

a. Students have the right to express their own individuality in their wearing apparel. The responsibility for what is worn by students is a matter to be determined by the students and their parents, provided that the dress does not present, in the judgment of the school principal, or his designee(s), a health or safety hazard and does not disturb the educational opportunities of other students or disrupt the educational program of the school.

b. Nothing may be worn that significantly detracts from the learning situation in the classroom by directing attention away from the learning activity and focusing it on the wearer. Likewise, nothing may be worn which interferes with school traffic or which constitutes a threat to the safety of the wearer or other students.

HC. THE RIGHT TO FREEDOM OF EXPRESSION AND PUBLICATION ——
DISSENT —— RIGHT TO PETITION

a. Students have the right orally, through symbols, and through publication, to express their opinions on issues and to express their beliefs. The atmosphere in school should be conducive to such expression in keeping with the position of the Detroit Public Schools that important areas of study involve issues on which differing positions are held by important individuals and groups. Study and discussion of these issues is frequently a necessary and appropriate part of education. Detroit schools thus encourage a scientific and unprejudiced study of pertinent issues in the classroom, many of which are patently controversial. The role of the teacher is that of the impartial moderator who does not attempt directly, or indirectly, to limit or control the students' judgment concerning controversial issues, but to make certain that full and fair consideration is given to many sides of an issue, and that facts are carefully examined as to their accuracy and interpretation.

*Preamble omitted and indexing added for this handbook.

On a lighter note, I hope that my book not only brings about vindication and justice to me and others who were in the same situation, but will also limit the suffering of those of us without a formal education and prevent such a failure of the school system from ever happening again.

The Administrative Handbook

This page of the Administrative Handbook reveals the provisions to be set aside for children with special needs. It appears, however, that dyslexia was not considered special enough – or well-known enough – during my formal school years.

II-G

Special Education
Selection, Transfer, Promotion, Release

Since 1883, the Detroit Public Schools have made special provisions for the education of handicapped children. Each handicapped child has a claim to a full education in accord with his own ability and limitations. The program is supervised by the Department of Special Education.*

GA. TYPES OF CLASSES

    a. The types of services that are available as part of the regular school program are listed in the accompanying table.

    b. Pupils will be assigned to special education programs only after examination by and upon recommendation of one of the several clinics and other agencies designated for that purpose.

(chart on pages 64-65)

*Division of Curriculum and Administrative Research.

It seems that despite the stipulations of The Administrative Handbook, no responsibility was taken for ensuring my education. It still makes me wonder why such consistently poor academic performances were not taken notice of during my formal school years.

The Administrative Handbook

This page was of the Administrative Handbook provides information for parents or teachers seeking assistance to ensure that all necessary educational opportunities are provided.

---

2. **Referral to School Social Work Service**

   The decision to request the services of the school social worker may originate with the classroom teacher, school administrator, other school personnel, community agencies, parents and/or children. When the request originates from school personnel, the following should be done:

   a. The school fills in Form 5006 which provides for the parents' consent for service to be given. It is imperative that parents work with the school in filling in this form in order to:

      (1) Protect the rights of the parents and children
      (2) Protect school personnel
      (3) Involve the parents from the inception of the request for service

      In certain situations a special conference including parents, school personnel, and the School Social Worker may be scheduled before service is requested. Such conferences should be jointly planned ahead of the time the parent is asked to participate. Clear decisions about the purpose of the conference should be mutually decided in advance. Conferences should be arranged through the region School Social Work Office.

   b. *Routing of Form 5006.*—After the school principal approves, he sends the completed Form 5006 to the school social work department head for the region in which the school is located.

   c. The region School Social Work department head reviews each 5006 with the school social worker in an effort to decide what method of help is needed and what priority should be given to the individual request. The regional department head is responsible for such follow-up services.

   d. The school social worker initiates service according to the needs of the child and school as considered in relation to his overall assignment.

   e. Referral of children in Special Education classes may be initiated in two ways:

      (1) From city-wide Special Education schools, Form 5006 is routed from the principal to the director of School Social Work Service.
      (2) From Special Education classes in regional schools, Form 5006, along with Form 1107, is routed to the Department of Special Education.

3. **Service Delivery**

   School Social Workers may use a variety of professional methodologies in meeting the needs of children, families and school communities.

   a. They may serve via casework counseling with the individual children and their families.

   b. They may work with groups of children and parents.

   c. They may work with community groups on behalf of children.

   d. They may offer consultation to teachers and administration regarding children, their problems, and resources available to meet their needs, with reference to individual situations or school crises.

4. **Responsibility**

   a. Department heads in the regions are responsible for the program provided by individual school social workers. They are responsible to the region superintendent, with consultative services provided by the Department of School Social Work Service.

   b. Overall responsibility for the quality of social work services rests centrally with the Department of School Social Work Services.

   c. For telephone numbers and addresses of department heads and School Social Work staff, and for their assignments, see listings in annual *Schools Directory,* contact the office of the region superintendent, or contact the office of the director.

CF. **DEPARTMENT OF EVALUATIVE SERVICES***

   The Department of Evaluative Services (Office of Pupil Personnel Services) supports the total educational

---

*See also II-HK-2, "Change in Age of Majority — Psychological Clinic Cases."

In retrospect, I believe that the intervention of a social worker during my formative school years, as outlined on the first three lines of item 3, could have provided the necessary start to ensure my education. But this was not done. I sincerely hope that this is not the case today. I hope that this book will serve as a call to ensure that things are done to ensure that each and every child gains the education they deserve.

Dos and Don'ts

Here's a collection of important dos and don'ts, respectfully presented to you on the basis of my personal struggles and experiences. I present these as suggestions and considerations to be mindful of: to help you as a parent to increase your ability to provide adequate assistant for a child challenged by a learning disability.

Do:

1. Once it has been discovered that your child is challenged by a learning disability, it is imperative that you educate yourself about learning disabilities so that you can better help your child as well as yourself.

2. Develop a first step action plan. Have your child tested for a learning disability as soon as you suspect from personal observation – or when a reliable source such as your child's teacher brings it to your attention – that something may be wrong with their academic performance. Treat poor academic marks as a red flag.

3. Before having your child tested for a learning disability, make sure you have your child examined by a physician to rule out any medical conditions or problems that could be mistaken for learning disabilities.

4. Teach your child; a learning disability doesn't mean they can't learn, but it may at times interfere with their learning. Despite interference, they have to keep trying to learn no matter what.

5. Refrain from physical punishment of poor academic performance in school. If your child is challenged by a hidden learning disability, tutoring and adequate teaching assistance will be far more effective than corporal punishment.

6. Get creative in helping your child academically: make sure that the next family field trip to the zoo, art museum or science museum can be treated as extra credit for the child after a request to the child's teacher.

7. Allow your child to become mad and angry sometimes in response to their learning disability challenge, and listen to them before lecturing.

8. When possible have the whole family participate in assisting and supporting any child with a learning disability.

9. Seek information and advice from other parents facing similar situations. This is particularly important if you find yourself not knowing what to do, feeling frustrated, overwhelmed, helpless and alone trying to help a child that happens to be challenged by a learning disability.

10. Make sure that your child don't feels less than their peers, regardless of their difficulties in learning, that they fit in with their peers. Make sure your child is treated as normal as possible at all times. It is particularly important that the child be placed in the mainstream school population if at all possible.

11. Encourage your child to build their confidence by doing things they have a talent in and that they like to do.

12. Check out your child's school's local community organization, and if they're not involved in learning disability support, find out why and then try to encourage them to get involved by showing them your involvement first.

13. Parents must challenge a teacher or the school system when necessary.

14. Do your job as parent, and make sure your child's school holds to their commitment to fairly and properly educate your children without prejudice.

15. Make the time to attend as many parent-teacher conferences as possible, and get involved in volunteering or joining a parent advocacy group, community organization or association pertaining to education.

16. If your child does receive poor marks, find the time to help them with the problem and schedule a meeting with their teacher.

17. Its imperative that you obtain a Student Code of Conduct Handbook in order to know what's expected of you and your child. Similarly, the school's Administrative Handbook will reveal the teachers', principal's and the overall school's responsibilities to you and your child. Use these booklets whenever a problem arises, they can prove invaluable in getting to grips with any problem.

18. Encourage your child to be as self-sufficient as possible.

19. Go to your child's school and don't be afraid to ask for help as soon as you discover your child performing academically poorly.

20. Form an alliance with your child's teachers to help with your child's overall needs.

21. Speak positively to your child in front of others, especially their peers.

22. View your child's education as a priority when helping your child challenged by learning disability; don't forget to be loving, caring and respectful in the process.

23. Its imperative that you be proactive in your child's educational process etc.

24. Create for your child a realistic daily schedule and area in the home for study, and eliminate all possible distractions to assist them to learn discipline.

25. Take the time to notice what your child possesses in other attributes, qualities and talents, and use them to ensure that their learning disability does not consume their whole identity and world.

26. Inform your child of the celebrities and famous people who are also challenged by learning disabilities – and if you don't know any, then make that an assignment for you and your child: research the many celebrities that live with learning disabilities, finding out what forms of learning disability they are challenged with, how they are handling it, and how they worked with their learning disability and still became a great success.

27. Try to be as understanding as possible; even if you don't understand or have no knowledge of a learning disability.

28. After your child has been tested for a learned disability and you now have the proper paperwork, you can now request a roundtable meeting with your child's teacher, principal and resource teacher to establish an Individualized Education Program (or IEP) that comes with the child having access to a Resource Room and teacher who will help to accommodate your child's overall educational needs. However, if you want other options and are not sure what to request, you should seek out information at your child's school or through one of those advocacy groups you're involved with.

29. Educate yourself regarding the many types of accommodation provided at GED testing centers after you have been tested for a learned disability. To initiate such accommodation you must ask for the proper form (L-15) at the GED testing center. Also, you must be over 18 years of age to take a GED test at the start.

30. You should make a conscious decision every day to pursue personal self development in knowledge, information, understanding and excellence: it is in these things that true wealth exists.

31. Make sure you take full advantage of your job's Parent Appreciation Day, when you are allowed to bring your children to work with you. When you do so, make sure your child's school is aware of this field trip so that your child can gain extra credit as well as improving their life experience.

32. "Seek and utilize when necessary the assistance of learning aids and other forms of technology, such as voice recognition software, spelling aid devices and computers, as well as the dictionary and tutorial assistance. Such devices and aids should be used to elevate your overall success in obtaining an education."

33. Make sure a dismissal from a learning institution or a place of employment doesn't pass without challenge if you believe your learning disability is the cause, particularly if you have already placed this information on your application before submission.

Don't:

1. Don't allow adulthood to stop you from being tested for a learning disability, because it's never too late to be tested.

2. Don't let a learning disability go ignored or untreated.

3. Don't ever give up in your search to find information that will help your child challenged by a learning disability to increase their chances of being successful in life.

4. Don't assume that all school dropouts dropped out by choice. So many children are denied an education after being failed by a lack of commitment by parents, teachers and the school system. It is only through the failings of others that children are left to fall through the proverbial cracks in society.

5. Words hurt: don't tell any child, especially one with a learning disability, that he or she is stupid, lazy, dumb, worthless, and will never amount to anything in life. Because all that simply does is crush a child's self-esteem, self-confidence and self-worth.

6. Don't allow your child to use their learning disability as a crutch to avoid school work or doing any other things they are capable of and responsible for doing.

7. Don't let your lack of knowledge regarding what to do or where to go for help paralyze your search in helping your child with any academic problems in school.

8. Don't let denial motivate your decision-making in regards to your child's learning disability.

9. Don't make the mistake of not being there for your child challenged by a learning disability when nobody else will.

10. Don't allow poor study habits to be the reason your child is performing poorly in school. Be on top of thing as the parent in asking the child almost daily how they're doing in school: their honesty will reveal how they are performing in school. The next action step will be to help them immediately with no exception.

11. Being frustrated, ashamed and embarrassed that your child is challenged by a learning disability is no good reason not to support them. Because little do you know, they are probably just as frustrated, and feeling overwhelmed, ashamed and embarrassed having to deal with a learning disability.

12. Don't forget to tell your child that they are just as good as everyone else and will someday be a great success, despite their being challenged by a learning disability.

13. Don't give up on your child when they are struggling to deal with a learning disability, especially when they are trying to the best of their ability and are still falling short academically in school. At that point they don't deserve punishment they deserve to be praised and appreciated and acknowledged for their efforts.

14. Don't allow your child to feel sorry for themselves because of their learning disability.

15. Don't treat your child's learning disability as a secret in the hopes that it will simply go away if you ignore it. Until a study shows otherwise, a learning disability is inherited and it's not going anywhere, it's primarily there for life – but this doesn't mean that your child still can't be a great success in life.

16. Don't allow your child to be taught to be an underachiever by anyone – that includes parents, teachers and the overall school system.

17. Don't use a child's report card and progress report only as a license to punish them. Their report card and progress report should be used as guideposts to identify problems your child may be experiencing so that a solution can follow instead of a punishment.

18. Don't allow your child to miss out on other alternative means and resources that can help them with their educational needs after high school, such as Community College, Vocational training, G.E.D etc.

19. Don't unnecessarily pressure the child to do better academically.

20. Don't let teachers or the school system make the final decision regarding your child's educational direction without your parental input.

21. Don't be so quick to use medication to control your child as a quick fix prescribed by your child's teacher. Being a child shouldn't be viewed and treated as a disorder, so trust your gut feeling and intuition and get a second opinion from a qualified physician that you have confidence in and actually cares about your children.

22. Don't let your child be cheated out of an education by bad decision-making, gross negligence and a lack of involvement or commitment on behalf of you, teachers or the overall school system, as it is your child who will ultimately have to deal with the legacy and burden of such decisions.

23. There are many other dos and don'ts that have not been covered here, and that doesn't mean they're not valid. You may want to create a few of your own that will work for you, and it probably wouldn't hurt if you shared them with others in a group of net-working parents in the community.

24. "Don't allow narrow-minded opinions to define who you are, or to dictate your's or your child's future- whether challenged with a learnimg disability or not. Remember that your're responsibilities for making decision about your future- you're responsible for giving up or taking up the power in your life."

25. Don't be afraid when asked 'what is your learning disability?' Get creative and speak in layman's terms. A little humor can also help to explain your condition. I like to use the analogy of being a dyslexic individual. I go on to compare dyslexia to computers with different operating systems, that will not process information not compatible with their particular operating system. So in conclusion, if you place that computer in a classroom with many others that process the information perfectly, then that one computer trying to process incompatible information will be viewed – mistakenly – as broken or dyslexic.

26. Don't dismiss a person with a learning disability by telling them that they look normal and that there isn't anything wrong with them.

27. By all means, don't forget to tell your child you love them and nothing is going to get in the way of that.

28. Don't take your child education's for granted, you want to lead by example in showing that education is important. Hopefully they will follow your lead.

29. Don't allow your child – or even you if you're an adult – to be discriminated against due to a learning disability you or they may have. There are legal consequences that can take place if you're denied special services to assist you as a student with your learning disability needs or if you are discriminated unfairly or illegally due to having a specific learning disability. If you do encounter any of the above, you should contact legal counsel and inquire about your rights under The Individuals with Disabilities Education act (IDEA), Section 504 of the Rehabilitation act of 1973 and the Americans with Disability Act (ADA) which defines the rights of students that are dyslexic or may be challenge by other specific learning disabilities.

30. Don't assume your child is going to be well educated without your support. Because in all due respect that is foolish thinking that will ultimately compromise your child's overall education.

31. Don't forget to inform your children that education and learning should not stop at any graduation: learning is life long.

32. Don't send your child to school without having a well balance breakfast.A hunger child don't learn well.

33. Once you have the proper documentation after being tested for a learning disability, don't make the mistake of not writing this information when necessary onto applications, such as a school enrollment applications and an employment applications etc.

"Parents and communities, lets take a pro-active role in
educating our children today."
By
Cornell Ray Amerson

Author's Commentary

This book has been a great accomplishment for me; a personal achievement in the face of my dyslexia. Yet despite this personal accomplishment, I believe strongly that this book will serve as a great source of information for parents, teachers, school systems – or indeed anyone with an interest in the topic – about dyslexia and learning disabilities. I want to bring an awareness to what people should do to ensure that their children are well educated. I sincerely hope that this book will not be considered an attempt to take cheap shots and bash teachers or the school system for no good reason; but I do believe that changes must take place. Mediocre teachers and inadequate systems must be exposed: there is simply too much at stake. I believe this book will serve as a wake-up call for parents in particular, helping them to realize how they must be involved in their child's education; they must monitor not only their child, but their child's teachers and the school system in general. Quite simply, we must recognize that problems that children may have with learning are not simply the child's fault alone: parents, teachers and the school system are all involved in what is going on. This leads me to the question "why Johnny can't read?" There is no simple answer to this question, but often the problem is that Johnny is not being taught by his teacher – for whatever reason – or that Johnny is challenged by some sort of undiagnosed learning disability.

But I wish to do more than expose a problem; I want solutions. One possible solution to the overall illiteracy crisis that we are having in this country pertains specifically to the GED preparation process. I suggest that GED classes run for adults be provided with special education instructors to assist those with learning disabilities; this will limit problems long before the actual test. On that note I hope to see more solutions emerge over time so that we can start the process of helping Johnny to read, as opposed to merely focusing on the fact that he can't read.

In closing, I would like to share some words of advice to any parent concerned about their children falling behind in school – whether they are challenged with a learning disability or not. "To reiterate my point once more, my advice to parents is that they can use extra credits to improve their child's academic shortcomings." Parents should utilize their creativity and call their child's school and inform the appropriate staff that their child is participating in extra credit activities, such as a 'bring you child to work day'. You could also utilize some cleverness and take your child on a family outing or a field trip to your local museum or science center. "After you have established the educational benefits of a field trip, you should call your child's school and make that extra credit request on behalf of your child's best interest. A couple of other strategies you could try include getting to know your child's principal and teacher by more than just their name, and seeking out other school staff such as the school counselor. By all means, make time to attend parent-teacher conferences and when possible joint a parent advocacy support group pertaining to educational matters. Making your present visible to the schools staff and your child's show you care. Remember parents, your child's education begins with you!"

Sincerely
Cornell Ray Amerson

Resource Pages

The purpose for this page and the one that follow is to reduce any time wastage in your search for help or basic knowledge pertaining to learning disabilities. Contact your state Dyslexia Foundation or surf the internet and write down their details cause someone may be counting on you!

Company name: _____

Contact person named: _____

Address_____City_____

Zip _____

P.O. Box_____

Phone: ( ) _____ Cell phone: ( ) _____

Fax: ( ) _____

E-mail _____

Web address _____

Company name: _____

Contact person named: _____

Address_____City_____

Zip _____

P.O. Box_____

Phone: ( ) _____ Cell phone: ( ) _____

Fax: ( ) _____

E-mail _____

Web address _____

Company name: _____

Contact person named: _____

Address_____City_____

Zip _____

P.O. Box_____

Phone: ( ) _____ Cell phone: ( ) _____

Fax: ( ) _____

E-mail _____

Web address _____

Company name: _____

Contact person named: _____

Address_____City_____

Zip _____

P.O. Box_____

Phone: ( ) _____ Cell phone: ( ) _____

Fax: ( ) _____

E-mail _____

Web address _____

Company name: _____

Contact person named: _____

Address_____City_____

Zip _____

P.O. Box_____

Phone: ( ) _____ Cell phone: ( ) _____

Fax: ( ) _____

E-mail _____

Web address _____

Chioma Inspirations Order Form

Ordering the book titled: THE JANITOR'S SECRET

3319 Greenfield Rd. #251
Dearborn
Michigan
48120-1212
USA

Chioma Inspirations is an online store that can best
be reached at: ChiomaInspirations@yahoo.com
Or Web-site: www. ChiomaInspirations.com

Name: _____

Address: _____

City: _____ State_____ Zip_____

How many books: _____ total book order price $._____

Make check or Money Order out to Chioma Inspirations
Book price $16.00 shipping& handling $7.00

Thanks for your Order!

Chioma Inspirations Order Form

Ordering the book titled: THE JANITOR'S SECRET

3319 Greenfield Rd. #251
Dearborn
Michigan
48120-1212
USA

Chioma Inspirations is an online store that can best
be reached at: ChiomaInspirations@yahoo.com
Or Web-site: www. ChiomaInspirations.com

Name: _____

Address: _____

City: _____ State_____ Zip_____

_____

How many books: _____ total book order price $._____

_____

Make check or Money Order out to Chioma Inspirations
Book price $16.00 shipping& handling $7.00

Thanks for your Order!